MW01170429

The LARKINS FAMILY ADVENTURES

By
Norma Wymore

My beautiful Granddaughter Mindi *Philippians 1:6 & 4:6* *With all My Love Grandma, Norma Wymore*

Copyright © 2012 by Norma Wymore

The Larkins Family Adventures
by Norma Wymore

Printed in the United States of America

ISBN 9781625092366

All rights reserved solely by the author. The author guarantees all contents are original and do not infringe upon the legal rights of any other person or work. No part of this book may be reproduced in any form without the permission of the author. The views expressed in this book are not necessarily those of the publisher.

www.xulonpress.com

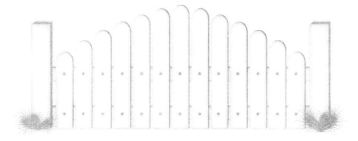

ACKNOWLEDGEMENTS

I want to praise Almighty God and thank Him for the story line He gave me and kept it coming until the book was finished.

I also want to thank my prayer partner Diane Lysiak for the many hours of prayer we, together; sent up to the throne of grace on behalf of this book. Without her encouragement & partnership in prayer, this book may not have been written. After reading the manuscript she also encouraged me by saying, "At times I laughed and at times I cried." I thought if it brings you joy and touches your heart it must be ok.

I also want to thank my husband Frank for standing by me and insisting that I get my book published.

I also want to thank Xulon Press for accepting this book and all the work they put into it to bring it to print and for all their prayers for me and this book. It means a lot to me.

PREFACE

After her husband was killed in a construction accident Tiffany was left with six children and one on the way. Two mounths after the baby was born, she put in her application as a surgical technician and registered nurse at hospitals around the state.

She knew she had to keep her family together somehow.

The story tells how their life unfolds and the people they meet after she accepts a job at a small hospital in a small town in Minnesota.

CHAPTER 1

THE LARKINS MEET MR. WOODARD

S he opened the door of our little church (the service had already started). She was the very picture of love; she was beautiful in appearance and graceful as a swan. She had blonde hair and the most beautiful blue eyes anyone had ever seen, and nestled in her arms was a little baby wrapped snugly in a soft, cuddly blanket. Behind her came six little children walking in a straight line just like little ducklings. She walked straight up to the last pew on the left side and began to take a place right next to old Mr. Woodard. Now Mr. Woodard was an old bachelor and had no time for children. But he stayed right in his place in the pew, almost like he was hypnotized. Those children sat as quiet as church mice and never moved a muscle. Mr. Woodard just sat there and almost could not move himself.

Well, anyway, when church was over, she came right up to Mr. Woodard and said "Hello, my name is Mrs. Tiffany Larkin." She continued, "and these are my children: Stephanie Marie, twelve years old, Gregory Shane, ten years old, Angela Nadine, eight years old, Jared Ross, six years old, Jordan Ra', four years old, Jackson Daniel, two years old, and the baby is a little boy, Blake Anthony, two months old." Now Stephanie was a small girl, not quite as tall as her mom. She stood about five feet tall, with long blond hair and blue eyes, just like her mom. Gregory was tall for his age, around five feet five inches, slender, and with features like his dad; everyone always said he was going to be big like his dad. Angela was also small and thin, and she had light brown hair and brown eyes.

Jared had broad shoulders and was built like a football player, with dark brown hair like his dad's and blue eyes like his mom. Jordan was a well-rounded, little girl who had not yet lost all her baby fat. She was a strawberry-blonde and her hair was curly; she had big brown eyes. Jackson was a precious little guy with a big smile like his Dad's and the biggest blue eyes you ever saw. He was a "tow-head." His hair was almost white; there was hardly any color to it. Little Blake was a chubby little guy with a toothless smile and big brown eyes, and he did not have any hair yet.

Mr. Woodard thought that her name sounded like a movie star and introduced himself. "I am Oliver Woodard; I have lived in this town and gone to this church all my life." Now Mr. Woodard was about sixty-five years old, and just retired.

Mrs. Larkin asked, "Is Mrs. Woodard ill that she is not in the church with you today?"

"Oh no," Mr. Woodard responded," I have never been married. I live alone."

"Well then," Mrs. Larkin said, "you must come home with us for dinner. It will be just great to have an adult to visit with. And I am sure you could use a nice home-cooked meal." Well, Mr. Woodard surely would have enjoyed a home-cooked meal all right, but he sure didn't think he could stand spending all afternoon around those seven children. He just didn't take to kids, but to be polite, Mr. Woodard accepted Mrs. Larkin's invitation and followed her and the children out to the parking lot of the church.

Now many people of the church came up to Mrs. Larkin and introduced themselves. And remarked how well behaved the children were in church. She thanked them graciously, and then she and her children got into their little car, and the children sat on each other's laps, so there would be room for Mr. Woodard. (Mr. Woodard thought to himself, this is really going to be some ride. I can just hear it now, "She is touching me." "You have a bony butt." "Mom, he is looking at me." "He stepped on my foot," and on and on as they drove to Mrs. Larkin's home.) But to his surprise, the children, and Mrs. Larkin began to sing Bible songs together. And it was such a pleasant time, he found himself joining right in. They all had a wonderful time, all the way home. Tiffany mentioned that they had tried a couple other churches, but none were as friendly as this one. The children were very orderly, getting out of the car and walking into the house with the older ones helping with the little ones. And when Mrs. Larkin opened the door, the most wonderful smells hit Mr. Woodard's nostrils: the smell of roast beef, homemade apple pie, and fresh bread. Mr. Woodard thought he had died and gone to heaven.

To be polite, he offered to help Mrs. Larkin set the table and get the dinner on. But she replied. "Thank you very much, but that is the children's job. They just love to help, and it is such a great help to me." Stephanie brought Mr. Woodard, a tall glass of ice water, while he patiently waited for the meal to be put on the table. Then she heated up Blake's bottle and fed him. While the rest got dinner on. Jordan and Jackson came up to him with a book and ask if he would please read it to them. Then they both sat very quietly, in front of him on the floor and waited very patiently with their legs crossed, and their chins in their hands. Mr. Woodard was so amazed at their good manners that he was happy to read to them. So he started the story, expecting them to get up and run off in a few minutes to find something else to do, but again, to his amazement, the children were gazing at him as he read. He actually began to enjoy himself and began to relax a little.

Before you knew it, Mrs. Larkin was calling them to dinner.

Each child knew exactly where they were supposed to sit, and everyone took their places. Mrs. Larkin said the blessing; she thanked the Lord for the food and the new church they had found and also for the very good new friend they had found in Mr. Woodard, and all the children said "Amen." And Mr. Woodard said "Amen" also. The children were so polite at the dinner table. They were seated so the older children could help the younger ones with their food and drinks. They never asked for anything without saying please and thank you, even the little ones. They had a lovely conversation with the children during dinner, where they went to school, what grades they were in, and what their hobbies were. Stephanie liked drama and dancing. She wanted to be an actress. Gregory liked drama also but wanted nothing to do with dancing. He liked music. He wanted to be a musician and to sing. Angela liked little children. She wanted to be a nurse and a mommy and have lots of kids. Jared liked football. He wanted to be a football player when he grew up. Jordan just loved her new baby brother, and she wanted to be a mommy, too. Jackson wanted to be an engineer and drive a big train when he got big. He loved trains. Mr. Woodard couldn't even imagine having so much fun with this many children in one room. When dinner was over Mrs. Larkin invited Mr. Woodard to the living room to have coffee and get acquainted.

Mrs. Larkin asked Mr. Woodard why he had never married in all these years. Of course he could not tell her it was because he could not stand children. So he just said, I guess I never found the right woman. Mrs. Larkin, being a fine Christian lady said "then I guess I had better start praying for you that the right woman comes along." They both had a good laugh. The children finished the dishes and cleaned up the kitchen and then asked if they may go outside to play. Mrs. Larkin told the older ones to be sure to look after the younger ones, and not let them run off somewhere. Their response was, "Yes Mother."

Mr. Woodard remarked how well-managed the children were, and how well behaved they were and asked; "How do you accomplish this on your own without any help?" Mrs. Larkin began to tell him her story about how her husband Gregory was killed in a construction accident eight months ago leaving her with six children, and one on the way. They had met in college. He was a tall man about 6'3". He was very handsome, had dark brown hair, big brown eyes, and a gracious smile. She showed him a picture of Gregory. He was going to be a civil engineer, and she was going to be a surgical technician and a registered nurse. They fell in love and married fourteen years ago. She finished college and started having babies. She told him how hard it was for her to go through the last months before the baby was born all by herself. Gregory's parents and her parents had both passed away, and they were both only children. I knew I had to keep my family together somehow. The children were in as much pain as I was going through. So after Blake was born, I started putting in applications to different hospitals around the state and was accepted here at the hospital in Wyoming.

After Gregory went to heaven to be with Jesus, she sat the children down and told them that they were a family and families stick together, work together, and play together. And Daddy would want them to do all they could to help their Mommy. So we went over everything that had to be done to keep a family together, and each one took on the jobs which were best suited to them for their age at the time. Responsibilities will change and be reviewed as they get older. Stephanie helps with cooking, some light cleaning, sorts cloths to wash, helps with the baby, and keeps her room clean. Gregory helps with the dishes, takes out the garbage, helps get Jackson dressed, keeps his room clean, and is teaching Jackson how to pick up his toys, and keep his room clean. Angela sets the table, and clears the table, keeps her room clean, and helps Jordan keep her room clean, and helps Jordan pick out her clothes,(with Mom's approval.) Jared keeps his room clean, and keeps his two younger siblings busy by playing with them. When he is at school they have to play together. They have been taught to just take out one toy at a time, and when they are done playing with it, they put it back before they take out another one. It is amazing how they have all pitched in to make it work so I could go to work. I am a surgical nurse at the hospital in town. I have Mrs. Pierce come in and stay with the three little ones, while I work. I am so grateful. Mrs. Pierce lives just down the road, and I am also so grateful to find this old farmhouse with plenty of room for the children to run and play.

All of a sudden, Jordan came running in from outside and came up to Mr. Woodard and ask," Are you going to be my grandpa?" "Jordan!" Mrs. Larkin said in a rather stern voice, "you should never come up to someone you just met with a question like that. Mr. Woodard is just a new friend we have found." Mr. Woodard said with a smile, "Oh! No harm done, she is just little. They don't understand these things." "But," Jordan said, "I don't have a grandpa, and I sure would like to have one." "Well," Mr. Woodard answered, "then I guess you have a new grandpa." Jordan jumped up on Mr. Woodard's lap and gave him the biggest hug and kiss he had ever had in his adult life. Then she took off running out the door. "We have a grandpa. We have a new grandpa." Well, I guess, the Larkin children have just broken the ice and melted Mr. Woodard's cold, hard heart.

CHAPTER 2

MR. WOODARD'S PROPOSAL

W ell, as Mr. Woodard got up to leave the children met him and their mother on the porch. The older children asked, "Are you really going to be our grandfather?" "Well," Mr. Woodard replied, "I am not really your grandfather, I mean not legally that is, but, I will be happy to be a grandfather to you all." They were so excited. One by one they came up and gave him a big hug and kiss. "Come, now children," Mother said, "We are going to give Mr. Woodard a ride home." Jordan asked, "Mommy, can't we call Mr. Woodard Grandpa Woodard now that he is our new grandpa?" "Well," Mom responded, "we should ask Mr. Woodard." Jared asked, "What do you think Mr. Woodard?" "Well," Mr. Woodard replied, "I think that would be just ducky." All the children got a big kick out of that. And they all had a good laugh.

On the way to take Grandpa Woodard home, (he lived just blocks from the church,). The children started asking questions in an orderly fashion, of course. Angela was the first one to speak. "Grandpa Woodard, do you have a car?" "Oh, yes," Grandpa Woodard said, "I have a big Lincoln town car." Jared asked, "Is it big enough for all of us to ride in?" "Oh yes," Grandpa Woodard said; "if we can all fit in your Moms car, we can all fit in my car." "Oh that's great;" Gregory said, "then you can come out and visit us sometime during the week." "That I can," Grandpa Woodard answered, "that I can."

When Mrs. Pierce, came to take care of the children on Monday, the two little ones, Jordan and Jackson were so excited, they could hardly stand it. Jordan said, "We have some good news." "Yeah," Jackson said, "we have a new grandpa." "You do?" Mrs. Pierce asked, "And who might this new grandpa be?" "Well," Jordan replied, "it is Grandpa Woodard. He lives by the church we go to in town. Mrs. Pierce asked, "Do you mean Oliver Woodard?" Jordan responded, "That's what he told my mommy his name was." Mrs. Pierce replied, "That is a little hard for me to believe." Jordan asked, "Why is it hard for you to believe?" Mrs. Pierce responded, "Because I have known Mr. Woodard all my life, and he never liked little children. Everybody knows that." "Well," Jackson and Jordan said, "He sure likes us."

Now Mrs. Pierce; Olivia, was her first name, lived in the great big house, just down the road from the Larkins. The children would sometimes take some cookies Mrs. Larkin made down to Mrs. Pierce and visit with her on Saturdays. They liked spending time with Mrs. Pierce. Now Mrs. Larkin had asked Mrs. Pierce many times to come to church with them, but she always said. "No, thank you." But this Friday, when Mrs. Larkin, came home from work, Mrs. Pierce asked, "Would you mind if I tagged along with you to church on Sunday?" Mrs. Larkin replied, "Heavens, no, we would love to have you come with us."

Now, Mrs. Pierce used to go to church all the time before her husband died, but she got angry with God when he took her husband to heaven. Anyway, I guess, she isn't angry with God anymore, because she is going to church on Sunday. Mrs. Larkin was sure happy that Mrs. Pierce was going to church. She had been praying for her ever since she had met her. When the Larkins drove up to Mrs. Pierce's house Gregory got out and went to walk her to the car. She looked just beautiful. She had on a royal blue suit, and with her white hair, she looked stunning. "Mrs. Pierce," Stephanie remarked, "you look beautiful." "Well. Thank you very much," Mrs. Pierce replied, "it has been a long time since I really dressed up for anything. When the Larkin's got to church, everyone was so happy to see Mrs. Pierce that they did not notice the look on Mr. Woodard's face, but Mrs. Larkin did. From that moment, she started to pray for Mr. Woodard and Mrs. Pierce that she might be the right woman for Mr. Woodard.

You should have seen the look on Mrs. Pierce's face when all the children, right there in church went up to Mr. Woodard and gave him a big hug and kiss before they took their seats. Mrs. Pierce could not believe the response that the children got from Mr. Woodard. Why he put both his arms around each of those children and gave each one a big bear hug and a big kiss on the cheek. The Larkin children had certainly melted old Mr. Woodard's heart after all. Mrs. Pierce had such a smile on her face she could hardly sing the hymns. Well! Mrs. Pierce just kept smiling all the while she was singing, and Mrs. Larkin couldn't help looking over at the two of them standing there side-by-side, singing joyful hymns to God.

After the church service was over, Mr. Woodard said "how about all of us going out to a restaurant for dinner?" Mrs. Larkin replied, "That is a lot to take all of us out to a restaurant." Mr. Woodard responded, "I never had a family before, and I would like to take my new family out to eat. I would like to invite you to go along, Mrs. Pierce." "Well then," Mrs. Larkin answered, "I guess it is settled. We shall all go out to dinner." The children were so excited. They had not been out to dinner since their daddy went to heaven. There was not enough money to take six hungry children out to a restaurant. They all had the time of their lives. Stephanie ordered a hamburger and fries and a cola, Gregory also had a hamburger, fries, and a cola. Angela ordered chicken nuggets, fries, and a cola. Jared wanted a hot dog with ketchup and hot chocolate and fries. Jordan ordered the macaroni and cheese with milk and toast. Jackson ordered a peanut-butter and jelly sandwich and milk. Grandpa Woodard insisted that Mrs. Larkin and Mrs. Pierce and he have steak, and so they did, and a wonderful time was had by all.

The days flew by so fast, and in a week school would be out and Mrs. Pierce would be at the house all day, five days a week, while Mrs. Larkin worked. The children were already thinking about what they would do with their Grandpa Woodard this summer. Stephanie wanted to go to the beach and have a picnic and swim. Gregory wanted to go fishing, (just him and his grandpa, all alone). Angela wanted to go to the beach to swim with her sister. Jared, Jordan, and Jackson wanted to go to the beach also, but they wanted to play on the jungle gym set and go on all the rides. Well, it looked like Grandpa Woodard would have his hands full trying to get in everything that everyone wanted to do.

Well, the second week the children were out of school, here came Grandpa Woodard down the driveway. All the children ran over to greet him. They were so happy to see him. "Well, children," Grandpa Woodard said, "what do you think I have planned for today?" They were so excited. They couldn't even think. Grandpa Woodard asked, "Well children, if we can get Mrs. Pierce to go with us, we can go to the lake and have a picnic and swim and play on the jungle gym. What do you say to that?" The children were praying all the way to the house that Mrs. Pierce would agree to go. And sure enough, she said "yes, let's go." Grandpa Woodard had brought the whole lunch for everyone except Blake, that is. Blake still had his bottle. Blake was about seven or eight months by now. So he could sit up and crawl around pretty well. So they all piled into Grandpa Woodard's, big car and headed for the lake. The children were so excited. They could hardly contain themselves. So they all started singing songs about Jesus and God. They always sang songs about Jesus and God. Grandpa Woodard said; "Now first, we are going to go to the picnic tables and have our picnic and then we will go to the jungle gym and play with the young ones. And then we will go down by the lake and the older ones can swim, while the younger ones play in the sand on the beach." The children were so well behaved that Grandpa Woodard and Mrs. Pierce didn't have to scold them at all. They were gone so long that they barely got home before Mrs. Larkin came home from work. The children had a hard time waiting for each one to tell about their day. The little ones were allowed to go first, because they were so excited. And the older children had fun just listening to the little ones tell their story. Then Mrs. Pierce stayed and helped Mrs. Larkin fix a bite to eat. And they had another picnic under the big oak tree in the big front yard. It sure was a busy day.

Well, Grandpa Woodard came out frequently during that first summer in the big farmhouse in the country. He took Gregory and Jared fishing a lot, and they caught some pretty big fish. Jared caught one fish that was longer than his arm, and Grandpa Woodard had to help him pull it in. Boy, was he excited! There were many picnics by the lake and long rides in the country. And Grandpa Woodard even took them into town for ice cream once in awhile. And all the while, Mrs. Pierce always went along to help with the children.

Almost as quickly as it had come, summer was over, and the older children had to go back to school. Jordan turned five and also started school. She was so excited, but she was also sad because she had to leave little Jackson home alone. Jackson wasn't all alone as he had little Blake, and Blake was almost a year old. So he was almost walking and getting into everything, including Jackson's toys. So Jackson had his hands full keeping Blake from getting into too much trouble.

Christmas would soon be here, and there was a Christmas play at church. They were really excited about that. Everyone in church had a part in the play. Stephanie was Mary, the mother of Jesus. Gregory was the shepherd boy. And Angela, Jared, Jordan, and Jackson were angels. They just stood there and sang songs about Jesus and God. They could do that really well. Little Blake was the baby Jesus, because he was the only baby in the church at this time. Mrs. Larkin told Blake he had to lie there in that manger, keep his eyes closed, pretend he was sleeping, and that he couldn't make a sound. So he just laid there with his little eyes shut and listened to all the children sing song about Jesus and God. It was a beautiful play. Mrs. Pierce's son came to visit her for Christmas and spent a week there. He was a doctor in a big hospital in Baltimore—wherever that is, far away, out east somewhere. Anyway, he was a big man, about 6'3" tall and dark hair and big brown eyes and a huge smile. He sure reminded the children of their Daddy. He seemed like a kind man, and he really liked children. He operated on children in the big hospital in that big city of Baltimore, wherever that it is. He was a neurosurgeon, and his name was Conrad Pierce. He had never married, because he had spent most of his time studying to be a doctor. He was about 37 years old, just a year or so older than Mrs. Larkin.

Mrs. Larkin invited Mrs. Pierce, Conrad Pierce, and Grandpa Woodard over for Christmas dinner. The children were so excited that they could hardly wait. They were excited about what they would get from Santa and what they would get from Grandpa Woodard and Mrs. Pierce and Mommy, but they were mostly excited about Dr. Pierce coming to their house. They never had a doctor in the house before. Well, the Christmas service was beautiful. It was all about the baby Jesus, and the children were glued to every word that talked about the baby Jesus. They just loved to hear about Jesus. After the service was over, some of the children wanted to ride with Grandpa Woodard. So Jared and Jordan went with Grandpa Woodard. Stephanie and Angela went with Mr. Pierce and Gregory, and Jackson and Blake rode home with Mrs. Larkin. They all sang about Jesus and God all the way home. Mr. Pierce opened the door for Mrs. Larkin, who was carrying little Blake, and the rest just followed in after them. The house smelled so good with Mrs. Larkin's roast beef in the oven, potatoes, carrots, and onions cooking right alongside. There were apple, rhubarb, and cherry pies sitting on the counter and homemade bread and rolls under the towel on the counter. Mrs. Pierce made a wonderful salad and a fruit bowl, while the rolls baked in the oven. It would be a beautiful Christmas dinner, thought Dr. Pierce. Dr. Pierce said he would help Mrs. Larkin get the dinner on. So the older children had a day off from setting the table. Boy, were they happy about that.

Gregory went over to the piano and started playing Christmas songs, and they all joined in while Mr. Pierce and Mrs. Larkin got the meal on the table. Before you knew it, it was time to eat, and Mrs. Larkin asked Dr. Pierce to say the blessing. It was a wonderful meal, and Dr. Pierce said he would help Mrs. Larkin with the dishes. But Grandpa Woodard said he and Mrs. Pierce would do them. So that's the way it was. Dr. Pierce and Mrs. Larkin and the children went into the living room and started putting a puzzle together. They were getting a good start on the puzzle when Grandpa Woodard and Mrs. Pierce came into the living room. That meant it was time to open gifts.

The children all sat down on the floor in a circle with the adults around them. Grandpa Woodard and Mrs. Pierce sat on the sofa. Dr. Pierce sat on the big overstuffed chair and mother sat on the Ottoman. The smaller ones opened their gifts first, starting with Blake. He didn't care about the gifts. He just wanted to tear open the paper. Everyone had fun just watching him. He got a little dog on a string to pull round, a big stuffed teddy bear, some wooden blocks, and a big truck to ride in. Next was Jackson's turn. He was so excited he could hardly keep this little fingers from shaking. He got a train set, and tracks to go with it, magnetic alphabet letters that go on the refrigerator, and a tool belt with all kinds of tools. Jordan was next, her first gift was a baby doll, and lots of clothes to go with it, a bunch of makeup, cloths to dress up in with heels and a purse, and a set of dishes. Jared was next; he got a baseball, a bat, and glove. Mother told him; "you can only play with that outside. No playing with it in the house." "Yes, Mom" Jared replied. He also received a game to teach him how to handle and save money and a baseball cap. Angela was next; her first gift was a Barbie doll with lots of clothes, an art set, and jewelry set to make jewelry. Gregory received a model airplane to put together and paint; he got a guitar, which was his favorite gift, a puzzle to put together, and a marble game. Stephanie got clothes, a Monopoly game, dominoes, and Bible character cards. Then it was Mrs. Larkin's turn, she got some driving gloves, a beautiful scarf, and the children all put their money together, and with a little help from Grandpa Woodard, bought her a beautiful pair of earrings. Jordan said, "Mommy, they look just like diamonds." Mommy said, "They are the most beautiful earrings I have ever gotten, thank you so much." Dr. Pierce said he didn't have any gifts for anyone, but he reached in his pants pocket and pulled out his wallet and gave each of the children a $10 bill. Wow! Were they ever excited, and he turned to Mrs. Larkin and said "I would be pleased if you would join me for a dinner out for your Christmas present." Well, how could she refuse?

So then it was Grandpa Woodard's turn, and he received a pair of driving gloves, a beautiful scarf, a new wallet, and a box of chocolates from the children. He said; "This is the best Christmas I have had since I was a young boy. I never realized how much I missed by not having a family, and now God has blessed me with you children and a beautiful daughter Tiffany and a good friend in Olivia, and I would like you to open your presents, Olivia." Olivia opened her first gift. It was an apron, and then some Christmas tapes and CDs, a box of chocolates from the children, and Grandpa Woodard said, "Olivia. I have one more gift for you," and he put his hand into his pocket and pulled out a little box wrapped in beautiful Christmas paper, with a little bow on the top and ribbon all-around. She took the box, and with shaky hands she undid the ribbon and removed the bow and the paper and opened the box. It was an engagement ring. Everyone was so excited and just then Grandpa Woodard said, "Olivia, would you marry me and make my life complete?" Mrs. Pierce, looked him right in the eye and said, "why, yes, Oliver, I certainly will!" Angela said in a loud voice, "does that mean Mrs. Pierce will be my grandma?" Everyone laughed, Conrad remarked, "that's a huge act to follow, and I was going to take you shopping, for Christmas Mom, but maybe you just want money, so you can take your time picking out your dress and whatever else you need for your wedding." "I will think about it for a little while," Olivia answered, "but thank you honey. You don't have to do all that." "Nonsense," Conrad said, "I would like to pay for the whole wedding if you would let me. I will also pay for the food and the hall. This is going to be so much fun, and I won't have to worry about you so much anymore; anyway, congratulations to both of you." And he got up and walked over and gave his Mom a big hug and kiss and he put his arms around Oliver and said, "Dad, this is going to be so neat." "Gee, Dr. Pierce," Jordan said, "now you will have a Dad. Are you ever lucky?" "I sure am lucky," Dr. Pierce said, as he bent down and gave her a big hug also. "So if my Mother is going to be your Grandmother Jordan, what does that make me?" "I don't know," Jordan said. "I guess you are still just Dr. Pierce."

Chapter 3

The Wedding

Now Mrs. Pierce didn't have any grandchildren, but she loved the Larkin children from the time she started to take care of them, so she said, "I would love to have you call me Grandma. But of course, not until after we are married." "Well," Grandpa Woodard said, "I guess we had better get married right away then." Conrad Pierce spoke up and said, "You can't get married without me here, because I intend to give the bride away." Mrs. Pierce got tears in her eyes, because she was so happy. And she knew that her son, Conrad would not be able to make it back home again before summer. She asked Oliver, if they could set the date when Conrad could come home in the summer. Grandpa Woodard agreed, and the date was set for Saturday, June 28th. That made everyone happy, except for the children, who thought June 28th was a long time to wait. Mother said, "But sometimes, we don't have control over when things happen." Well in the meantime, they still had Mrs. Pierce with them during the week and they all went to church together and had dinner together on Sundays.

The children talked it over and thought back to how lonely they were after their Daddy went to heaven to be with Jesus. And how God had given them a Grandpa, and now a Grandma to be with them and take care of them and play with them, and they all prayed and thanked God for all He had done for them: the fact that He had brought so much happiness into their lives and also the fact that their Mother was able to work and take care of them.

The children were very excited; because Grandpa Woodard and Mrs. Pierce agreed to help drive the children home from their activities that they had after school such as: two nights a week Gregory took drama in school, and took guitar and singing lessons after school. Stephanie took drama in the school and took dancing after school two nights a week. Grandpa Woodard saw to it that they both got home on those nights. The rest of the children came home on the bus and Mrs. Pierce took care of them till Mrs. Larkin came home from work. The children were so happy that they were able to do the things they liked to do, and the time seemed to go by so fast. Before you knew it, the snow was gone and spring was here, and summer was just around the corner.

Everyone in town was so excited about Grandpa Woodard and Mrs. Pierce's wedding. The whole town wanted to come to the wedding. Now that presented some problems, because the church was quite small, but Grandpa Woodard just said, "If it is a nice day we will just bring the wedding outside and have it on the church lawn." Well, the children had a good laugh, because they had never seen anyone get married outside. Where would the music come from? The church-yard wasn't much bigger than the church building. The children wondered what the big worry was all about. God would take care of it all, because after all, it was God who gave them Grandpa Woodard, and He would make sure that this would work out too. So the children got together and started to pray to God that He would take care of everything, and left it up to Him. And so it came to be that the day the children had waited for so long; the day that they thought would never come finally arrived. And guess what? God did indeed take care of everything. It was a beautiful day, the sun was shining, and there was a slight breeze. It was the most beautiful day of the summer, I believe. Gregory sure would have liked to go fishing with Grandpa Woodard, and the girls and the young ones sure would have liked to have gone to the lake, swimming and playing on the jungle gym. But they all knew that they had prayed for this beautiful day for a purpose, and now the time had come for the wedding.

The churchyard was beautiful, ladies from all around the church within six or seven blocks, brought pots of beautiful flowers and lined both sides of the sidewalk, going up to the church steps and on up the steps on both sides. There were hanging flowers people had put on both sides of Grandpa Woodard and Mrs. Pierce and behind the Pastor. The children had never seen anything like that outside a church before and said so. They also had wheeled the piano out onto the porch of the church, and it was just behind the Pastor on the right side. Jordan remarked, "So, there is going to be music, God thought of everything." The children just smiled at each other when they saw the piano.

Mrs. Larkin had taken the children shopping and bought them all new clothes and a new dress for herself. Now Stephanie had on a powder blue dress and wore her hair flowing down over her shoulders and had on white sandals. Jared said, "You sure look beautiful, Stephanie." Stephanie answered in a very loving way; "Thank you very much, Jared." Gregory had on a light brown suit and a white shirt with a multicolored tie, new brown shoes which kind of hurt his feet, because this was the first time he wore them. He sure wished he had his tennis shoes on. Jordan said she thought he was handsome, just like their daddy. Gregory smiled at her with a little tear in his eye and said, "Thank you, little sis." Angela wore a bright yellow summer dress with large dark blue flowers on it and Navy sandals. Her hair hung over her shoulders and pulled back above her ears with barrettes. She looked a lot like her mother and Stephanie, only with brown hair. She also had a navy ribbon in her hair with a big bow at the top. She had bangs, which came down over her forehead. Grandpa Woodard told her she looked just like an angel. Jared was dressed in a black suit, a white shirt, and black and white striped tie, black leather shoes. He also wished he could have worn his old tennis shoes. Stephanie told him he was a handsome little man, which made him feel a little bit better. He said, "thank you Stephanie, you look pretty too." Stephanie said, "Thank you, little Bro." Jordan wore a beautiful red dress with a full skirt that stuck out like a wedding dress all around, and a band with a big red bow in the back. She had red barrettes in her hair and black satin shoes with buckles. Dr. Pierce came up to her and bent down and took her hands in his and said, "Jordan, you look just like a bride yourself." Her face got almost as red as her dress, and she said, "Awe, I'm not a bride." Everyone had a hearty laugh, she was so cute. Little Jackson looked just like a tiny little man with his new black suit with a white shirt, and a tie with different colored balloons on it. He really liked his tie. Mrs. Larkin said he was her precious little man. Little Blake was dressed in a dark brown suit and a white shirt and a bow tie and a pair of black dress shoes. He wanted to take his tie off, and he was walking all over by now, and everyone had to take their turn, keeping track of him. He was as cute as a bug's ear. Mrs. Larkin had on a royal blue dress with a full skirt with a band that fastened tight around her waist. It had short sleeves and a soft curved neckline, very plain. She wore a single strand of pearls around her neck and royal blue shoes. She looked like she stepped right out of heaven. And you should have seen Dr. Pierce when he first saw her. His eyes got a little bigger, his mouth dropped just a little, and he just stared at her. She didn't see him, because she was helping little Jordan with her big bow in the back of her dress, but all the other children saw how Dr. Pierce looked at their mother, and they looked at each other,(at least the older ones did) and their minds started thinking.

It seemed like forever that the children were standing outside the little church. They had to be there for pictures before the wedding, and there would be more pictures with Grandpa and Grandma Woodard after the wedding, but the children were very patient, because after all, this was the big day they had waited for almost all year. Then all of a sudden the music began to play, and around the corner came Grandpa Woodard's big town car with Dr. Pierce driving. Dr. Pierce got out and opened the back door and reached in and took Mrs. Pierce by the hand and helped her out of the car. She was just beautiful. She had on a two-piece rose colored suit with a small white handbag, white gloves, and white heels. She had tiny bright roses in her beautiful white hair, which flowed beautifully around her face, and in her left hand she had a beautiful bouquet of white and tiny bright roses. She was absolutely stunning. Grandpa Woodard's eyes were fixed on Mrs. Pierce, and there were tears in his eyes, as her son Conrad began to walk her up the sidewalk of the church to where Grandpa Woodard and Pastor Tom Parker stood. Everyone stood in amazement as they watched her walk up the sidewalk. She was beautiful. The Larkin children were really getting excited now. Pretty soon they would have a new Grandma. The children were sure excited about how God worked all this out, and the day was just perfect. Most of the town turned out for the wedding. No one wanted to miss Mr. Woodard's and Mrs. Pierce's wedding, after all, they both lived in that town all their lives. The children were really surprised that the wedding didn't take very long. They were so excited. Little Jackson ran up to the newlyweds and said, "Grandpa Woodard, Grandma Pierce." Everyone started laughing, and they stopped and explained that now, Mrs. Pierce's last name was Woodard. So Grandpa and Grandma Woodard stopped right there and took Jackson, Jordan, and Jared aside and explained that when a man and a woman get married the woman usually takes the man's last name as her own and from then on, they could call her Grandma Woodard. They said that was a lot easier than having to say two different names.

After the rest of the pictures were taken, we left to go to the VFW hall for the wedding dinner or reception, as most people call it. There was really a lot of food. The children had a hard time picking out what they wanted. They were always told not to take more than they could eat, but they could always have seconds. So Pastor Parker said the blessing, and Grandpa and Grandma Woodard went first. Then came the Pastor, then Dr. Pierce went with Mrs. Larkin, who was carrying Little Blake in one arm. Dr. Pierce carried two plates, while Mrs. Larkin served the food on both plates with her free hand. They had two tables with food, and people went on both sides of each table. Stephanie went next with Jackson and helped him fill his plate. And then Gregory went with Jordan and helped her with her plate. And then Angela went next and helped Jared with his plate. Grandpa and Grandma Woodard sure were proud of their grandchildren, how they behaved, and how well mannered they were with "No thanks, I don't want that" or "Yes, please, I would like some of that." As always, the children sat in an order so that the older ones could help the younger ones, and Blake sat beside Mrs. Larkin. Grandpa and Grandma Woodard sat in the center of the long table with Mrs. Larkin and Dr. Pierce on either side of them, and the children on both sides. They were all facing the people. The children sure felt funny, setting in front of all the people. But it was a wonderful dinner, and the children all found enough food they liked to fill them up. They were reminded to leave room for cake.

Jared said, "Grandpa and Grandma Woodard are you going to be living in Grandma's big house by us?" "Yes," Grandpa Woodard said. Jared asked, "Then can I ride home with you tonight?" Grandpa Woodard responded, "Well, we are not going home tonight. We are going on a honeymoon."

Jordan asked, "What's a honeymoon?" "Well," Grandpa Woodard said, "When people get married, they go away some place to get to know one another a little better for a few days. Then they come home to spend time with the rest of the family." Jared said, "But you already know each other—if you didn't know each other, you would not have gotten married." Everyone got a little chuckle out of that.

Jackson asked, "Who is going to take care of us, while you are gone?" Mother responded, "I am taking a few days off work, and Dr. Pierce is also going to be staying at Grandma Woodard's for a few days before he goes back to Baltimore next Friday. So he will be here to help out if we need him." The older children looked at one another and thought, we are going to have to have a meeting when we get home.

After the dinner was over, everyone said their goodbyes to Grandpa and Grandma Woodard. As they drove off in Grandpa Woodard's big town car there were tin cans, hanging behind it. Jackson remarked, "I can't understand why they fastened tin cans to Grandpa Woodard's car." We all started off for home too. The four little ones were so tired from such a long day, they fell fast asleep. Dr. Pierce had to help Mrs. Larkin carry the little ones in, so Mrs. Larkin asked Dr. Pierce if he would like a cup of coffee. Dr. Pierce answered, "That would be wonderful, and that big house of my Mother's will take some getting used to. It will be a little lonely up there all by myself." Stephanie said to Gregory, "we need to have a meeting." So Stephanie, Gregory, and Angela met in Stephanie's bedroom. Angela said, "What's going on?" "Well," Stephanie responded, "remember when Mom had a meeting with us and said we should all pray that Grandpa Woodard and Mrs. Pierce would get together and get married, because she said she thought that was what God wanted for them." Angela answered, "And she was right, it sure looks like God did a good job." "Well, anyway," Stephanie replied, "did you see the way Dr. Pierce looked at our Mom at Grandpa and Grandma's wedding? Well, I think maybe that is what God wants for Dr. Pierce and Mom." "Oh, my gosh," Angela asked, "How would they ever get to know one another? Dr. Pierce lives clear out east in Baltimore, and Mom is here in Minnesota." "Well, I don't know," Gregory mentioned, "but that is God's problem. Maybe we should start praying right now, while Dr. Pierce is still here." "That's a good idea," Stephanie said, "that's why I called you up here." And so the three children got down on their knees and prayed to God that He would work a miracle with Dr. Pierce and their mom. After their prayer, they got up and went to the dining room where Dr. Pierce and their mother was talking and having coffee. They were looking at each other and smiling. They said goodnight to Dr. Pierce and gave their Mother a big hug and kiss and told her that they had already said their prayers and were off to bed.

The week went by so fast; the children could hardly believe it was time for Dr. Pierce to leave. They had had so much fun, they went swimming at least three times and went on picnics. Dr. Pierce took the older boys fishing, and he even took the three older children bowling. That was so much fun; they had never been bowling before. Stephanie, Gregory, and Angela were so excited when they got home. They almost woke up the younger children. They all started talking at once, and Mother had to quiet them down and only allow one of them to talk at a time. Well, anyway, after the children finished telling their Mother all about their bowling and how they all went to eat burgers and fries and cola and then they went for ice cream. Mrs. Larkin thought that Dr. Pierce was spoiling the children. The children went upstairs and said their prayers and went right off to bed and slept right through the night.

The little ones were up bright and early on Friday morning, and someone knocked at the door just before breakfast. Mrs. Larkin told Jared to answer the door and

Jordan, Jackson, and little Blake all ran after Jared, almost beating him to the door. The children were so excited, because Grandpa and Grandma Woodard were back from their honeymoon. Jackson said, "I guess, by now you got to know each other." Grandpa and Grandma Woodard and Mother laughed. Grandpa Woodard said; "we figured Conrad would still be sleeping in on his last day here and we knew you would be up early with the children, so we stopped here first." Grandma and Grandpa Woodard asked, "Did you miss us?" Jackson answered, "We sure did miss you, but we sure had fun with Dr. Pierce while you were gone."

The three older children, heard all the noise and laughing and had to come and find out what was going on. Stephanie, Gregory, and Angela were very happy to see that their Grandparents were back. Everyone had a lot to talk about. Everyone was so excited to tell everyone else, what they did all week that Mother had to quiet the children down and let Grandpa and Grandma Woodard talk first. After all, they were the ones who had just returned from their honeymoon. Now that they knew one another better, they had lots to say, I guess. Just about the time the last one was done talking, and that would have been Stephanie, (because the little ones always went first,) someone knocked at the door. Jared said, "I know who that is," as he opened the door, and sure enough, it was Dr. Pierce. Mom and Grandma Woodard were busy making breakfast. Mom said, "You children come help me and let Grandma go in the living room with Grandpa and Dr. Pierce to tell him about their trip." "Trip," Jared said, "I thought it was a honeymoon." Everyone got a chuckle out of that comment. After breakfast, Dr. Pierce and Grandpa and Grandma Woodard went back to the big house. Grandpa and Grandma Woodard had to get unpacked and Dr. Pierce had to pack, because he had to leave that night to go back to Baltimore. As Dr. Pierce went out the door, he turned and asked Mrs. Larkin, if she would go out to dinner with him before he left for the plane. Grandpa and Grandma Woodard said they would watch the children. Mrs. Larkin said, "I would love to." Jordan asked, "Why is Dr. Pierce taking Mama out to dinner in July, it can't be a Christmas present in July." They all had a good laugh over that comment.

The day went by fast for the Larkin children; there was so much to do outside in the summer. Before you knew it, Grandpa and Grandma Woodard's big town car came pulling into the driveway. Grandpa and Grandma Woodard got out and went toward the house. They sat down on the big porch swing and Mrs. Larkin came out onto the porch. She had on a pink flowered dress, and pink shoes to match. She had a light, white sweater draped over one arm, just in case she got cool later on. The older children were looking at Dr. Pierce. As he turned around from giving Jackson a big hug goodbye, and when his eyes looked into their mother's eyes, the children looked at each other and smiled. Dr. Pierce quickly gave the rest of the children a big hug and kiss goodbye and gave Grandpa Woodard a handshake, and he also shook hands with Gregory, then he bent over and gave Grandma Woodard, a big hug and a kiss on the cheek, and said, "Goodbye Mom, I guess I will see you around Christmas." "Christmas;" Jordan remarked, "That's a long time away. First we had to wait for Christmas last year. Then we had to wait for the wedding, and now we have to wait for Christmas again, that's a long time away." "The time will go by fast," Dr. Pierce said, "you just wait and see."

CHAPTER 4

SUMMER WITH GRANDMA AND GRANDPA WOODARD

Grandpa and Grandma Woodard, sat on the big porch swing and called all the children together around them and Grandpa Woodard said, "Well now,(Grandpa said well a lot), each of you have to tell us when your birthdays are, so we can write them down so we won't forget them. Our memory is not as good as it used to be. Jordan said, "What happened to your memory?" "Well," Grandpa Woodard said, "Grandma and I are just getting old." "I am old too," Jordan said, "I am six years old." Grandpa Woodard remarked, "You are getting big, let's start with Blake. How old is Blake." Stephanie answered, "Blake will be two years old on October 25th." Jordan said, "My birthday is before Blake's, I will be six on July 23rd." Grandma Woodard replied, "Boy, that is soon." Grandpa asked, "Whose birthday is next?" Jackson said; "My birthday is September 15th, and I will be four." Grandma Woodard said, "Boy, you really are getting big, aren't you?" Jackson answered with, "Next year after summer is over, I will be going to school." Jordan said, "Well, I am going to school all day long this year." Grandma Woodard replied, "You are a big girl." Jared said, "I already had my birthday, it was May 18th, and I am eight years old." Grandma Woodard asked, "How did we miss your birthday?" "Well," Jared replied, "Mama said you and Grandpa Woodard was so busy getting ready for your wedding that we just had a quiet birthday party like we used to do before." Grandpa Woodard said, "Well, we will see that you get a present anyway." "Okay," Grandma Woodard remarked, "who is next?" Angela mentioned, "My birthday was April 28th, and I am 10 years old." Grandma Woodard replied, "My, you are really growing up fast; we should really try and catch up on all these birthdays that took place early in the year."

The older children sure were excited about the fact that they were going to get a birthday present, even if it was late. Grandpa Woodard asked, "Well, what about you, Gregory?" Gregory replied, "My birthday was February 24th, and I am 12 years old." Grandpa Woodard said, "You are getting to be quite a young man." Grandma Woodard remarked, "Stephanie it's your turn." Stephanie answered with, "I was 14 years old on January 30th." "Okay," Grandpa Woodard said, "now all of you will have to go inside and get a pen and paper and write down a couple or three things you would like to have, and we will see what we will get for you." The children were really excited, so all the children and Grandpa and Grandma Woodard went into the house. The small ones went and sat at the dining room table, and patiently waited while Angela, Gregory, and Stephanie got paper and pens to write out their list. Stephanie helped Blake, Gregory helped Jackson, and Angela helped Jordan. Jared was eight years old; he was big enough to write down what he wanted by himself. While the children were busy writing, Grandma and Grandpa Woodard got busy in the kitchen getting cookies ready and making Kool-Aid. After their lists were done, they all had cookies and Kool-Aid. Then they got out the money game that Jared got for Christmas last year and had a wonderful time learning how to spend and save money.

By the time Mrs. Larkin got home, all the children were fast asleep, and Grandma and Grandpa Woodard were relaxing at the dining room table playing Dominoes with the Dominoes Stephanie got for Christmas last year.

Before you knew it, it was almost Jordan's birthday. Mrs. Larkin said she could have her birthday party at the lake, and they could have a picnic and a cake, and she could invite one friend. Boy was she ever excited about that. She would invite her friend from Sunday school, Jill Hanson. She could hardly wait till she finished making her invitation, so she could give it to Jill in Sunday school. Stephanie helped her with the cutting and some coloring. Jordan's birthday finally came. It was a beautiful day. All the children were busy getting their bathing suits, towels, and toys together to take with them to the lake. They took Frisbees, bat and ball, little pails, and shovels for playing in the sand for Jackson and Blake. Grandpa Woodard said he would leave early and take Jackson, Jordan, Angela and Grandma with him to pick up Jill. He said he knew right where she lived. He also took quite a bit of the stuff they needed for the picnic, dishes, cold drinks, coals for the fire, and the hamburgers. He said he would get the hamburgers started, so they could eat when Tiffany got there. Little Blake really wanted to go with Grandma and Grandpa Woodard, but he was really good about it when Mommy said he would have to wait. Jared was real good about keeping Blake busy, while Stephanie and Gregory helped Mommy get ready. All of a sudden Mommy said, "It's time to go." Jared got Little Blake in his car seat while Stephanie and Gregory helped Mom pack the car, and off they went. Jared said, "I hope we didn't forget anything." Mom replied, "I believe we have everything." Stephanie responded with, "I checked off everything on the list." They no sooner got out of the driveway than they started singing Bible songs. Before you knew it they were at the lake. Grandpa Woodard had gotten a picnic table right by the sandy beach, just off the water.

The children were so excited they could hardly wait, especially Jordan, because it was her birthday. Things started happening right away. By the time Mommy and Grandma Woodard and Stephanie got the table ready, Grandpa Woodard had the hamburgers and hot dogs cooked. Mrs. Larkin had a kind of highchair, which fit right at the end of the picnic table for Blake, and as always, the children sat the same way they did at home, so the bigger ones could help the little ones. Grandpa Woodard had to get an extra table, because there were so many of them and Tiffany had brought a special tablecloth, plates, cups, and napkins, because Jordan's favorite thing was "The Little Mermaid". Jordan said, "That's because we're having my party by the lake." They had a wonderful birthday dinner, and then it was time for cake. "Boy," Jackson said, "Mom sure is good at building cakes." They all had a good laugh, and they all had a lot of good cake. Everyone sang "Happy Birthday" to Jordan. Then it was time to open up gifts before they could go swimming, or on the jungle gym, or whatever Mom said they were going to do first. The first gift Jordan opened was from her very best friend Jill. Jill gave Jordan a "Little Mermaid" doll. Jordan was so happy. Blake said, "Open mine, open mine, I wrapped it myself." It was wrapped in blue paper, and it was a big box. Blake said, "Hurry, hurry." I believe Blake was more excited than Jordan, anyway; Jordan finally got the box open; it was bright red beach ball. She said, "thank you so much Blake, I just love it." "Open ours next," Jackson said, "It's from Jared and me. We wrapped it together." It was wrapped in bright red paper, because they knew Jordan liked red best. Jordan finally got it open, and it was a jump rope and a set of Jack's. "Oh! Thank you, Jared and Jackson; we will really have fun with those today." Angela's gift was next. Her gift was wrapped in green paper with different colored balloons and happy birthday, written on it. Jordan was hurrying to get the paper off, and then she had to open the box. It was a ring-toss game. "Boy, will this really be fun," Jordan said, "thank you Angela." Now Gregory and Stephanie went together and got her a gift. It was wrapped in "Little Mermaid" paper and tied with a big bow. Jordan said, "That is just beautiful." Inside was three Bible story books, and two Bible activity books, some color crayons, some colored pencils and a first-grade workbook. "Oh, boy," Jordan said, "this will be so much fun. We can all read the Bible story books together. Thank you so much Stephanie and Gregory." Then she went over and gave each one of her brothers and sisters, a big hug and kiss. Then she opened her gift from Grandpa and Grandma Woodard. It was a small package, about eight or 10 inches long, 1 inch high, and about 5 inches wide. It was wrapped in "Little Mermaid" paper also with a small pink bow. Jordan was very careful opening it. It was almost like she was afraid something was going to jump out at her. There was tissue paper inside, and when Jordan pulled back the tissue paper, there was just silence. She looked out at Grandpa and Grandma with a blank stare. Everyone was so quiet. Jackson said, "What is it? What is it?" "Well," Jordan replied, "it is a picture of a bicycle, a bright red bicycle. "Do you mean?" That's about as far as Jordan got because Grandpa said, "I sure do. In my garage there is a big red bicycle that looks just like that picture." "Oh!" Tiffany said, "Now that is way too much, way too much." "Now," Grandpa Woodard said, "I never had any children or grandchildren before, so you just let me have a little fun." I think Grandpa Woodard was just as excited as Jordan. Jordan said, "Oh, Grandpa and Grandma, I am so happy I could burst." "Oh, you can't do that," Grandpa Woodard said, "Who would ride your bike when we get home?" Everyone laughed. Well, there were more gifts to open. The last one was from Mom, which was a big box wrapped in "guess what"? "The Little Mermaid" paper, and had a big red bow on it. She took her time opening this gift. She got the paper off and opened the box and peeled back the tissue paper, and there was a beautiful blue dress with little mermaid's sewed into the skirt. Jordan looked up at her Mom with tears in her eyes. "Oh Mamma, I just love it. Did you make it just for me?" "Yes," Mother said, "just for my little girl." There were also two short sets just for the summer and some bows for her hair. Jordan said, "This was my best birthday ever." With that Mother said, "We had better get over to the jungle gyms, right away." And off they went. Grandpa Woodard remarked, "I will start putting some of these things in the trunk."

By the time the children were done playing on the jungle gyms. Grandpa Woodard had almost all the presents and other boxes put in the trunk. And Grandpa and Grandma and Mom sat at the picnic table and watched as the children played in the lake. Blake and Jackson mostly played in the sand with their pails and shovels. Tiffany looked at the children playing and having so much fun, and she looked at Grandpa and Grandma Woodard, who was also watching the children and Tiffany said, "God has been so good to me; I just thank and praise Him for bringing both of you into my life. The children are so happy." She had tears in her eyes as she spoke. Grandma Woodard said, "I feel the same way. I didn't notice how lonely I was out here all by myself, till you moved in next door with your children, and you, my dear Oliver, have made my life almost complete. The only thing that could make my life more complete would be to have Conrad living closer to me, so I could see him more often."

It was getting late, and they had to drop off Jill before they went home. So, Tiffany called the children and had them go and change clothes in the shower room at the beach. When they started to get into the cars, Grandpa Woodard remarked; "We haven't had any ice cream yet. You can't have a birthday party and not have any ice cream, can you?" "Oh, no," the children said, altogether. "Okay," Mother replied. So off they went to get ice cream. Well it looks like that was a grand day for sure.

Sure enough, the summer just flew by. Grandpa Woodard, Gregory, and Jared went fishing at the end of August and caught the biggest bunch of Walleyes you ever saw. They must have had 20 or 30 fish. Grandpa and Grandma Woodard had a big fish fry at their big farmhouse. Grandpa invited some friends from church over just to help eat up all the fish. Grandma Woodard and Mom did all the frying and Grandpa and some of the other men did the cleaning. And the other ladies brought all kinds of food to go with the fish. Blake and Jackson said they didn't like fish, but once they took one bite of Mamma and Grandma Woodard's fried fish, they couldn't get enough.

Time has a way of going on and on and on, and before you knew it, it was time to go back to school. The children were excited about that. Especially Jordan was going to be going to school all day long. Jordan was so excited to come home and play school with Jackson, and Jackson was just as excited when Jordan came home from school. But one day Jordan came home from school, and Jackson couldn't play with her. He was sick. Grandma Woodard said, "Jackson has a real sore throat, he can hardly swallow." Mother said she would take him to the doctor, first thing in the morning. After all the children got on the bus for school, Mother put Jackson in her car and off they went to the doctor's office. Jackson couldn't remember ever being in the doctor's office before. He wished he felt better, so he could have enjoyed playing with all the toys in the doctor's office.

Mother mentioned, "Dr. Larson is the doctor you are going to see, he is a very nice man." Jackson replied, "I don't want to see Dr. Larson, I want to see Dr. Pierce." "Oh Jackson," Mother answered, "Dr. Pierce is very far away. He is in Baltimore." Jackson said, "Wherever that is." Then all of a sudden, a very pretty lady said, "Jackson Larkin."

Jackson lifted his head up off his mother's lap and Mother said, "We have to go in and see the doctor now, Jackson." Mrs. Larkin picked up Jackson and carried him into the doctor's examination room. There was a long bed in there and it was really high off the floor. Mommy laid Jackson on the bed and took his hand in hers. Mommy started to tell Jackson what would happen when Dr. Larson came into the room. "The doctor is going to take your temperature. That tells the doctor how warm or cold your body is." Mother went on to tell Jackson that the doctor would ask him to open his mouth real wide and say ah. "Can you do that Jackson?" Jackson said, "Yes", and he opened his mouth real wide. Mother replied, "That's really good Jackson, you did a good job." And right then, in walked Dr. Larson. Dr. Larson was kind of short; he sure didn't look like Dr. Pierce. He said, "Hello, Jackson." Jackson said. "How do you know my name?" "Well," Dr. Larson answered, "It's right here on my chart." Jackson asked, "What's a chart?" "Well," Dr. Larson remarked, "a chart is where I write down everything I do to you and everything I find out about you." Jackson asked, "Like how old I am?" "Why yes," Dr. Larson replied, "I have your age, right here. You are three years old, is that right?" "Well," Jackson answered, "next week I'm going to be four years old." "Boy," Dr. Larson said, "you are getting bigger, just while you are sitting here." Mommy smiled. Dr. Larson asked, "Now, Jackson, can you open your mouth wide in say ah for me please," Jackson opened his mouth real wide and said ah. Dr. Larson put a flat stick on Jackson's tongue and pressed down. "My," Dr. Larson said, "his tonsils are really swollen. I am going to give him some penicillin to take care of the infection, but they are going to have to come out as soon as possible. The penicillin will take care of the infection by the middle of next week. And I believe we should operate by next Friday, or it will just come back again. You can call and schedule an appointment with my secretary in a day or so." Tiffany said, "Thank you." Jackson asked, "Are you going to see if I am hot or cold?" Tiffany smiled and said. "He wants to know if you are going to take his temperature." Dr. Larson remarked, "I really don't need to Jackson; the medicine I gave your mother will take care of any fever if there is one. Your mother can take your temperature at home, if she needs to." "Okay," Jackson said. On the way home, Jackson was very quiet. Mother asked him what he was thinking about. He said, "I want Dr. Pierce to operate on me." Mother responded, "Dr. Pierce is a long way away, and he probably is too busy to take time off work to come here. Besides, he operates on people's brains, not on their tonsils." Jackson never said another word all the way home. "Well," Grandpa Woodard said when they got home, "What did the doctor say?" Tiffany answered, "Jackson has to have his tonsils out, probably next week, maybe Friday." Jackson said, "I want to have Dr. Pierce operate on me." Tiffany remarked, "I tried to tell him that wasn't possible." "Well," Grandma Woodard replied, "we don't know for sure that that is impossible, now do we?"

CHAPTER 5

JACKSON'S OPERATION

M ost everyone thought Dr. Pierce could not make it
clear to Minnesota from Baltimore, (wherever that
is) to operate on Jackson, but that didn't deter Jackson from
taking the matter to God. Jackson thought, "After all, God
can do anything." So he decided that he had better start
praying that Dr. Pierce would be able to come, and somehow
God would work it out. Grandma Woodard stayed and fixed
supper, while Mommy spent her time rocking and com-
forting Jackson in the big living room. Jackson could only
have some soup and juice, because his throat hurt so much.
All the children talked about Jackson's operation. They had
never known anyone who had an operation before, except for
Gregory, who broke his arm when he was five years old. And
really the only ones who remembered that were Gregory and
Stephanie because Angela and Jared were too young, and
Jordan and Jackson and Blake weren't even born yet. After
dinner, Grandpa and Grandma gave all the children goodbye
hugs and kisses and left to go home. The children cleaned up
the kitchen and came and consoled Jackson. The time went
by fast, and before long, it was time to go to bed.

After Grandma and Grandpa Woodard got home,
Grandma Woodard called Dr. Pierce as soon as possible.
Hardly before she got her jacket off, she was on the phone.

"Well, hello Mother," Conrad asked, "what brings you to call during the week?" Grandma Woodard always called Dr. Pierce on weekends because it was cheaper, you know. Grandma Woodard started to tell Dr. Pierce about little Jackson needing to have his tonsils out, possibly next Friday, and how Jackson didn't want Dr. Larson to operate on him. He wanted Dr. Pierce to come out here from Baltimore, (wherever that is) Jackson said. "Well," Conrad said with a hardy laugh, "it looks like I have myself a fan. Now, how can we let the little guy down, I am going to have to do some checking around and see if I am going to be busy next week. Oh, and don't say anything to Jackson or Tiffany, I would like to surprise them both, and just in case I can't make it, I don't want to disappoint them, either. Oh, and I will need to call Dr. Larson and see what he says about all of this." "Okay," Olivia responded, "you can call me back on Monday or Tuesday." "Okay," Conrad replied, and he said goodbye and told his mom he loved her.

The weekend was pretty quiet, because all the children stayed in the house to give Jackson some company, so he wouldn't get lonely. Gregory and Stephanie helped Mom around the house, and Angela and Jared took turns reading to the little ones while they sat on the floor around Jackson, feeling sorry for him. Grandpa and Grandma Woodard took the five older children to church, but Blake wanted to stay home with Mommy and Jackson, and keep him company. The Sunday school teacher prayed for Jackson, and that made all the children feel good. When Grandpa and Grandma Woodard and all the other children got home, Mommy had dinner ready for them. Boy, were they ever hungry. Jackson was feeling a little better and could eat a little easier by Sunday. The children had to tell Jackson that all the teachers at church prayed for him in the Sunday school classes. Jackson smiled a great big smile. He was praying too, but not for him to get well. Grandpa Woodard said the blessing and prayed that Jackson would be well enough to get his tonsils out on Friday. They had already decided that Grandpa and Grandma Woodard would stay over the weekend with all the other children and Mommy would stay at the hospital with Jackson throughout the weekend. Wednesday night, Grandpa Woodard called and told Tiffany that they would be gone all morning Thursday, but they would be home by noon. The children didn't have school on Thursday, so Tiffany said, "well then, let's have a big meal at noon, because Jackson can't have anything to eat after 1:00 on Thursday afternoon, and nothing to drink after midnight."

Dr. Larson called on Thursday morning and asks how Jackson was doing, and said, "Everything is all ready for the operation Friday morning. So if you could be here by 7:00 a.m. that would be fine." Mrs. Larkin said, "We will be there at 7:00 a.m." The children didn't have school on Friday, either. There was a teacher's conference on both Thursday and Friday. The children were excited that they had four whole days off from school, but they were also kind of sad that Jackson would be in the hospital all four days. They didn't like that. Jackson was excited that he would have his Mama all to himself for four days. Dr. Larson had barely hung up the phone, when Jackson asked Mommy, if she would pray for him for his operation. Mommy said, "Yes, of course." She and all the children (even two year-old Blake), folded his little hands and prayed with the others. Mommy started the prayer. "Dear God in heaven, we ask that You will be with Jackson tomorrow and give him peace and comfort about his operation," and Mommy went on and prayed a lot of things for Jackson and for Dr. Larson, but Jackson was praying a whole different prayer. Jackson was praying to himself. "Dear God, I know I am just little, but Mommy says You hear all our prayers, so God, I need You to hear my prayer today. Dear God, I don't ask for much, but would You please get Dr. Pierce here in time for my operation. I sure would like to have him for my doctor, and there is still time God because the operation isn't till tomorrow, and that's enough time for him to get here from Baltimore, wherever that is. So God, that's all I'm going to ask You for, Amen." Mother finished her prayer just about the same time, Jackson ended his prayer and all the children said, "Amen." Jordan asked, "Are you scared, Jackson?" Jackson answered, "Not anymore, because Mommy says God hears all our prayers, and He answers them. Isn't that right Mommy?" "Why yes, Jackson," Mommy replied, "He sure does." Jordan, Jackson, and Blake played very quietly coloring pictures, while Angela and Jared set the table for a big lunch, because Grandpa and Grandma were coming for lunch. Stephanie and Gregory were helping Mommy fix the big lunch. It seemed odd that they were eating a big lunch in the middle of the day, but it was going to be special because it was the last meal Jackson could eat until after his operation. The meal was just about ready. Mommy had made Jackson's favorite meal of fried chicken, mashed potatoes and gravy, corn, carrots, and a salad. Jackson really loved salad because he got to have his favorite dressing, (ranch dressing). Mommy said they were going to have chocolate cake and ice cream for dessert. Dr. Larson told Jackson he could have all the ice cream he wanted after his surgery. He was getting really excited about that because he will be really hungry.

All of a sudden, the children heard Grandpa Woodard's car come down the driveway. They all ran out of the house almost at the same time, except Stephanie and Gregory, who were helping Mommy put the food on the table. "Grandpa and Grandma, you're back," all the children said at once. Jackson remarked, "We're having fried chicken, that's my favorite." Grandpa Woodard answered, "That's my favorite, too," as he picked up Jackson and held him up so he could see into the back seat of the car. Lying down so the children couldn't see him was Dr. Pierce. Jackson could hardly stand it, he was so happy he almost jumped right out of Grandpa Woodard's arms. They finally got the back door opened, and Jackson jumped right into Dr. Pierce's arms. Jackson was so excited, he shouted, "I knew you would come, I knew you would come, because I have been praying that God would bring you, and He did, He did. Thank You God, thank You God." Angela, Jared, Jordan and Blake ran for the house as fast as their feet could carry them. They even beat Grandma Woodard. "Dr. Pierce is here, Dr. Pierce is here," they all said at the same time. Mother responded, "That can't be." So Mother, Stephanie, and Gregory all went to the door at the same time, and coming up the steps of the big front porch was Dr. Pierce, carrying Jackson in his arms, with Grandpa and Grandma Woodard coming behind him. Mommy opened the door, and Jackson said with a big smile on his face, "I knew God would get him here, you were right Mama; God did answer my prayers." "Well," Grandpa Woodard remarked to Grandma Woodard, "I guess we are just not that important anymore." And they both laughed. While they were still standing in the doorway, Dr. Pierce bent over and put his arm around Tiffany and gave her a big kiss on the cheek. Tiffany put her arm around Dr. Pierce too, and Jackson asked. "Are you happy that Dr. Pierce came too, Mommy?" With tears in her eyes, Mommy responded, "yes, I sure am." Stephanie said, "mommies and grandmas always have tears in their eyes when they are happy." Tiffany said, "Stephanie, you had better set another plate for dinner." While the children were washing up for dinner, the adults were discussing how all this came to be. As they sat down to eat, Dr. Pierce told how Grandma Woodard had called him last weekend and told him what was going on; how Jackson wanted him to come and operate on him and that he said he would see what he could do. Grandma Woodard said: "Well; you see what you can do, and we will start praying." Jackson said, "And

God did the rest." And everyone said "Amen." Dr. Pierce said the blessing, and Jackson ate all he could possibly eat. Just then Mommy walked in from the kitchen with a big chocolate cake with a big train engine on it and 4 candles. Jackson said, "Oh my gosh; I forgot all about my birthday. I was so busy praying that God would get Dr. Pierce here in time for my operation." Everyone laughed. It seemed everyone knew about his birthday party except him. They all went into the living room, and Jackson sat in the middle of the room, and everyone sat around him in a circle, except little Blake, who wanted to be right in front of Jackson. Mommy picked Blake up and set him on her lap. Everyone brought in their presents and set them in front of Jackson. He didn't know where to start. Blake said, "Open mine," so Jackson opened Blake's first. It was a big boat for Jackson to take in the bathtub when they took a bath. Jackson said, "Thank you Blake, it floats." Jordan's gift was next. Jackson opened it in a hurry. It was little people who fit on the little boat, and they floated also. Jackson said, "Oh, thank you Jordan, These will be so much fun." "Yah," Blake said, "we can play with them when we take a bath together." Jared's gift was next. It was a small box and Jared wrapped it himself. Jackson quickly tore the paper off, and it was another train to go with the train set and tracks he got last Christmas. Jackson said, "Oh, this is great, thank you so much, Jared." Angela's gift was next. It was some colored crayons and coloring books of trains. There was also a pop-up book of trains. "Thank you Angela, this will be great while I am sick. I can color in bed." Gregory's gift was the next one Jackson opened. He got two more train pieces and another section of track for his set. Jackson said, "Oh boy, I can make a bigger track. Thank you so much Gregory." Stephanie's gift was next. It was wrapped in blue paper with trains on it. Jackson just tore it open as fast as he could. It was two more train cars, and four more sections of track. Jackson looked at

Stephanie and said, "Oh, boy, thank you Stephanie, I am really going to have fun playing with my train set next week after my operation." Jackson said, "I want to open your gift next Mommy." Mommy's gift was also wrapped in blue paper with trains on it. Jackson opened it up so fast; there were two pairs of pajamas to wear at the hospital, two blue shirts with a pair of bib overhauls with a train on the front, and an engineer's cap. Jackson was so excited. He put on the cap, and replied, "Now I will be a real engineer, thank you so much Mommy." Tiffany took a picture of her little engineer. "Well," Grandpa Woodard remarked, "I believe there is one more gift out in the car. Maybe Dr. Pierce and I should go out and bring it in. Could you hold the door open for us, Jackson please?" "Oh yes," Jackson answered, as he headed for the door. Mommy told him, "You don't open the door Jackson, till Grandpa Woodard gets right up here on the porch, okay?" "Okay Mommy," Jackson answered, with his little nose pressed tight against the glass on the door. Jackson said with a shout, "Oh Mommy come quickly, this gift is really big, I may need some help." As Grandpa Woodard and Dr. Pierce carried the gift into the house Grandpa Woodard remarked. "This gift is from Grandpa and Grandma and Dr. Pierce." Jackson followed Grandpa and Dr. Pierce into the living room, and stopped just as they set it down on the floor. "Well," Grandpa asked, "are you going to open it, or are you going to just look at it?" Everyone laughed. Everyone said "go," and Jackson just started tearing off the paper. "Oh, my gosh," Jackson shouted. There it was, a big large table with a green pad on top with trees, streams, and a lake on the top, and you could put a train track right on top of it. Jackson couldn't even speak for a few minutes. Then he saw the drawers underneath. "This is so cool," he said, "I can put my trains right in the drawers." He opened one of the drawers, and inside it was full of Lincoln logs, more Lincoln logs than he had ever seen. "Jared, this is so cool, you can help me

make a whole town. Wow, this is my best birthday ever."
Jackson got up and gave everyone a big hug. Dr. Pierce said,
"This was the best idea about having his birthday today, it
sure is taking his mind off the operation." Just about that
time Gregory, Grandpa, and Dr. Pierce got the tracks and the
trains put on the table, Jared and Jackson had made a couple
or three Lincoln log houses to put on top. It sure looked neat
when it was done. There were railroad crossings, bridges,
tunnels, and train yards where you could park the trains.
Angela, Jordan, and Blake built a railroad station out of
Lincoln logs. By the time they got it all put together, it was
evening and suppertime. "Well Tiffany," Dr. Pierce said, "as
long as everything is taken care of here for tonight, I think I
should take you out to dinner." "You two go right ahead and
relax a little," Grandma Woodard said, "Grandpa and I will
hold down the fort." "This is not a fort," Jackson remarked,
"It's a railroad yard." Everyone had a good laugh. "Jackson,"
Dr. Pierce mentioned, "you do not have to worry about
staying at the hospital all weekend either. As soon as your
medication wears off after your operation, your Mother and
I are going to bring you right back home. And you will have
your own private doctor and nurse to take care of you, right
here at home, how about that?" "Wow," Jackson replied,
"My own doctor and nurse right here at home. That will be
super." "Yes," Grandma Woodard said, "the other children
will come and stay with Grandpa and I for the weekend, and
it will be real quiet here so you can get lots of rest." Jackson
said, "My own doctor and nurse right here," as Mommy and
Dr. Pierce walked out of the door. Grandpa and the children
were busy playing with the train set, While Stephanie and
Grandma were busy putting together a light supper. Jackson
couldn't eat anything he could only have a glass of water. All
of the children were pretty tired by the time Dr. Pierce and
Mommy got home from dinner. Jackson could not figure out
why it took them so long to eat dinner. Dr. Pierce carried

little Blake out to Grandpa's car and Jordan and the rest of the children walked to Grandma's house down the path, and through the woods. Jackson was the only one who stayed home with his Mother. Mommy mentioned, "Dr. Pierce will pick us up in the morning with Grandpa Woodard's big car, and we will go to the hospital." Jackson was so tired he didn't even care. He didn't care in the morning either, because he slept all the way to the hospital.

It didn't take long to get the operating room ready either. Jackson barely woke up before Dr. Pierce and Mommy both walked in. Mommy was in her uniform, and Dr. Pierce was in his uniform. They had already put the needle in his arm while he was sleeping, and Dr. Pierce asked, "Jackson can you hear me?" Jackson's shook his head yes, he was very sleepy. His mommy was holding his hand. "Jackson, I am going to count to five and by the time I am done you will be sleeping again, okay?" Jackson shook his head yes. Dr. Pierce started to count, "one, two, three," and Jackson was fast asleep. Dr. Pierce looked at Tiffany and smiled. Tiffany smiled back. It seemed like only a couple minutes before Jackson woke up. Mommy said, "Well, hello there, sweetheart, you had quite a sleep. You will be ready to go home in a few minutes." All of a sudden, Dr. Pierce was carrying Jackson into his own house, and laying him down in his own bed. Mommy told him, "We are going to stay right here by your side, you can go right back to sleep. We will not leave you." Jackson gave his Mommy, a tiny grin and went right back to sleep. He felt very safe. Jackson was just so happy that God sent Dr. Pierce. Tiffany called Grandpa and Grandma, and told them and the children that they were home, and that Jackson was doing fine. She told Grandma to tell the children that they could come down on Saturday and see Jackson.

Dr. Pierce took a little break on Saturday and went down to Grandma and Grandpa Woodard's house to see how everything was going. Olivia assured him, "Everything is going fine, but you had better take some food back to Tiffany for supper. The children and Grandpa and I will be down after supper, to see Jackson." The children were so happy to see Jackson. Each one had made a get-well card for him. Mommy read all the cards to Jackson. Then she pinned them up on a bulletin board, which Grandpa had put at the end of his bed on the wall. Jackson said he was hungry, so Mommy got him some ice cream. He loved ice cream. But he had a hard time swallowing it. Dr. Pierce told him, "You can have all the ice cream, you want Jackson." Jackson smiled a little smile.

By Tuesday, Jackson was feeling much better, and Dr. Pierce told him he was going to have to go back to Baltimore and take care of all his other patients. Jackson responded with, "I will miss you. I would like you to stay here, Dr. Pierce." Dr. Pierce looked across the bed at Tiffany and said. "You have the best nurse in the world taking care of you, and I will be back for Christmas. You will be all better by then, and I might add, you have the most beautiful nurse in the world too." Jackson said, "That's my mommy." They both laughed. On Wednesday morning, Grandma and Grandpa Woodard and Dr. Pierce drove in the driveway. The children were getting ready to catch the bus for school. They all ran outside including Jackson. Blake and Tiffany followed them out. Dr. Pierce said, "Well, I am off to catch the plane." Blake said, "We don't want you to go." Dr. Pierce told him, "Before you know it, I will be back." Blake asked, "Are you coming for my birthday?" "Blake," Mommy remarked, "Baltimore is a long way away, and Dr. Pierce cannot be coming out here every couple months." "Yeah," Jackson said, "wherever Baltimore is, but we can pray, Blake. God can do anything." Dr. Pierce and Tiffany smiled at each other.

CHAPTER 6

BLAKE'S SURPRISE

Jackson's tonsils were healing very well, and Mommy had to take him back to Dr. Larson for a checkup just to make sure everything was healing okay. Dr. Larson said, "Well, hello there Jackson. Boy, I don't know what kind of pull you have to get a big-name doctor like Dr. Pierce to come all the way from Baltimore clear out here to perform your operation. How did you manage that?" Jackson replied, "I just prayed to God, and He did the rest." "Well, Dr. Larson replied, "then maybe I had better start praying right away, because we could really use a doctor like Dr. Pierce working full-time in our small hospital." Jackson responded, "You could? Then I had better start praying too, because we sure would like Dr. Pierce to come back here to live. Wouldn't we Mama?" "Well," Mrs. Larkin answered, "I guess that would be really nice." Jackson asked, "Would Dr. Pierce really be able to operate in this hospital, Dr. Larson?" Dr. Larson answered, "We sure could use him here all right. He would be a great asset to this hospital, but I am not sure you could get him to make the move. Coming here to do a surgery, and moving here are two different things." "Well," Jackson replied, "maybe we cannot get him to come, but God sure can. He can do anything. He is a big God." Dr. Larson said with a smile, "Well, I'll tell you, what Jackson, we will both pray and see what happens, but if God decides not to send Dr. Pierce here to live, we have to accept that, okay?" Jackson answered, "Okay." "Wow, Mommy," Jackson remarked on the way out to the car. "Wouldn't that be cool if Dr. Pierce really came here to live and work in this hospital? You could work with him every day." Mother responded with, "That sure would be nice."

The rest of the children were home from school, when Mommy and Jackson drove in the driveway, and Jackson could hardly wait to tell them what Dr. Larson and he had talked about at the doctor's office. Jackson told everyone about the conversation. "Oh my," said Grandma Woodard, (who was watching the other children for Tiffany) "that would be a tall order for God to work out." Stephanie said with a smile, "Yes, it would, but God can do anything. And we will start praying right away." They all went into the living room, and knelt down by the couch and began to pray. Grandma Woodard thought to herself, it's time to make another phone call.

The next weekend, Olivia called Conrad. "Hello Conrad, how are things in Baltimore?" "Things are pretty normal here, Mom. How is Jackson doing?" "Oh, Jackson is just fine. In fact, he has started praying again, and so have the rest of the children." Conrad remarked, "And what, may I ask, are they praying for now?" Olivia answered, "I'm not sure you want to know, but here goes. It seems Dr. Larson and Jackson had quite a conversation about you, in his office." And Olivia continued to tell her son Conrad, the entire conversation between Jackson and Dr. Larson. She also mentioned that as soon as the other kids heard the conversation, they all went into the living room, got down on their knees and started praying. "Tiffany, Oliver, and I didn't quite know what to do. The children have been praying, ever since." Dr. Pierce started to laugh. "When those kids get something in their minds, no one can change it. I think they have an agenda." "Well," Olivia stated, "I just thought you should know what they're up to; by the way, how are things going between you and Tiffany, or shouldn't I ask?" "I really like her a lot. I think she is a wonderful person, but I don't believe she would ever be interested in moving to the big city again. I mean, the children like it here too, especially with you and their Grandpa Woodard, living out there, I don't believe they would want to leave you, either. There are a lot of things to think about and pray about. Maybe I should come out for Blake's birthday, and Tiffany and I could spend some time talking and see how things go." Olivia responded, "That sounds fine to me, do you want it to be a surprise?" Conrad remarked, "Oh yes, that was so much fun last time. Just to see the look on their faces was worth it." Olivia made the remark, "Maybe we could all come to Baltimore for Christmas, the children have two weeks off school and Tiffany has not had a vacation, since she moved here, except when Jackson had his surgery. Oliver and I could watch the children, so you and Tiffany would have more time to spend together." "That is certainly something else to think about. I'm glad you brought that up Mom, but we will have to deal with Blake's birthday first." Olivia answered with, "Of course, I understand there are a lot of details to be worked out, but it is never too early to start thinking about it." "You're right Mom; it's good to start thinking about it early. That will give me more time to plan what I would like for them to do and see while they are here, just in case I decide you all should come. There is my work schedule, of course, and I would have to get somewhere for you all to stay. Let me think about it a while, and we will discuss it at Blake's birthday. I love you Mom. Give my love to Oliver, Tiffany, and the children. Be sure not to say anything about Blake's birthday, I will call you next week." Olivia said, "Goodbye for now, Honey, I will wait to hear from you, love you too."

"Well," Oliver remarked, "that was some conversation." "Well," Olivia replied, "there were a lot of things to talk about. Conrad said to give you his love." She gave him a big smile. Oliver said, "I suppose we had better start praying, too." Olivia answered with, "I believe we should start praying right now. God has a lot of work to do to sort all this out." "He sure does," Oliver remarked, "let's pray."

Time has a way of going on and on and on, and before you knew it; Blake's birthday was next—Saturday, October 25th. Boy, was he excited! But there was a little problem, because Stephanie and Gregory were both going to be in a play on Saturday at school, and everyone was going to go. Mommy told Blake, they would have to have the birthday party on Sunday after church. Blake said, "Okay," he didn't have a problem with that. He didn't know what day his birthday was on anyway. Stephanie helped Blake make up a list of what he wanted for his birthday. That's all he could talk about all week. Grandpa Woodard's big car pulled out of their driveway just about the time the children caught the bus for school on Friday morning. Jared asked, "Where is Grandpa Woodard going so early in the morning?" Angela replied, "I don't know, Grandma didn't say anything about Grandpa Woodard having to go anywhere special today." Gregory remarked, "Grandpa usually isn't even up this early." Stephanie mentioned, "Maybe he had a doctor's appointment." Jordan asked, "Is Grandpa Woodard sick?" "No," Gregory responded, "he probably just had an appointment for a checkup." Jordan said, "I sure wouldn't want Grandpa Woodard to be sick." Jared replied, "Me neither."

It was just about lunchtime when Grandpa Woodard's car drove into the driveway. Jackson and Blake were excited to see Grandpa Woodard. They were just going to open the door and stand there and wait for Grandpa to come in, but Grandma Woodard told them to close the door, they were letting all the cold air in. And Grandma Woodard told them to go wash their hands for lunch and by the time they got back Grandpa would be in the house. So the little ones went into the bathroom to wash up, and when they came out and got to the living room door, who do you suppose was standing in the living room with Grandpa Woodard, but Dr. Pierce. Jackson and Blake were so excited; they forgot how hungry they were. They ran up to Dr. Pierce, and he bent down and picked both of them up at once and turned them around and around and around. When Dr. Pierce, put them down, they were so dizzy they couldn't stand up, they just kept falling over. Just about that time, Grandma Woodard called them for lunch. Jackson said, "I get to sit by Dr. Pierce." Blake said, "Me too," as they took their places on either side of Dr. Pierce. "Well," Grandpa Woodard remarked, "some people don't even care if I'm around anymore," in a teasing way. Jackson assured him, "I do Grandpa, and you can sit on my other side." Grandpa responded, "I feel so much better now." Blake remarked, "And you can sit by me, Grandma." Everyone laughed. Jackson and Blake decided they weren't very hungry and wanted to get down and play with Dr. Pierce. But Dr. Pierce told them, "I am very hungry, and I really like Grandma Woodard's cooking." So the boys sat real quiet and ate lunch with Dr. Pierce and Grandpa and Grandma Woodard.

After lunch, Blake had to take a nap and little Jackson would not let Dr. Pierce visit with Grandpa and Grandma Woodard. Jackson had a whole lot of questions to ask Dr. Pierce. Dr. Pierce hardly had time to answer one question when Jackson asked him another question. What kind of house do you live in? How do you get to work? What you do all weekend by yourself? Do you ever get lonely, not having anyone else to talk to? Have you ever lived in the country? Would you like to live in the country? Dr. Pierce looked at Olivia and smiled, she smiled back. Dr. Pierce knew what all Jackson's questions were leading up to. Grandma Woodard told Jackson he had better let Dr. Pierce rest for a while, and he should go play with his train set. Jackson responded with, "Okay, boy, Mommy and the other children are really going to be surprised when they get home."

Olivia, Oliver, and Conrad had a really nice conversation. The afternoon went by so fast. Before you knew it Blake was up from his nap, and playing with Jackson with his train set. The bus drove up, just as Tiffany was going to turn into the driveway. The children decided to race her to the house. They lost, of course. It was all Grandpa and Grandma Woodard could do to convince the little ones that they had to stay in Jackson's bedroom and play with his train set, finally Dr. Pierce told them he would stay in there and play with them. Grandma Woodard assured them she would find some reason to have their Mother and the children come into Jackson's room. When they all got inside and took their coats off, Grandma told them; "you all have to go and see what Jackson and Blake are building with the train set, and the Lincoln Logs." The children beat their Mother up the stairs, of course. And when they got in the room, they let out a squeal, and Dr. Pierce motioned for them not to say anything till Tiffany got in the room. Mother asked, "What in the world are you guys building in here?" As she came through the door, she remarked, "Oh! my gosh." Her eyes were big and her mouth fell open as she said, "you could give a person a heart attack, Conrad." "Well," Dr. Pierce replied, "at least there's a doctor here." All the children laughed. Then the children all ran up to Dr. Pierce and gave him hugs, then he reached out and took Tiffany in his arms, and held her close. Dr. Pierce asked, "I was wondering if you would like to go to dinner with me?" Tiffany responded, "I have to fix dinner for the children, but I would be happy to have you stay for dinner." Just about that time, Grandpa and Grandma Woodard walked in the bedroom. Grandma said, "I heard that, I already have dinner in the oven and

Stephanie can help me make a salad, so it is all taken care of." Dr. Pierce replied, "Well then, is there any other reason we can't go out to dinner?" "Well, no," Tiffany responded, "I will just need a few minutes to clean up and change clothes." Stephanie remarked, "I'll go start the salad." Gregory said, "I'll go set the table." Angela answered with, "I'll help you, Gregory," and they all took off down the stairs with smiles on their faces and a prayer in their hearts. Jared and Jordan followed close behind. Jackson said, "You can't be taking my Mommy to dinner for a Christmas present again because it isn't Christmas." Dr. Pierce responded, "No, I would just like to spend a little time with your mom alone, if that's okay with you." Jackson answered with, "Oh! That is just fine with me," as he took Dr. Pierce's hand and walked him down the stairs. When Tiffany walked downstairs, all dressed up, the little ones said how pretty she was, and the older ones just looked at Dr. Pierce's face and watched him look at their Mother. Everyone just smiled. Tiffany gave each of the children a big hug and kiss, and told them they had better be good for Grandpa and Grandma Woodard. "Oh, we will Mama, you can bet on that," the children answered with smiles on their faces. Dr. Pierce and Tiffany were just driving down the driveway when all the children took off for Stephanie's bedroom, and all knelt down around her bed and began to pray. When they got through praying, they all filed downstairs and had dinner with Grandpa and Grandma Woodard.

Saturday morning came quickly. Mommy remarked that they had a lot to do to get ready for Blake's birthday party, and get Stephanie and Gregory to the school early enough for practice in the afternoon. She mentioned, "We are just going to have a light snack for lunch, because Dr. Pierce is going to take all of us out to dinner after the play tonight." Angela asked, "Where are we going?" Mother replied, "I don't know, Dr. Pierce said it would be up to Stephanie and Gregory, because it would be in their honor." Jackson asked,

"What does that mean?" Mother answered, "It means, we are taking Stephanie and Gregory out to dinner, because of the good job they will do in the play." Jordan responded, "They haven't even had the play yet, how do we know they will do a good job?" Mommy replied, "Oh, we know they will do a good job; we don't have to worry about that. They have been practicing for a long time." Jordan and Jackson remarked, "Oh good," as they went to ask Stephanie and Gregory, where they would like to go to eat, after the play.

The play was about a family who lived in the country and went to visit their grandparents in the big city for a vacation. It was really funny, and the children's tummies' hurt from laughing so much. Angela said, "You were both very good." Everyone agreed with her and gave Stephanie and Gregory big hugs and kisses. Then, off they went to the restaurant. The children were very well behaved in the restaurant, each taking their places, just like they do at home, with the older ones sitting so they can help the younger ones. Mother ordered for Jordan, Jackson, and Blake, and the rest got to place their orders themselves. Jackson asked if he could please have hot cocoa, because he really liked that. The waitress answered with, "I think we can handle that," so Blake and he both had hot cocoa. While they were waiting for their food, the little ones colored on the coloring sheets the waitress gave them, and the rest kept busy talking about the play. Since the play had been about going to the big city on vacation, Jared asked Dr. Pierce if he was going to come back here for Christmas.

All of a sudden, it got very quiet. All the children looked at Dr. Pierce, and Dr. Pierce was the first one to talk. "Well now, if I told you, it wouldn't be a surprise, now would it?" Jordan answered with, "No, it wouldn't, but we want to know, if you are going to be here or not." Gregory remarked, "We never get to buy you anything for Christmas, because we never know if you are coming or not." Dr. Pierce looked at their Mother with that look in his eye again, and he replied. "Well, your mother and I discussed that very thing last night over dinner, and we couldn't decide whether you children would want me to come here for Christmas, or if you all would like to come to Baltimore to see me for Christmas." The children's eyes got real big, and their mouths were wide open. The adults all started to laugh, because the children all looked so funny. "Well," Dr. Pierce remarked, "who is going to talk first?" Grandpa Woodard replied, "I believe the cat has got their tongues." "Oh my," they all said at once. Mom told them, "Wait a minute, I think we should only have one speak at a time, and we will start with Stephanie, that way the little ones will have a little more time to think about what they want to say." Stephanie started with, "I would love to go to Baltimore; they have plays there, and it would be so much fun." Gregory added, "Yah, and maybe we could go to a concert and listen to some music. I love music." Angela said, "I would love to go window shopping, and look at all the beautiful decorations and get our pictures taken with Santa Claus." Jared replied, "I would like to go to a football game." Jordan remarked, "I wonder if they have a store there that sells doll houses, if they do, I would like to go and look at them, and I would like to go skating in the park." Jackson added, "They must have trains there, I would like to ride on a train." Mommy asked, "What about you Blake, what would you like to do?" Blake said, "Me go bye-bye, go to a toy store." Everyone laughed; his response was so cute. Dr. Pierce remarked, "Wow that would be a full schedule, if we did all that in two weeks." Angela replied, "Two weeks— how would we get there?" Dr. Pierce responded with, "Well, Grandpa and Grandma Woodard would drive out a week early, with Jordan, Jackson, and Blake. It would take around three days for them to get there. Your mom, and you four older children, would fly out on the 17th of December." Gregory remarked, "Oh that is just four days till Mom's birthday." "Well," Dr. Pierce replied as he looked at Tiffany, "that is news to me." Mother remarked, "You should not have brought that up, Gregory." Gregory apologized, "I'm sorry Mom, but it just came out." Dr. Pierce continued with, "Well, we will talk it over and decide what we are going to do, but first we have to concentrate on Blake's birthday tomorrow, isn't that right Blake?" Blake said, "Yah," with a smile on his face. They had a very nice dinner, and it was a very full day. The little ones fell fast asleep on the way home.

Morning came very early, or so Blake thought anyway. He was up extra early and was so excited; he could hardly eat his breakfast. Mommy was very busy getting dinner ready and in the oven before they went to church, and the last thing she did was decorate the birthday cake. Gregory, Angela, and Jared helped get the little ones ready for church, and Stephanie made the salad, put it in the refrigerator, and then set the table for lunch. Mother remarked, "Angela, Jared, and Jordan will ride with Grandpa and Grandma Woodard, and Dr. Pierce will drive my car, and the other children will go with us." Dr. Pierce called from Grandma Woodard's house and said they were ready to leave; they would be over in just a couple minutes.

Church was a lot of fun, and everyone enjoyed going there. The children really liked Sunday school. They all got treats, and Blake's Sunday school class sang "Happy Birthday" to him. He really liked that. On the ride home, they all sang Bible songs. It already was a beautiful day, and it had hardly started. When they got home, Dr. Pierce picked up Jackson and Blake, one in each arm and carried them to the house. They were both having a wonderful time. Grandma and Grandpa Woodard stopped at their house and picked up a Jell-O salad and ice cream for the birthday cake. They all washed up for dinner and took their places at the table. Mother asked Dr. Pierce to say a prayer for the food. They had a wonderful dinner; ham, and a potato hot dish, carrots, corn, lettuce salad, Jell-O salad, homemade bread and butter, and hot cocoa. What a wonderful birthday dinner. They were all Blake's favorites.

After dinner they gathered around the dining room table to sing Happy Birthday to Blake. Dr. Pierce lit the candles, and Blake blew them out, all two of them. Afterward, Mommy, Grandma, Stephanie, and Gregory finished cleaning up the kitchen. They all sat down in the living room with Blake as the center of attention, because he was the birthday boy. Jackson's gift was the first one Blake opened. It was a toy, a semi truck. Blake was so excited; he loved big trucks. Next he opened Jordan's present. He just tore into that one. It was a really neat boat for the bathtub. Blake said, "Now we both have a boat for the tub, Jackson." He thanked both Jackson and Jordan, and then came Jared's gift. This was a bigger box. Blake was really getting excited. He opened it quickly. It was a toy jet plane. Blake thanked Jared and quickly went to the next gift, which was Angela's. It was a little book of children's prayers, and a Noah's ark book. Blake really liked books, he thanked Angela very much. Then he went straight to the next gift, which was from Gregory and Stephanie. They had put their money together and bought Blake's gift. It was a good sized box. Blake tore off the paper and opened the package. It was a really nice tool belt with a screwdriver, hammer, pliers, a drill and a saw that each made noise, and some bolts and nuts. "Wow," Blake remarked, "now I can fix Mommy's stuff that breaks." Dr. Pierce added, "Way to go." Blake said with a big smile, "Thanks much Stephanie and Gregory, me likes this a lot." Mommy's gift came next. Blake was in a hurry to open that one. He tore away the paper and ripped open the box, inside was two pairs of bib overhauls, two shirts, four pairs of socks, and a hard hat. "Now me can go to work." He put on his hard hat and tool belt and off he went. Grandpa Woodard remarked, "Wait a minute, you still have one more gift to open." Blake answered, "Really?" "Yes," Grandpa Woodard replied, "I will get it out of my car." Dr. Pierce remarked, "I will go and bring it in." Blake and Jackson went to the door to wait for Dr. Pierce. Blake said, "Boy is that ever big." Gregory had to help them hold the door open. The box was taller than Blake. Blake tore away at the paper, and there was a picture of a big toolbox on the box. Blake could hardly speak. His eyes were wide open, and his mouth was open, and he just stood there and looked at the picture on the box. Grandpa Woodard asked, "Do you need some help to open it?" Blake responded with, "Oh yes, please." He could still hardly talk. He was so excited. Grandma Woodard told him, "It is from Grandpa and Grandma and Dr. Pierce." "Oh, thank you so much Gampa and Gamma and Dr. Pierce. I just love it. Now Jackson and I can both go to work." Blake went and gave everyone hugs and kisses and thanked them again. By the time Grandpa Woodard, Dr. Pierce, and Gregory got the toolbox put together, it was time for supper. They just had a light snack, because they had such a big dinner after church. Before you knew it, it was time for the children to go to bed.

Dr. Pierce said, "I have to leave in the morning to go back to Baltimore." Jackson asked, "Will you come down and tell us goodbye?" Dr. Pierce answered, "Of course I will; Grandpa Woodard is going to take me to the airport." Jared asked, "Are you coming for Christmas?" Dr. Pierce replied, "I really don't know yet, either I will come here, or you will all come to Baltimore. Your mother and I haven't decided which way it will be yet." Jackson answered him with, "Well, that is a long time to wait." Mommy remarked, "Oh it is not that long. Now you children say goodnight to Dr. Pierce and Grandma and Grandpa Woodard and run along to bed. I will be up there in a few minutes to tuck you in. Be sure to say your prayers. They all looked at each other and smiled, "we sure will."

CHAPTER 7

THANKSGIVING

T he children were having a hard time doing their homework and thinking about what was going to happen at
Christmas. Angela remarked, "Just about two whole months
and I can hardly wait. "Well," Mother replied, "we have no
choice, but time will go by fast. Just wait till the first snow
comes, you will be having so much fun outside, you'll not
think about Christmas at all."

Before the children knew it, it was Thanksgiving vacation, with two days off school, and four days off altogether.
On Wednesday morning, the day before Thanksgiving, the
children got up and came downstairs. Mommy was in the
kitchen making coffee as she mentioned, "You children can
go back upstairs and sleep for another couple hours, we have
2 feet of snow, and school is closed." Jared and Jordan were
so excited. They had to go open the front door and see for
themselves. There was no going back to sleep for them. They
were going to get dressed and get outside and make snowmen.
"Not so fast," Mommy said, "it's still dark out there and the
snow is too deep. You can't even walk out there. Go and get
Gregory and Stephanie up. Gregory can start blowing the
snow with the snow blower right now before breakfast, and
Stephanie can help me get breakfast on the table. We'll have
a nice big breakfast and then Stephanie, Gregory, and I will

take turns cleaning the driveway. After we get a path cleared out, you kids can go out to play in the snow. We also have to clear out the path over to Grandma and Grandpa's house." Jared remarked, "I will help Gregory with the shoveling. I can clear off the porch and the steps." Mom replied, "That would be very nice." Jordan chimed in, "I will help Blake get dressed.". Angela replied "I will get dressed and then set the table for you, Mom." Jackson said with a big smile, "I will get dressed, and make my bed." Mother answered, "You children are so good to help out, but you all need to make your beds before you come back downstairs. By the time we're done getting dressed and eating breakfast, it should be light enough to go outside." "Boy," Angela said excitedly, "we get five days off of school now. This is really going to be fun."

Tiffany called Grandma Woodard, and told her that they would have the path cleared over to their house in a couple of hours. She mentioned, "It is a good thing I have everything I need for my Thanksgiving dinner tomorrow." Grandma Woodard remarked, "I will make the pies. By the way, Mrs. Peters called to say that they are so upset; they were supposed to fly to California today to spend the holiday with their son Jim and his family. They had to call and tell them they couldn't even get to the airport. I don't imagine they have anything to fix for dinner tomorrow either, because they weren't planning on being here." Tiffany told Grandma to call Mrs. Peters back and let her know that we could all use our snow blowers, and Grandpa Woodard's four-wheeler, we should be able to be down to their house by late this afternoon. Grandpa can make a few trips and bring them and their luggage back to your house on the four-wheeler, and they can vacation at your house and come down here for supper tonight and dinner tomorrow. "Maybe by Friday the roads will be opened, and they will be able to fly out to California then." Grandma replied with a smile,

"Tiffany, that sounds like a wonderful idea. I would just love the company, and Grandpa would love to have another man around to visit with."

Breakfast was just about ready so Tiffany asked Stephanie to go call Gregory for breakfast. As Gregory walked in and stomped the snow off his feet, he mentioned that he had just finished clearing the path to Grandpa and Grandma's house. Just then the phone rang. It was Grandma Woodard, saying that she had just got off the phone with Mrs. Peters, and she was so happy for the invitation. "Emily told me they just cleaned out the refrigerator yesterday, because they were going to be gone for two weeks, and they would be pretty hungry by tonight." Tiffany remarked, "By the way, Gregory was just here to let us know he cleaned out the path to your house. Why don't Grandpa and you ride down on the four-wheeler and have breakfast with us, then you could stay with the little ones while Grandpa, Gregory, Stephanie, and I work on the snow." "Sounds great," Olivia answered, "And I will bring down my makings for my pies and bake them at your house; we are going to eat them there anyway."

By 11:00 a.m. Grandpa Woodard was well on his way down the road to Mr. Peter's house. He wanted to make a path wide enough for the 4-wheeler to get through, and then he could let the snowplow finish the work on Thursday or Friday, whenever they could come by. Grandpa Woodard had to make two trips: one to pick up Mrs. Peters and her luggage, and one to pick up Mr. Peters and his luggage.

By the time Grandpa Woodard came back with Mrs. Peters, the children were all outside having a blast in the snow. They were busy playing with each other; the older ones helping the little ones make snowmen. They had gotten a few carrots from Mommy for the big long noses. And they put buttons on for eyes, and buttons going down their front. And they each had put a scarf around the necks of the snowmen, but they didn't know where they were going to get all the hats. They needed five hats. Angela asked, "Do you have any hats, Grandpa?" Mrs. Peters said, "We have three hats. And what about caps, can you use caps? We have two caps." "Oh yes," Jackson answered, "they will keep the sun out of their eyes." "Wonderful," Mrs. Peters remarked, "three hats and two caps, it is then. Oliver, tell Mr. Peters to bring the three hats and two caps in the front hall closet. Just tell him we have need of them." "Right on," Grandpa Woodard replied, as he took off down the path to go pick up Mr. Peters, "we shall be back in a flash, three hats, and two caps coming right up." The children got a kick out of that, and they let out a hearty laugh. Angela went inside and came back with a whole bunch of large, black buttons, and they made the biggest smiley faces they could on all five of their snowmen. By the time Grandpa Woodard and Mr. Peters got back, the snowmen were all finished except for the hats and caps. The children all ran up to the four-wheeler before they even got it stopped. Mr. Peters asked, "What are all these hats and caps for?" Jackson answered, "These are for our snowmen, and I get a cap." Blake said, "Me too." Jordan replied, "We will take the hats." Angela asked, "There now, don't they look just super?" Mr. Peters answered, "They sure do, and they look like they could come alive." "Aw," Blake mentioned, "they're just made of snow." Everyone laughed.

Grandpa Woodard remarked, "Let's go inside and warm up." Gregory replied, "Sounds like a good idea to me," since he had been helping the other children after his work was done. They opened the door, and the smell of chocolate chip cookies and hot cocoa hit them. Angela mentioned, "Boy, does that smell good!" They didn't realize how cold and hungry they were. The children were having so much fun. Mother was on the phone when they all came in from outside, she had told the people at the county garage that whoever was going to plow their road on Thanksgiving day should stop in for Thanksgiving dinner. They heard her say, no one should have to work on a holiday and not have a good meal. After they had their snack of cookies and hot cocoa, Grandpa Woodard took pictures of all the children with their snowmen.

They all had such a wonderful time. Mr. and Mrs. Peters stayed for supper with them, and then they played games and sang songs and then Grandpa and Grandma Woodard, and Mr. and Mrs. Peters went home to Grandma's house to spend the night. The children got ready for bed. It had been a full day, and what an exciting day it was. And there were four more days left. The little ones thought they wouldn't be able to get to sleep, because they were so excited about playing in the snow tomorrow, but they were sleeping before Mommy made it all the way downstairs.

The little ones were up early the next morning; they didn't beat Mommy up, though. Mommy was already getting the turkey in the oven, when they came downstairs. She remarked, "We are going to have a light breakfast this morning, because we are going to eat a big dinner early today." Jordan asked, "Can we go outside, right away?" "No," Mommy said, "you have to wait for the other children to get up." Jackson whispered, "Blake, Then let's go and wake them up." "Oh, no you don't," Mommy remarked, "You just come and sit down and have something to eat and let them sleep." Jackson replied, "Darn." It seemed like ages before the older children got up.

Stephanie stayed inside to help Mother with the Thanksgiving dinner, and Angela set the table before she went outside with the other children. Gregory pulled the little ones on the sled up and down the driveway; which was just wide enough for a four-wheeler to get through, because it wasn't cleared all the way across; but it was a lot of fun. Before long, Grandpa Woodard came down the path between their houses with Mrs. Peters. It took Grandpa three trips to get everyone over to Tiffany's. As the children watched, they thought how cool it would be; if Grandpa would consider taking them for a ride on his four-wheeler. Grandpa must have read their minds, because just before he went in the house, he told them that after dinner he would give them a ride. Just then, they were called to come in and get washed up for dinner. They just started for the house when all of a sudden they heard the big snow plow coming down the road, only instead of going right on past, he turned into their driveway, and started to come right for the house. The little ones got so scared; they ran right up on the porch and leaned right against the house. That plow just kept coming, he got almost to the house, and just then he turned that plow, and plowed all that snow to the right of the driveway. "Boy," Jared remarked, "I thought all our snowmen were dead meat." Just then the man turned the motor off, and climbed out of the snow plow and saw the look on the children's faces. He asked with a smile, "Did you think I was going to plow down your snowmen? Aw, I saw those snowmen there. I would not have hit them, and I know how important they are. My children made some of them yesterday too." The children were relieved. This man was a pretty nice man, after all. They all walked into the house together.

They all stopped and washed their hands for dinner. All the children took their places, and there were special places for Mr. and Mrs. Peters and the special guest, the snow plow driver. His name was Mr. Jim Jacobs. He lived clear on the other side of the county, over by Sand Creek. He had four little children. The children thought about how Mrs. Jacobs and her children had to spend the holiday without their Daddy home, and they felt sad for them, so Angela asked if she could say a special prayer for Mr. Jacobs children. After Grandpa Woodard said the blessing and thanked God for his new family and everything else He had given him, it was Angela's turn to pray. She asked God to bless Mr. Jacobs's children, and make it so they would not miss their Daddy so much, especially today. Mr. Jacobs said he didn't think the children would miss him too much, because their Grandma and Grandpa, Aunt, and Uncle, and four cousins had all come down Tuesday night to spend the holidays with us. And all the children have been playing outside in the snow ever since Wednesday morning. Mr. Peters mentioned how they were supposed to go to California and spend the holiday with their son and his family too, but they got snowed in, and none of the planes were flying. Even if they were, they couldn't get out of their driveway. Mr. Jacobs replied. "Oh well, I can plow you out of your driveway so you can get to the airport." Tiffany remarked, "You can use our phone to call the airport to find out how soon you can get a plane out to California." Mrs. Peters got almost too excited to eat.

It was such a wonderful Thanksgiving dinner, everyone told at least one thing they were thankful for. Grandpa Woodard already said what he was thankful for when he gave the blessing. Grandma was thankful that God had brought Grandpa Woodard and Tiffany and all the children into her life. Mrs. Peters was so thankful that Tiffany had invited them over for Thanksgiving dinner, since they didn't have any food at home, and also for Grandma and Grandpa Woodard, who let them stay overnight. Mr. Peters was very thankful that Mr. Jacobs was going to plow out his driveway for him, because that was always a big job for him to do. Mr. Jacobs was very thankful to Tiffany's invitation to dinner; it made him not feel so alone on Thanksgiving. And the children were very thankful for all the snow and the extra day off of school. Stephanie and Gregory were also thankful that Mr. Jacobs plowed out the rest of the driveway, so they didn't have to do it. The little ones were thankful that Mr. Jacobs did not plow down their snowmen. Jackson remarked, "I only wished that Dr. Pierce was here." Tiffany was so thankful for all the new friends she had just met, for her job, for all her children, and for Grandpa and Grandma Woodard, who had come into her life. It was a beautiful Thanksgiving dinner with all the trimmings. After dinner was over, Mr. Jacobs had to leave right away and get back to work. The first thing he did was plow the road out down as far as the Peters farm. And then he turned into their driveway, and plowed out the whole driveway. Then he drove back out to the road and continued plowing.

Mrs. Peters went right to the phone and called the airport. There was a flight leaving for California at 8:00 a.m. tomorrow morning. Mr. and Mrs. Peters were so excited. Tiffany said they could stay and have supper with them tonight, and then she would drive them home. Mrs. Peters replied, "Thank you so very much." They all went into the living room, except for Mrs. Peters, Grandma Woodard, Stephanie, and Gregory, who cleaned up the kitchen and put the food away. Tiffany played the piano while the rest sang, including those in the kitchen. They all had a wonderful time. Mrs. Peters said they had better be getting home, because they had to get up early in the morning to catch the plane. She added, "We will eat breakfast at the airport, since we have to wait for two hours before the plane leaves anyway. That will give us something to do while we're waiting." Grandpa Woodard said he would take the four-wheeler home and pick up his car and the Peters's luggage and then he would give them a ride home. Tiffany replied, "Thank you so much Oliver, I really appreciate that."

Grandma Woodard stayed at Tiffany's, until Grandpa came back. Grandpa Woodard walked in and remarked, "I sure could use a piece of pie and a cup of coffee." Olivia replied, "You could always use a piece of pie, and a cup of coffee." Everyone laughed. They were all having pie, Oliver, Olivia, and Tiffany were having coffee, and the children were having hot cocoa milk, as Blake calls it. Just then the phone rang. Tiffany answered the phone. Tiffany answered, "Well hello there, we are so happy you called." Jackson asked, "Its Dr. Pierce, isn't it?" "Isn't it?" Mommy replied, "Yes, yes." Well I guess that made everyone's day complete, well, almost complete, after all, Dr. Pierce was only on the phone, he wasn't really here. The children could hardly contain themselves, which one of them would Mommy let talk to Dr. Pierce first? Jackson remarked, "We always go from smallest to biggest." Gregory replied, "That's only when we are opening presents." "Now, now," Grandma Woodard mentioned, "maybe we should draw straws." Jackson responded, "We don't have any straws." Grandpa Woodard answered, "Well, we have toothpicks. I will break one in half, and the one who chooses that one out of all the others will talk first, then we will throw one toothpick away and the one who chooses the short one the next time will be the next one and so on until everyone has had a chance to talk to Dr. Pierce." So anyway, Stephanie quickly got out seven toothpicks and handed them to Grandpa. Grandpa broke one in half and then held them in his hand so the children couldn't see which one was the shortest, then he put out his hand, and they started to each choose one. Angela was the first one to get the short toothpick. She was so excited. Just as the others were drawing the second time to see who would be the second one to talk to Dr. Pierce, Mommy came into the kitchen. "But; Mom," Angela remarked, "we were drawing straws to find out who would be first to talk to Dr. Pierce and I won." "I'm so sorry," Mother replied, "but Dr. Pierce had to hang up." Angela and the children's eyes got wet with tears. Tiffany felt just heartbroken. "But," she said, with a smile on her face, "who would like to go with me, and Grandpa and Grandma Woodard to pick up Dr. Pierce at the airport?" "The children and Grandma Woodard got so excited that their eyes overflowed with tears, and they let out a holler and jumped up and down, and Mommy couldn't tell them to quiet down, because she felt like jumping up and down too. "Well, I'll be," Grandpa Woodard remarked, "that man sure enough likes to surprise people, could've given his mother a heart attack." "Oh," Grandma Woodard remarked, "it is so much fun to be on the other end of a surprise once in a while." "Okay," Mother replied we had better get going; we do not want to keep Dr. Pierce waiting." So they got into two cars and off they went.

There was no arguing or fussing on the long ride. They all sang songs and the children looked at each other with grins on their faces. God had again answered their prayers. Dr. Pierce was waiting for them when they drove up. Oliver opened the trunk of his big car, and they put Dr. Pierce's luggage in, and then Dr. Pierce knocked on the driver's door of Tiffany's car, and motioned for her to move over, and he got in, and off they went. The little ones were going to stay awake all the way home, but before they were off the freeway, they were fast asleep. When they got home, the little ones woke up, and Dr. Pierce carried them in. When they got in the house, Dr. Pierce mentioned, "I could sure use some turkey and dressing and all the trimmings." He had not had his Thanksgiving dinner yet. Tiffany replied, "Coming right up, as she went and dished up his supper. Grandpa, Grandma and Tiffany sat at the table and had coffee with Dr. Pierce, and all the children stood around the table and watched him eat. They all stayed up late into the night and talked and talked and talked. Mommy said it would be okay, because they did not have school the next morning, and they all could sleep in. It was the best Thanksgiving any of them had ever had that they could even remember. Dr. Pierce carried the two little ones upstairs, and Mommy tucked them in. Then Grandpa and Grandma and Dr. Pierce, drove over to Grandpa and Grandma's house. Stephanie, Gregory, and Tiffany cleaned up the kitchen, went into Stephanie's room, and knelt and gave thanks to God for Dr. Pierce, and then they all went to bed with smiles on their faces.

All the children were still sleeping at 8:30 a.m. when Tiffany got up to put the coffee on. She was saying her prayers and reading her Bible, when someone knocked at the kitchen door. She opened the door, and Conrad said, "I could smell your coffee all the way down at Mom's, and since I was too lazy to make my own, I jogged all the way down here to bum a cup." "Do come in," Tiffany remarked, "I just made it." Conrad mentioned, "It is so nice and warm in here too, and it is so quiet yet too." "Yes," Tiffany replied, "I wonder how long they will sleep, the teenagers will sleep till noon, if I let them, but I don't know how long the little ones will sleep, they are not used to being up that late." Conrad mentioned, "Maybe we should make a bet, the one who guesses the closest to the right time the first one wakes up, gets to throw the other one into the snow bank, how's that?" "Well, it sounds okay to me," Tiffany answered, "if you will let me throw you in, I sure couldn't do it by myself." "I'm always a good sport," Conrad said with a smile, "but I have another idea. Maybe the looser should have to run around the house in their bare feet, at least three times." Tiffany replied, "Thank goodness the snow is too deep for that, you would have to come and pull me out." "That," Conrad remarked, "would be worth my whole trip out here." They both laughed. Conrad said, "So what time do you want Tiffany?" "I'll take 9:25 a.m." Conrad looked at his watch. It was 9:15 a.m. He replied, "I think I'll take 9:35 a.m." Tiffany remarked, "Well done," and she got up from the table, got a frying pan out of the cupboard, and set it down hard on the stove. Dr. Pierce jumped up from the table, and before Tiffany knew it, he had put his big arms around her, and picked her up, and turned her around away from the stove, and said, "Ta,Ta,Ta, no help with extra noise from the kitchen," and he started carrying her towards the kitchen door. Just then the door opened up, and Oliver stepped in, "My, my, my, what do we have here?" He had a big grin on his face. Dr. Pierce looked at Tiffany, and Tiffany looked at Dr. Pierce. Her face was beet red. And they both looked at Grandpa Woodard. Just then all the children, who were watching from the stair steps standing there, one on each step—they looked like stair steps themselves, anyway—let out with a big laugh, and Dr. Pierce turned around to look at the stairs. Conrad looked at his watch, then looked at Tiffany, and had a big grin on his face. He knew what he had to do, and Tiffany knew what he was going to do. "No!" Tiffany squealed as Dr. Pierce turned around and headed for the kitchen door, which was still open, and out they went, right past Grandpa Woodard and down the steps, with the children, and Grandpa right behind them. Tiffany was hanging on to Conrad's neck for dear life, and her feet were swinging, and she was yelling at the top of her lungs. All the children were standing on the porch in their pajamas and bare feet, while Grandpa Woodward just stared as Dr. Pierce tried to throw Mama in the snow bank. Mama would not let go of Dr. Pierce's neck, so down they both went right into that two feet of snow. They sunk right on down till they were half covered up. About that time, Grandma Woodard was running down the path, about halfway to our house; she didn't know what was going on, because of all Mama's screaming. By the time Grandma Woodard got there, the children and Grandpa Woodard were laughing so hard, and Grandma just stood there looking at the children, Grandpa Woodard, Mama, and Dr. Pierce. Mama and Dr. Pierce were still lying in the snow, and all of a sudden, Grandma started laughing and said "this is a crazy household; I have never seen anything like this." Grandpa Woodard had to help Mama up out of the snow, because she was on top of Dr. Pierce, and he was pretty much buried. Mama tried to explain, but she didn't really know where to start. Grandma Woodard said, "I suppose Grandpa Woodard didn't tell you that I was making breakfast at our house, and it is almost ready." "Well," Grandpa Woodard remarked, "I was going to tell them, but I barely got in the door and ..." "Oh, never mind," Grandma Woodard replied, "breakfast is in fifteen minutes." She could hardly keep from laughing herself. And off she went back down the path. Dr. Pierce stated, "I had better get some dry clothes on." Mommy replied, "Me too, and you children have ten minutes to get dressed, also." Grandpa said, "And I had better just go and help Grandma."

Grandma Woodard had everything on the table, when everyone walked in the door. Tiffany remarked, "It sure smells good, thank you so much Olivia for doing this, I really appreciate it." Grandpa Woodard could hardly say the blessing, because he could hardly hold a straight face. So after everyone got their food, Dr. Pierce stated, "I believe your mother and I owe you all an explanation of what just happened this morning." Olivia remarked, "That would be a good idea." "Yes, Sir, it would," the children said, almost at the same time. Tiffany could just feel her face getting red all over again. Dr. Pierce looked across the table at Tiffany, and started to tell his story from the time he knocked on the door. The children started laughing when they found out their mother had tried to make a lot of noise to wake them up, and they continued to laugh harder when they found out why Dr. Pierce was holding their Mother in his arms. "So when I turned around and saw the kitchen door was still open, I knew what I had to do and so did your mother and you know the rest of the story. Angela stated, "This is the most fun I've ever had on Thanksgiving vacation." "Well," Dr. Pierce remarked, "our vacation has just started."

CHAPTER 8

THE ACCIDENT

I t was the morning after Thanksgiving, and Dr. Pierce's
holiday had barely got started. Right after breakfast, Dr.
Pierce asked Grandpa Woodard if he wanted to do a little
snowmobiling with him. "I could rent a couple of snowmobiles, and you, Stephanie, Gregory and I could go for a little
ride." Stephanie and Gregory were really excited. They had
never been on a snowmobile before. So they all got bundled
up, and off they went in Grandpa Woodard's big car to see
if they could rent some snowmobiles. Jackson and Blake
asked if they could stay and play at Grandma Woodard's
house, and she said that would be fine, with her, she didn't
have anything special that she was going to do anyway, so
Mommy said it was okay with her, too. Angela, Jared, and
Jordan wanted to stay outside and play, so they did. "That's
fine with me," Tiffany replied, "I'm still a little cold." So she
went home and curled up on the couch with a blanket and a
good book.

About two hours later, she got up to get a cup of coffee,
and just then the phone rang. "Hello," she said, as she picked
up the receiver. It was Dr. Larson, who called to say that
there had been an accident in the south end of the county on
Highway 15, a bad head injury, "I hate to bother you Tiffany,
but I may need you. Do you think you could come in? It's

a really bad head injury; it sure would be nice if Dr. Pierce was here. We may have to send him to the cities." Tiffany replied, "I'll leave right away, and about Dr. Pierce, I'll see what I can do." And she hung up before Dr. Larson could say anything. Tiffany called Olivia and told her there had been a bad accident, and she had to go in to work. It was a very bad head injury, and she asked Olivia if she had Dr. Pierce's cell phone number. Olivia responded with, "Why, yes I do and just tell the children to come down here and play. We will all be just fine." Tiffany thanked her and immediately called Dr. Pierce and left her cell phone number, got her coat, and headed for the hospital.

Dr. Pierce had his cell phone set to vibrate when somebody called. When the phone went off Dr. Pierce stopped his machine. "Oh no," Dr. Pierce thought, I thought I was far enough away from Baltimore they wouldn't be able to find me. Dr. Pierce mentioned, "Oliver, do you know where there might be a phone around here; I am not getting very good reception, this looks like it might be local phone number." Stephanie looked at the number on the phone and said "that's Mom's cell phone, I wonder what happened. She wouldn't call unless something was really wrong." Grandpa Woodard replied, "We had better take a minute to pray first." Dr. Pierce stated, "Good idea about praying, Oliver, but we had better pray while were driving, "we don't want to waste any time." Oliver remarked, "Follow me. There is a house about a mile from here, just where the road crosses the river, just down from the river bridge; pray that someone there will be home." It seemed like forever before they got to the river bridge, and there was a pickup just pulling out of the driveway when they pulled up. "Sorry to bother you," Dr. Pierce mentioned, "but we need to use your phone if we can. I'm a doctor and I just received a call on my cell phone, and there could be something wrong. I can't get good reception out here in the woods." Mr. Stevens replied, "Sure, no problem." Mr. Stevens unlocked the door and pointed to the phone on the wall in the kitchen. Dr. Pierce said, "Thank you very much." His hands were shaking as he dialed the phone number. Tiffany answered, "Well hello there, Dr. Pierce, How would you like to go to work?" Dr. Pierce responded with, "What do you mean by that, you had us scared to death." Tiffany apologized, "I am so sorry, I didn't mean to scare you. It's just that Dr. Larson called me, and said there was a bad accident in the south end of the county. He asked if I could come into work. They might need me, and he mentioned that it is a bad head injury, and they may need to operate. He also said it sure would be nice if Dr. Pierce were here. He said he was not too keen on head injuries. They may have to send the patient to the cities. I told him I would see what I could do." Dr. Pierce asked, "How much time do we have?" "Well," Tiffany responded, "I am about five minutes from the hospital; the ambulance should be there in approximately ten to fifteen minutes. Where are you?" Dr. Pierce asked, "How far are we from the hospital?" Mr. Stevens replied, "About five to seven minutes, if we take my truck." "Good enough," Dr. Pierce stated. "We are about ten to twelve minutes by the time we put the snowmobiles in this man's garage, so I will see you there. Have everything ready to take an x-ray, an MRI, and a CAT scan, whatever you have." Tiffany responded, "Yes boss, over and out." Conrad had to smile at how serious and professional Tiffany could be, and yet he remembered the beautiful time they had this morning, and how very personal, loving, and jolly she was. "Your mother has been called into work," Dr. Pierce stated, "she wants me there just in case they need me, it's a bad head injury, I guess." Mr. Stevens asked, "Are you that big doctor who keeps coming here from out east?" "Yes he is," Stephanie remarked, "he and my mom are going to work together today, and we get to pray." Mr. Stevens mentioned, "We'll just put those snowmobiles in the garage. I'll open the door if you two will drive them in. You kids can get in the truck, and start praying. Then everyone will be doing their jobs." Dr. Pierce stated, "Sounds like we have a team here." And off they went. Grandpa Woodard remarked, "We rented those snowmobiles from the gas station downtown, "would be much obliged if you could help me return them, Mr. Stevens, and I will pick up my car at the station and come back to the hospital." Mr. Stevens responded, "No problem, it's good as done." Stephanie and Gregory were praying that the person would not need an operation.

Now that is a very nice prayer, and we hope it is in God's will. Well, they arrived at the hospital at the same time as Mom. Dr. Larson was really happy when he saw Dr. Pierce. He asked Tiffany, "Now, how did you manage this?" "Well," Tiffany remarked with a smile, "Dr. Pierce is in town visiting his mother for the holidays, so I just asked him to come along." Dr. Larson responded with, "That sure makes me feel better, serious head injuries are something I do not know much about." Dr. Larson and Dr. Pierce were all scrubbed up, when the patient arrived a few minutes later. They rushed him in for an MRI, x-rays, and a CAT scan. He was in pretty bad shape. Stephanie and Gregory were still praying that he would not need surgery. Then Dr. Larson came in and told the children they might want to find a ride home, that he would have to have surgery, and it could be a long wait. Gregory stated, "Our Grandfather will pick us up after he takes the snowmobiles back, and picks up his car; meanwhile, we will continue to pray for the man in surgery." Dr. Larson, remarked, "By the way, the man's name is Mr. George Snyder. It would be easier for you to pray for him by name."

And when Grandpa Woodard arrived, the children told him about how hard they had prayed that Mr. Snyder would not need surgery, but he needed surgery anyway. Grandpa Woodard remarked, "Now, you both feel like God let you down, is that right? Let's sit down and examine your prayer.

Praying that Mr. Snyder would not have to have surgery is a noble prayer, but what were your motives for praying that prayer?" "Well," Stephanie remarked, as she and Gregory looked at each other. Grandpa Woodard knew there was something wrong. Grandpa Woodard responded, "So, what is the problem?" They told him they were praying that Mr. Snyder would not need surgery, so they could go back and snowmobile for the rest of the day. Grandpa Woodard replied, "That was a very selfish prayer. You were both more concerned about yourselves and what you wanted then you were about poor Mr. Snyder. God is not happy when we try to use Him to get our own way. We have to have a right attitude in our hearts when we pray. Both of you should ask God to forgive you for your sin, then we will continue to pray for Mr. Snyder, Dr. Pierce, and Dr. Larson, that God will guide their hands during the surgery, and give them wisdom and discernment in knowing exactly what to do. That kind of prayer will honor God, and give Him the glory." Mrs. Snyder and the children, Sam and Ginny, arrived right after Mr. Snyder went into surgery. It seemed like hours before Dr. Pierce, Dr. Larson, and mother came out of the operating room, and indeed it was. Twelve hours to be exact. Mr. Snyder's wife, Emily, and his two children were all there praying with Grandpa Woodard, Stephanie, and Gregory. Dr. Pierce and Dr. Larson went into a private room with Mrs. Snyder, and talked with her about Mr. Snyder's condition. He would be in the hospital two or three weeks, and then he would need some therapy, depending on how well his brain healed. For the next few days, they were going to keep him in a medically induced coma, so his brain would have time to heal, and would not swell. Dr. Pierce said;" The surgery went very well, and if there were no complications, he should heal very well. I will be here through the weekend, but then Dr. Larson will be taking over." Mrs. Snyder and the children were so thankful for everything. Sammy and

Ginny were so thankful that Stephanie and Gregory had chosen to stay and pray with them for their father instead of going home. Sammy and Ginny offered Stephanie and Gregory their tickets to the movies, which was playing at the theater downtown. "We were supposed to go tonight, but then the accident happened, and we would rather be here with Mom, than go to the movies, (By then it was the wee hours of the morning), please take them and use them." Mrs. Snyder remarked, "Give them Dads and mine too; maybe they have some brothers and sisters." Sammy took the tickets, and gave them to Stephanie and Gregory. They thanked him and Mrs. Snyder for the tickets and gave them a big hug. Grandpa Woodard remarked, "You see how good God is, when we are willing to give up something for others, God always gives us back a blessing."

After mother and Dr. Pierce went to clean up and change clothes, Stephanie said to Mrs. Snyder, "your husband was very lucky that the accident happened this weekend, because Dr. Pierce is a very well-known neurosurgeon in a big hospital in Baltimore. He just happened to be here on vacation for the holidays." "Yes," Grandpa Woodard mentioned, "he probably would have had to be flown to the cities or the Mayo Clinic in Rochester, and that would have taken precious time, which he did not have." "That's correct," Dr. Larson stated, "we sure could use someone like Dr. Pierce on our staff. How is it that he comes back here so often?" "Well," Oliver responded, "his mother lives here; in fact, I'm married to his mother." "Well! You don't say," Dr. Larson remarked, "no wonder Tiffany said she would see what she could do today when I mentioned I sure wished Dr. Pierce was here. I will have to have a serious talk with him before he leaves here." "God is so good," Mrs. Snyder responded, "we will have to thank Him for sending Dr. Pierce home for a visit this weekend. He may very well have saved my husband's life. God sure knows how to take something sad and bring good out of it." They all stood there and held hands, and all prayed again, and thanked God for His goodness, and His faithfulness. When Dr. Pierce and Tiffany were ready to leave, Dr. Pierce told Dr. Larson, "I will be staying at my mother's for the rest of this weekend. If there is any change in Mr. Snyder of any kind, please call me at once; otherwise, I will stop and look in on him tomorrow. I want him kept in a comatose state for a few days, so his brain can heal. I will give you my cell phone number, Dr. Larson."

Grandpa and the children started for home in Grandpa Woodard's big car. Dr. Pierce and Tiffany went in Tiffany's car. It was around 3:30 a.m. by the time they got home. Mother stated, "We sure appreciate you children staying and playing with the Snyder children, they were pretty scared. We are very proud of you." "Likewise," Dr. Pierce remarked, "I am very proud of both of you too." Stephanie remarked, "Just don't wake us up in the morning Mom, and no bets on how long we will sleep or when we will wake up." They all had a hearty laugh. "Don't worry about that," Mother replied, "I have learned a valuable lesson on betting." They all laughed again. "Oh," Dr. Pierce mentioned, "your mother just doesn't have a very good sense of humor." "Well," Grandpa Woodard stated, "I thought it was very humorous; in fact, it was the funniest thing I had seen in years. In fact, Olivia said she was disappointed that she didn't get to see the two of you land in the snow bank" "Yah," Stephanie remarked, "I thought it was a blast." "Yah," Gregory mentioned, "it's too bad we didn't have time to get the camera." "Oh! But I did," Grandpa Woodard responded. "I saw the camera on top of the refrigerator, just as the two of you sailed past me, and out the door. In fact, I got three pictures before it was over." "Well," Tiffany replied, "right now I am too tired to even care. Come on children, we better get those two guys on their way home. We'll see you guys tomorrow afternoon. Tell Olivia thanks for taking the children, I really appreciate it." "On second thought," Grandpa Woodard remarked, "I think maybe Dr. Pierce and I should just bunk in over here, I think we will get a much better day's sleep." "Yah," Gregory replied, "you two can sleep in Blake's and Jackson's beds, but be careful your feet might hang over." "Oh, is that right?" Dr. Pierce remarked, "I hear that Gregory's bed is very comfortable," and off they went. Dr. Pierce, leading the way taking two steps at a time with Gregory right on his heels. Tiffany looked at Grandpa Woodard and said, "oh my, and to think how quiet it used to be here." "Yes," Grandpa Woodard stated, "but that was before you had a teenager and a 39-year-old running through the house." They both had a good laugh as they walked up the stairs. Tiffany called Grandma Woodard's house, and left a message on her phone about Grandpa Woodard and Conrad sleeping over, and then she got into bed and fell fast asleep.

It was about 10:00 a.m., when Tiffany came downstairs. She asked, "What smells so good?" As she came into the kitchen, there was Grandpa Woodard and Conrad with her aprons on, standing in the kitchen fixing breakfast. "My," Tiffany stated, "it looks like someone has taken over my kitchen." "Well," Conrad replied, "I thought I should pay for my room, so I got Oliver to help me, and before you knew it there were pancakes, eggs, bacon, and toast, and, oh yes, coffee." Tiffany mentioned, "Will the miracles never seem to cease around here?" As she sat down at the kitchen table she said, "And by the way, how did you and Gregory enjoy sleeping in the same bed Conrad?" "Oh," Conrad replied, "he made such a fuss I had to let him have the bed, mostly because he beat me to it because I didn't know which way to go after I got to the top of the stairs. But, I found a pretty little pink bedroom, with a pink bed, with pink covers, and I climbed in there and slept like a baby." Tiffany remarked, "Oh that was Angela's room. She will be happy to know that you slept in her room." "Well, look who's up," Dr. Pierce remarked, as the two children came bouncing down the stairs. They both said, "It sure smells good down here." Gregory stated, "Wow! Look who's making breakfast." Mom mentioned, "Come sit down, and put your order in." Dr. Pierce asked, "Which will it be, pancakes, eggs, or bacon?" Both children stated, "Yes, please." Grandpa Woodard let out a big laugh as he flipped a pancake, "I think that means some of each Conrad." Stephanie remarked, "And I will have some cocoa milk as Blake would call it. I could get used to this, Mom, how about you?" Tiffany remarked, "This is just like as if I died and went to heaven. What are my two cooks fixing for lunch?"

Just then, there was a knock at the door. Before anyone could answer it, it flew open and in rushed Blake, Jackson, Jordan, Jared, and Angela, and following right behind them, was Grandma Woodard. The little ones ran to Mommy and then to Dr. Pierce. Blake said, "You were gone a long time." Dr. Pierce mentioned, "It was a long operation, twelve hours, in fact, but I believe Mr. Snyder will be just fine in a month or so." Olivia asked, "You don't mean George Snyder, do you?" "Why yes," Conrad remarked, "do you know him?" Olivia responded, "He is the son of very good and dear friends, Arnold and Nancy Snyder." Oliver stated, "I remember them, but they moved away years ago. The boy was just a child. Where did they move to?" Olivia answered, "They bought a small house in Carson Creek. Arnold was a school teacher there until he retired, then they moved to Florida. I lost track of them after that." Conrad stated, "Well, I believe George must still live in Carson Creek, because the accident happened just outside of town, at the railroad crossing. Guess the lights were out or something. We have to wait until he wakes up to find out exactly what happened." Olivia mentioned, "Well, when you go into the hospital this afternoon, Conrad, you let Mrs. Snyder know that they are welcome to stay here as long as George is in the hospital, and if they need anything, be sure to let us know." So Dr.

Pierce and Grandpa Woodard made breakfast for the whole crew. And Stephanie and Gregory cleaned up the kitchen and did the dishes. Tiffany said; "this is the best holiday, I have ever had; no cooking, no cleaning, and no dishes." Conrad remarked, "And, you are off the hook for supper too. I will give the four older children money to get a hot dog or whatever else they want at the theater, and the rest of us are going out for dinner and ice cream while they are at the movies." All the children were really excited about that. Conrad continued, "But first, Tiffany, I would like you to run into the hospital with me this afternoon and see how our patient is doing. Then I will have a talk with Mrs. Snyder." Tiffany said, "That's fine with me.

After Dr. Pierce and Tiffany left for the hospital, Stephanie and Gregory went up to Grandpa Woodard and said, "Grandpa, is it a bad attitude in our hearts to pray that Dr. Pierce will ask our mother to marry him? Because you know we really would like him to be our dad." "Oh! I see," said Grandpa Woodard, "Praying a prayer like that and letting God know what you want is okay and good as long as you remember to add at the end, 'but Lord, we want your will for their lives to be done, not ours.' Then you are putting them in God's hands and He will do His will in their lives." "Okay," Stephanie said, "That is how we will continue to pray then." The children have learned a valuable lesson in knowing how to pray.

Mr. Snyder seem to be doing just fine; there didn't seem to be any swelling in the brain or any other problems. They had a very nice visit with Mrs. Snyder, and she agreed to stay with Grandpa and Grandma Woodard while George was in the hospital, at least part of the time. The children wanted to be near their mother, so she said she would agree that Mr. Woodard could drive the children home Monday morning to pick up clothes for all of them and get their homework from school, at least for the next week. Then she would let them stay with her. Tiffany said the children could come to her house for two or three hours in the evenings to spend some time with Stephanie and Gregory. Sam and Ginny were really happy about that. Tiffany stated, "I could take them home with me when I leave work, they can have supper with us or Oliver and Olivia." Mrs. Snyder replied, "You are all so kind, how can I ever repay you for all you are doing?" Tiffany responded, "You don't owe us anything, we are more than happy to help out the children of some very dear friends of Olivia's." "By the way," Mrs. Snyder remarked, "Mom and Dad Snyder are driving up from Florida. They should be here sometime by Monday afternoon." Dr. Pierce replied, "I may stick around and meet them, I should check in on George Monday morning before I leave anyway. Would you children want to change your minds and go to the movies with the others?" "Oh no," Sam answered, "we will stay right here with Mom, at least till Grandpa and Grandma Snyder get here."

Tiffany said, "We will bring you some turkey sandwiches, dressing, cranberry sauce, and pumpkin pie, when we come in to take the children to the movies." Mrs. Snyder answered, "Oh, thank you so much, hospital food can be expensive for an extended length of time."

As they were leaving the hospital, Dr. Larson stopped them and said he would like to get together with Dr. Pierce on Monday morning, before he left to go back to Baltimore. "That's fine," Dr. Pierce remarked, "I was going to stop in to see Mr. Snyder anyway before I left on Monday. I just have to make sure I can still catch my plane on time."

Conrad and Tiffany had a really nice time visiting on the way back home. They had just about enough time to change clothes, and make some sandwiches and pack a nice picnic lunch and pop for the Snyders at the hospital, and be on their way back to town. The movie was "Black Beauty." Angela just loves horses, so she was really excited. Stephanie and

Gregory were reminded to take very good care of Angela and Jared, and make sure they bought a hot dog as well as popcorn, or candy and pop. Mother remarked, "And make sure the younger ones sit between you older children, and if they have to go to the bathroom, make sure one of you goes with them." "Yes, Mother," Stephanie and Gregory both answered. And with that said, the children were left at the theater.

The next stop was the hospital. Tiffany quickly ran the food in to the Snyders in the family waiting room, and then they were off to have supper, and then ice cream. The children were very good and ate all their dinner. When they got to the ice cream place, they couldn't decide what they wanted. Blake got a small dish of vanilla ice cream with chocolate sauce on it. Jackson wanted one of those big vanilla ice creams on a stick, dipped in chocolate, and Jordan, wanted a vanilla ice cream sundae with bananas and chocolate sauce and a big cherry on top. Tiffany remarked, "I don't know where they are putting all this food." Tiffany and Olivia both got the same thing Blake had, and Oliver and Dr. Pierce got a big banana split with the works. The children were so full, and so tired by the time they reached the theater, they fell fast asleep. Grandpa Woodard told Tiffany, they would wait for the children, and that she could just take the little ones home and get them to bed. Tiffany responded, "Sounds good to me." So she and Dr. Pierce drove off with the three little sleeping angels in the back seat.

Tiffany and Dr. Pierce had just finished putting the little ones to bed, when Grandpa and Grandma Woodard drove up with the other children. "Oh, Mommy," Angela remarked," Black beauty is such a beautiful horse; I wished I could have a horse." Mother responded, "A horse would be very expensive to keep. They eat a lot of food, which we would have to buy." Gregory stated, "I would like to have one too." Jared mentioned, "me too. Mother asked, "Why don't we buy a whole herd of horses?" Jared stated, "We don't have room for a whole herd of horses, we just want three of them." Everyone gave a hearty laugh. "Well," Mother remarked, "if and when my ship comes in, we will get you your horses." Jared asked, "What do you mean by that? You don't even have a ship." Everyone started laughing again. "Jared," Dr. Pierce replied, "it means when your mother gets rich, she will get horses for you." "Well," Jared remarked, "I guess we can forget about our horses, because I don't think our mom is ever going to be rich." "Well," Mother responded, "you children had better get upstairs and get to bed. Maybe you will dream you have a herd of horses. Sweet dreams, sleep fast, morning will come soon enough, and we have church tomorrow." Dr. Pierce and Grandpa and Grandma Woodard said goodnight and left. Tiffany and the children almost ran up the stairs. They were all very tired. It was the end of another beautiful day. Mother laid out the children's clothes for church before she went to sleep. She told the children they were going to have a light breakfast, because Grandma Woodard was having all of them down to her house for dinner after church.

The children all wanted to sit by Dr. Pierce at every meal, so they had been drawing straws to see whose turn it would be at each meal. Gregory and Jordan got to sit by him at breakfast, and Stephanie and Angela would sit by him at church, and Jared and Jackson would sit by him at dinner at Grandma's house. At church, everyone prayed for Mr. Snyder and Mrs. Snyder and the children, and they prayed for Grandpa and Grandma Snyder on their drive and their safety on the way home from Florida. Everyone in town had heard about the big accident, and everyone was praying for Mr. Snyder. After church, Grandma and Grandpa Woodard headed right on home with the four oldest children to help get ready for dinner. Tiffany and Dr. Pierce and the younger children went right on over to the hospital. Between Dr. Pierce, Dr. Larson, and Tiffany, they convinced Mrs. Snyder to go with Dr. Pierce and Tiffany, have a nice hot meal, take a shower, change clothes, and get a few hours rest. It will do you and the children a world of good, and Mr. Snyder will be just fine with all the nurses to look after him. If anything happens, we promise we will call you right away. Mrs. Snyder mentioned, "I'll follow you all in my car, then I will learn how to come and go on my own." So off they went. They had a wonderful meal, and Mrs. Snyder had a nice hot bath, as did Sam and Ginny, and Mrs. Snyder slept for about four hours. Sam and Ginny had a wonderful time with Gregory and Stephanie. After a supper of turkey soup, salad, and homemade bread, Mrs. Snyder stated, "I will stay at the hospital tonight, but I think you children should stay here and get a good night's rest." Then she left for the hospital. That's exactly what they did. They rode in with Tiffany when she went to work Monday morning. As soon as the children left for school, Grandpa and Grandma Woodard drove in to take the children to Carson Creek to get their homework, and more clothes. Dr. Pierce spent most of the morning in a meeting with Dr. Larson, and then he stopped in to check on Mr. Snyder, who was doing very well. Dr. Larson stated, "There is still no swelling in the brain, which is a good sign, and Mrs. Larkin can have time off to take Dr. Pierce to the airport." So off they went.

CHAPTER 9

THE LONG WAIT

Even though the children had a wonderful time on their Thanksgiving vacation, they were glad to get back to school, especially Stephanie and Gregory. The sooner they got back to school, the sooner they would be on Christmas vacation (two whole weeks). They could hardly wait. They were counting the days, fifteen more days of school. The children still didn't know whether they were going to go be going to Baltimore, or whether Dr. Pierce was coming here for Christmas, but either way they knew they would have a wonderful time being with Dr. Pierce no matter where they were. Every night they would pray that Dr. Pierce would ask their mother to marry him. They would add, but; Father God, not our will, but Yours be done.

All the children were home from school, when Tiffany pulled into the driveway. The children had forgotten that Sam and Ginny Snyder were going to come home with Mom for supper and to stay overnight. Gregory and Stephanie were really glad to see them. Sam and Ginny had some homework to do, so they all four went upstairs and started on their homework. Mrs. Snyder came about one hour later. Tiffany answered the door. "We're so happy to see you, Mrs. Snyder. "Supper will be ready in just a few minutes; do sit down and have a cup of coffee." Mrs. Snyder thanked Tiffany and said, "I'll only be staying a couple or three hours, then I will go back to the hospital and stay through the night. Mom and Dad Snyder will come out and stay the night at Mr. and Mrs. Woodard's. They really need their rest after their long trip. They will come back to the hospital tomorrow, and then we will take turns every other night, so George will always have someone with him. That way the children can ride back and forth with one of us, and you will not have to worry about them." Tiffany replied, "It was no problem at all, but, whatever you think is best. So when did Mr. and Mrs. Snyder get here?" Mrs. Snyder answered, "Around 2:30 p.m. They really looked drained and tired out. I wished I could do something for them." Tiffany responded, "You are doing all you can for them, by letting them get a good night's rest. The fact that George is showing improvement every day is enough to give them hope. Dr. Pierce will call every day and check in on him, and Dr. Larson will give you all an update every day also. Other than that, there is nothing for us to do but pray, and wait. And I know waiting is the hardest part. Angela, would you please go and let Stephanie, Gregory, and the Snyder children know supper is ready?" Angela answered, "Yes, Mom," as she started up the stairs. Olivia mentioned, "Tomorrow night supper will be on us." "That would be super," Tiffany remarked, "and Stephanie, Gregory, and Angela, you children can help Grandma Woodard with supper tomorrow night." Ginny and Sam said, "We would like to help tomorrow night too." "That's a good idea," Mrs. Snyder remarked, "and you two children can do the dishes and cleanup tonight also." Ginny and Sam replied, "Yes, Mother." Stephanie remarked, "We will help also, that is our job." Tiffany mentioned, "As long as there will be so much help in the kitchen tomorrow night, Angela, you can help with the younger children at Grandma Woodard's, when you get home from school." Angela replied, "Good, I really enjoy playing with the little ones. They always like to play school, and I get to be the teacher." Mrs. Snyder remarked, what a wonderful dinner it was, but she would like to go over to Mrs. Woodard's and lie down for a couple hours before she had to go back to the hospital. Olivia said, "That's fine with me, I could stand to sit down and rest a bit myself." Everyone retired early as they were still a little tired from the long weekend. Grandpa Woodard said he would wait up for Mr. and Mrs. Snyder. Tiffany remarked, "I will bring the little ones down in the morning so Olivia can visit with the Snyder's a little while before they go back to the hospital, and I will send some dinner down for the Snyders so they can have supper, when they get there tonight."

By the end of the week, Mr. Snyder was doing much better. Dr. Pierce had said that Dr. Larson could start taking him out of the coma very slowly, and see how his brain reacts. He mentioned, "I want to be notified of even the slightest change, no matter how small." "Okay," Dr. Larson replied, "we will start taking him off the medication, first thing in the morning. And if there is any sign of swelling in the brain, or anything else, I will call you at once." The Snyder family did not want to leave the hospital in case Mr. Snyder started to move or respond to anything, but Dr. Larson told them, "there is much danger of him getting excited by seeing all of you here at once, so we don't want more than one or two here at any one time. We don't want him to make any sudden moves, or get upset if he should see his parents here. He may think things are really serious, if they've come all the way from Florida. Until we see how he responds and understands what happened, I think it would be best if just his wife were here."

Mr. and Mrs. Snyder went to stay with the Woodard's, and Sam and Ginny went to stay at the Larkin's house. That helped a great deal. By Wednesday evening, Mr. Larkin was moving his hands and feet a little, and his eyes would open and close, and he was looking around a little bit. They were all really good signs. The MRI showed no swelling in the brain, another really good sign. Everyone was so excited; they were thanking God for the positive signs and the progress, and asking him to continue to heal Mr. Snyder.

On Wednesday, December 8th, Grandpa and Grandma Woodard and Tiffany sat down at the table, and discussed their trip. Grandpa and Grandma Woodard, Jordan, Jackson, and Blake would leave on December 14th, in the morning. Oliver stated, "That is less than a week away, we have to convince the Snyders that they should continue to use our house, while we are gone." "Leave that to me," Olivia replied, "I will talk to Arnold and Nancy tonight when they get here. Everything will be fine." "Okay," Oliver remarked. Tiffany mentioned, "I will have the children's clothes packed and ready to go by Sunday evening; you can pack them in your trunk Monday, if you want to, and there will be one special bag to take in with you when you stop overnight. I would appreciate it if you would call me collect every evening, wherever you stop, and here is some money for food for the children." "No deal," Oliver responded, "Conrad bought us a cell phone; he said he would not have us traveling without one. And he also left plenty of money for food and lodging before he left. He said this trip is on him. If Olivia was not so scared to fly, he would've had everyone fly. So when are you flying out?" Tiffany replied, "The children get out of school at 2:00 p.m. on the 17th, and I will be at the school to pick them up. The plane leaves at 5:00 p.m. we should have time to check in and get something to eat before the plane takes off. We should be in Baltimore by 7:30 or 8:00 p.m. at the latest. Conrad is going to send the tickets by Federal Express to the hospital on Friday the 10th, so everything should be pretty well set." "Well," Oliver stated, "we should all be there to pick you up. We should be there by Friday afternoon, (early around one or two o'clock,)"

Tiffany arrived home from work just after the children got off the bus. As she walked in the house, she mentioned that Mr. and Mrs. Snyder were bringing supper home tonight. They are picking up Chinese. Jackson asked, "I don't know what Chinese is." Jordan replied, "Don't be silly; it is the kind of food the Chinese people eat, the kind they have in China." Jackson asked, "Where is China?" Angela replied, "It's way across the ocean." Jackson asked, "Is that further than Baltimore?" Everyone burst out laughing. "Jackson," Stephanie remarked, "it is time you learned that Baltimore is in Maryland. Right here in the good old USA." Jackson asked, "What is the good old USA?" "Jackson," Stephanie responded, "it means the United States of America, the USA, it's where we live." Jackson answered, "I thought we lived in Minnesota!" "I give up," Stephanie remarked, "You will learn more, Jackson, once you start school." "Good," Jackson replied, "then I will find out where Baltimore is." Everyone laughed. Just then the Snyders drove in. Jackson said, "good, now we'll find out what Chinese food is." Mommy stated, "You will also be polite and eat it, too, won't you." Jackson replied, "Yes, I will." Everyone really liked the Chinese food, and just for fun, the Snyder's brought chopsticks to eat with. The children never had so much fun trying to eat in their lives, only Jackson couldn't quite handle the chopsticks, so Mommy finally gave him a spoon and Mommy had to help little Blake also. Angela mentioned, "We should have this more often. It is really good." Tiffany invited the Snyder children to stay with them overnight, and Grandpa and Grandma Snyder said they could, so all the children were happy. The Snyders went over to Oliver and Olivia's early so they could get a good night's sleep. Olivia put on a pot of coffee when they got to her house, and they sat down and started talking. Olivia explained about the trip and how they would like the Snyder's to continue to stay at their house, and watch it for them while they were gone on the trip. The Snyders said that they would be happy to help out. They said they would all stay at the house except one person would constantly be at the hospital with George, so he would not be alone.

Before you knew it, it was Sunday, December 12th. Tiffany had invited the whole Snyder family to church. Since George Snyder was completely awake and alert, they all said they would go. Everyone at church was so happy to see them and to find out that George was doing so much better. The whole church started praising God, because they had been praying for Mr. Snyder for a long time. Mrs. Snyder's eyes filled with tears, because she was so thankful for all the prayers, and thankful to God for all He had done. It was a beautiful sermon, and a wonderful service altogether. After church, Arnold and Nancy Snyder said, "Oliver, you and your family have been so kind and good to us these past two weeks, we want to take all of you out to dinner." Oliver stated, "Oh, that's way too much." "Not at all," Nancy Snyder replied, "I insist." Jackson asked, "Can we have Chinese again? I love Chinese." Nancy Snyder said with a smile, "Why, yes, of course." So Chinese it was, and it was just as good as it was last week. Olivia and Oliver went in to see George Snyder, on Monday before they left on their trip. He was completely off his medication, so he was saying a few words. He could not sit up for very long, though. Tuesday they would start therapy, but he was in good spirits and had a good sense of humor. Dr. Pierce had been calling every day just to see how he was doing. "Well," Oliver remarked, "we are leaving on a trip out east, and we would like you to be able to be staying at the house by the time we get back, and having a therapist coming out there to see you." Mrs. Snyder replied, "That would be a miracle" "Well," Oliver mentioned, "miracles are what God does best." "That He does," Mrs. Snyder remarked, "that He does." Oliver said a prayer for Mr. Snyder and then they went to leave. Emily Snyder said, "Your family has been so good to us, we can't ever repay you. "Well," Oliver stated, "from what I hear your in-laws were very good friends to Olivia, and after all, that's what good friends are for, to help one another out."

Tuesday morning, December 14th, came quickly. The older children were getting ready for school, and Mommy was getting everything ready for the little ones to leave. Grandpa and Grandma Woodard drove down the driveway, and Grandpa parked the car right up as close to the house as he could. They got out of the car and came in. The little ones were so excited; they were all ready to go, and one by one they gave all the other children hugs and kisses, and the other children gave Grandpa and Grandma Woodard hugs and kisses too. Mommy had tears in her eyes, and said; "are you sure you will be okay?" "Oh, heavens yes," Grandpa Woodard remarked, "we are only going to go about 300 miles a day, and we will have plenty of stops to stretch our legs. We have about 1,125 miles to go, so three and one half days should do it, more or less." Mommy strapped little Blake in his car seat, and strapped Jackson and Jordan in, and gave each one a big hug and kiss and said; "you had better go, or I may change my mind." So she got their cell phone number and off they went. They no more than left, when the school bus came, and Tiffany also had to leave for work. Her first stop was to see how Mr. Snyder was doing. Dr. Larson stated, "He is doing just great." Tiffany replied, "That is just wonderful." Then she left and went about her duties.

The time flew by fast, and before you knew it, it was Friday, the 17th of December. The children were up extra early and had all their things packed in the car. They each had as many bags as they could take. Gregory remarked, "I don't know how I'm going to get any schoolwork done today, I am so excited I can hardly think." Jared stated, "Me too." Mother told them, "Just make sure you guys are in the office and ready to go at 2:00 p.m." The children couldn't even remember being on an airplane before. Mother stated, "Only Stephanie and Gregory were on an airplane before, and they were very young."

The day went by so slowly. Mr. Snyder was being sent home to Grandpa and Grandma Woodard's house, just after lunch, and they were going to start therapy first thing Saturday morning.

Dr. Pierce called to find out how he was doing, and when he got the news, he was overjoyed. "By the way," Conrad remarked, "Mom, Oliver and the children just arrived at the hospital, so I will be leaving in just a few minutes to go home. We will stop for lunch on the way. We will be at the airport around 7:00 p.m., so we will see you soon." Tiffany answered, "Thank you so much, Conrad, for telling me that, I am so relieved to know they got there okay, I will let the other children know. Dr. Larson told me I could leave at 1:00 p.m., so I am going to call the school and make sure the children are ready to go. So we will see you soon." Conrad mentioned, "We will go out for dinner tonight, since I don't have a maid; although I might hire one for the next two weeks, so we don't have to worry about it." They both laughed.

Mother was at school at 1:15 p.m. Gregory asked, "Boy, Mom, why are you so early?" Mother remarked, "Dr. Larson gave me a little extra time, just in case we needed it." "Well, here we go," Stephanie replied, "we are finally on our vacation." They said a prayer for the trip on the way to the airport and thanked God that Grandpa and Grandma Woodard made it to Baltimore safely, that Mr. Snyder was going to leave the hospital, and that they would make it to the airport on time.

They made it to the airport in plenty of time, parked the car at one of those "park and ride" places, and got a shuttle bus over to the airport terminal where they got a cart to put their luggage on. Since they already had their tickets, they just had to check in their luggage. Then they found a place to get something to eat. It was just five minutes from where they were to board the plane. Praise God for that. After they ate, they went to the boarding gate. People with little children boarded first. Because Mom had four children, they told her to go in right away. As the children sat on the plane they thought they were already way above the ground.

The pilot said over the intercom, "It will be another twenty minutes before the plane actually takes off, but we should leave right on time." In a few minutes, the pilot came back on the intercom. "Well," he said, "we are leaving a few minutes early, and we will be having a good tailwind, so we should be arriving in Baltimore about twenty minutes early. Thank you for traveling with us today, and we should have a very smooth flight." The children were really happy about that.

As they started to back out of the terminal, the stewardess came on the monitor and gave them a very important message about safety: that they should keep their seat belts fastened until the pilot tells you it is safe to unbuckle them. She also mentioned about the exit doors in case they had to evacuate the plane. Now that made the children nervous. Ever so slowly, they went down the runway to their starting position. Then the pilot revved up the engines until the whole plane shook. All of a sudden, they started to move forward faster and faster and faster until the ground started to look further and further away. Jared stated "We are in the air." Jared and Angela got to sit by the window on the way to Baltimore, and Gregory and Stephanie would get to sit there on the way home. They were so excited to see the ground so far away, and all the tiny little roads and tiny cars and trucks driving on them. The fields were all square, or rectangular, or round and a patch of woods was so perfectly round or square. The houses looked so small too.

The stewardess asked them if they wanted some pop and pretzels. They all answered her at the same time. Mother mentioned, "One at a time." All of a sudden, the pilot came back on the intercom. "We have reached a cruising altitude and are leveling off at 40,000 feet. It looks like we will have a very smooth trip. You can unbuckle your seat belts now: if it's going to get rough, I will let you know. Now sit back and enjoy your trip, and thank you for traveling with us." The children each brought a book to read, but they couldn't help looking out the windows at all the beautiful blue sky and white fluffy clouds and all the fields, and woods and lakes and rivers all laid out in a neat pattern. Mother decided she was going to take a nap, but the children were too excited to sleep. It seemed like they had just taken off when the pilot came back on the speaker and said. "Would you please fasten your seat belts? We are entering the landing pattern of the Baltimore airport; we should be landing in about ten minutes. Thank you for flying with us today, and enjoy your stay in Baltimore. Have a good evening. The temperature in Baltimore is 41°. It should be a beautiful day tomorrow. And it is going to be a beautiful night tonight also, thought Tiffany, and she smiled. The steward said, "Please keep your seat belts fastened until the plane comes to a complete stop, families with children will be the first ones off."

The plane came to a complete stop. Gregory stood up, got their carry-on luggage down from the overhead bins and handed it to everyone else. Mother went first, and then Jared, Angela, and Stephanie, with Gregory last. Mother said, "We must all stay together." They went to retrieve the rest of their luggage, and as they came to the end of the walkway where it went to the luggage pickup; there was Grandpa and Grandma Woodard, Blake, Jackson, Jordan, and Dr. Pierce. "Mommy, Mommy, Mommy," the little ones all hollered at once, and off they ran. They all said, "We missed you, we missed you." Mommy replied, "We missed you too," and bent down and gave each of them big hugs and kisses. Dr. Pierce just picked up Tiffany and swung her around, and gave her a great big kiss right in front of everyone. "Boy," Jordan remarked, "Dr. Pierce must have really missed our mama a whole lot," and everyone laughed. Conrad replied, "I sure did." Tiffany thought she had better change the subject, so she said. "How in the world did all of you get past security this far, clear up here? No one without a boarding pass is allowed in here." Conrad replied, "I have a little pull, I know all the security at the airport. I am always having to go someplace in a hurry, in an emergency. They're always letting me go through, I have a special pass." Gregory remarked, "Sounds exciting." Dr. Pierce answered, "Well, study real hard, Gregory, and maybe someday you can be a doctor too." Gregory remarked, "I don't know, it sounds like you have to stay in school for a long time." "You sure do," Dr. Pierce replied, "but we had better get over to the baggage pickup, and get our luggage before someone thinks we forgot it, and they take it and put it away someplace." Stephanie said, "We can't let that happen, all my good clothes are in there." "Well," Dr. Pierce replied, "we had better hurry then," and they took off. He knew right where to go.

Conrad remarked, "We took a cab over here from my apartment. I told Oliver, there is no need in him trying to find his way around Baltimore, especially during the holidays. It gets pretty wild around here. In fact most of the time, I take a helicopter to and from the hospital. There is a heliport on the roof of our apartment building. Jackson, you think Grandpa Woodard's car is big, wait till you see this car." When they reached the outside of the building, one of those big, long stretch limos pulled up front. It looked to Jackson like two or three of Grandpa Woodard's big old Lincoln town cars could fit right inside. Neither Jackson, nor any of the other children for that matter, had ever seen a car that long. They couldn't even speak. They just stood there and stared at it. The driver had all the luggage loaded in the big trunk, and was just standing there with the door open, waiting for someone to get in. Mother remarked, "Well children, are you going to get in, or are you going to just stare at the car?" They still just stood there, like they were hypnotized. Mother walked around in front of the children, carrying little Blake, and got in the car, and the rest of the children followed one by one. When everyone was in, the driver said, "There are some sodas in the refrigerator and some extra cups, if anyone would like one." "Thank you," Dr. Pierce remarked. Between Dr. Pierce and Grandpa Woodard, they got everybody served in a short time. The children didn't even notice the big city, which was going past them on the outside. They had all they could do to take in all the things that were inside the car. Tiffany stated, "I have a feeling the children will talk about this trip for years to come." Grandpa Woodard replied, "And just wait till the little ones start telling you both about their trip out here." "By the way," Dr. Pierce added, "I forgot to tell you about my apartment. It is rather small. I have only two bedrooms, and two baths and a small kitchen, and a small living room." Now it was Mother's turn to get very quiet, and her eyes got big, and her mouth dropped open. "But," Dr. Pierce continued, "don't worry, I was going to rent a suite for you and the children, but some very good friends of mine insisted you stay in their apartment, across the hall from mine. They have six bedrooms, five bathrooms, and a very large kitchen and dining room, a huge living room, a family room, and a great room; we can spend most of our time over there too." "And," Tiffany mentioned; "where are these very good friends of yours staying, while we will be using their apartment?" "Well," Conrad replied, "they always go to Hawaii for the winter months. In fact, they just left on Wednesday and will be gone till the middle of March. Oh, I almost forgot, they are keeping their maid and their cook on, through the time you are going to be here, so you will have your own maid service. And your cook, or should I say our cook, will be cooking for us, too. I told them that I would pay them, whatever they wanted, plus a bonus for the maid and cook, and she said, "no way! You have done so much for us since we moved in here, now it is our turn to do a favor for you. "Just pass it on," that's what she said." "Well," Grandpa Woodard remarked, "I believe you have already passed it on, Tiffany." Tiffany asked, "What do you mean?" "Well," Grandma Woodard replied, "you have already done a lot for the Snyders, and so has Dr. Pierce. I would say you both have passed it on already."

Time went by so fast since they left the airport, that they were all surprised when the driver pulled over to the curb and got out. He opened the door, reached in, and took Tiffany's hand and helped her out. Then he reached in and helped Grandma Woodard. When it came Stephanie's turn, she felt just like a princess. After he helped Angela out, he reached in and picked up Jordan and turned her around and put her on the sidewalk. Then he bowed and tipped his hat. She just looked at Mommy and didn't know what to do. When everyone was out of the car he opened the trunk, and two men with uniforms came up to the car with a big cart on wheels and loaded all of the luggage on it. Dr. Pierce gave them some money and a key and off they went with the entire luggage. "Hey, Mom," Jared said, "those two men just stole our luggage." "Jared, it's OK," Dr. Pierce answered, "they didn't steal your luggage. They are taking it up to your apartment for you." Angela asked, "How do they know where to go?" Dr. Pierce replied, "I just told them. They know everyone who lives in this apartment building, and Sally and Jim already told them that my family was going to be using their apartment for few weeks." Angela said, "Oh, I see." All the children caught that little bit about (my family was going to be using the apartment). So did Mother, but they were all wise, and didn't mention anything about it.

Dr. Pierce gave the chauffer some money, and then he said; "we are going to go into the restaurant in our building for supper tonight, because your cook has already left for the day. It is getting late and the children must be very hungry." Tiffany stated, "Sounds good to me, we need to feed them before they fall asleep on their plates." Gregory answered, "Oh, Mom." "Honey," Mother replied, "I was talking about the little ones; they are very tired."

The restaurant was just beautiful. Angela stated, "This must be very expensive." Mother remarked, "Angela!" Conrad replied, "Oh, it's okay, this is all very new and exciting for the children. They are not used to these kinds of things." Olivia said, "Neither am I." Tiffany remarked, "We will order something that doesn't take very long to fix, because the children are so tired." When the waiter came to the table, he said, "Good evening, Dr. Pierce, this must be your family you have been talking about." There it was again, the word (family). Everyone caught it that time also. But again, no one said anything. While the waiter was taking their orders; Stephanie was looking at the waiter. He was tall and very good-looking. He had brown hair and deep brown eyes. He looked very handsome in his waiter uniform, and he had a towel draped over his arm. All of a sudden, she noticed he was talking to her. "What about you, young lady, what would you have?" She felt so embarrassed, she quickly said, "the same thing Gregory is having." The waiter replied, "Ma'am, I do not know which one is Gregory." Gregory replied, "I am Gregory." The waiter stated, "Now I know what you will have, and my name is Todd. I will be your waiter for the evening. If there is anything you need, please let me know." Stephanie remarked, "Why, yes Sir." The waiter walked away.

Jared asked, "How come he was just looking at Stephanie, when he was talking?" Dr. Pierce replied, "Why, I never noticed that." Mother responded, "Me either," Stephanie stated, "That's enough." In a few minutes he was back with their drinks, and when he served Stephanie, he bowed as he set her drink down, and off he went. "See," Jared said, "he did it again." "Okay Jared," Mother replied, "that's enough." "Well," Jared remarked, "I'm going to keep my eye on him." Dr. Pierce replied, "That's quite a protector you have there, Stephanie."

Dr. Pierce went on to tell about the apartment. "The cook will come in at 7:30 a.m. to start breakfast. The maid will be in around 7:45 a.m. to help get breakfast on. If you want them to serve you in bed, just leave them a note the night before you go to sleep. Also, if you want anything special, you have to let them know; otherwise, you have to eat what they fix. We will be coming over for breakfast also, they already know that. They already have your towels and other things laid out for your bath or shower, so enjoy yourselves. Emma is the cook, and Carrie is the maid. "Boy," Stephanie stated, "this is going to be the best vacation I have ever had. Gregory replied, "Me too." Mother mentioned, "Just remember, you will have to come back down to earth when we get home." Jordan asked, "What does that mean?" Mother replied, "That means, you will all have your work to do when we get home, so don't get too used to being waited on, and giving orders for what you want to eat." Grandma Woodard replied, "Oh, let them have some fun, Tiffany. The children need a break and so do you. Just enjoy yourselves for a couple of weeks; reality will settle in soon enough. I know I am going to enjoy being waited on." Tiffany answered, "Well, maybe you are right; I know I am going to enjoy a nice hot bath, once I get the little ones put to bed." Stephanie mentioned, "Me too." "Well," Conrad remarked, "I think you are all going to be quite surprised when you get upstairs and see this apartment. Shall we go?" Dr. Pierce had motioned for the waiter, and signed his name on the receipt for dinner. Dr. Pierce replied, "Thank you Todd." Todd remarked, "I hope you all have a wonderful Christmas here in Baltimore."

CHAPTER 10

THE BIG APARTMENT

D r. Pierce pushed the button on the elevator, the door opened, and there was another man wearing a very sharp uniform sitting inside the elevator who said, "Good evening, Dr. Pierce, you are home early tonight." "Yes sir," Dr. Pierce replied, "I would like you to meet the rest of my family, Walter. You've already met my mother, Oliver, and the three little children. This is Tiffany Larkin and her four oldest children, Stephanie, Gregory, Angela, and Jared." Walter remarked, "Please to meet you all, now, they are going to be staying in Sally and Jim's apartment is that correct?" Dr. Pierce stated, "That's correct." Walter said, "You children will just love that apartment, it is super! Well, here is the twenty-fifth floor, you have a good visit, and I'll see you in the morning." The children's mouths kind of fell open. Jared stated, "The twenty-fifth floor." "Jared," Dr. Pierce replied, "Your nose will probably start to bleed from the high altitude. We will look at my apartment tomorrow, but for now, we will stop at your apartment and get the little ones settled in." Jackson mentioned, "We already saw your apartment. It is pretty small."

Dr. Pierce took out a key and turned it in the lock, and then he stepped inside and pushed open the door. Tiffany entered right behind Dr. Pierce. As the others entered the room, Dr.

Pierce said, "Just wait right there and I will get the lights."
Just as Grandpa and Grandma Woodard entered the room, the
lights came on. Dr. Pierce stated, "Sorry about taking so long
to find the lights," as he turned around to see everyone just
gazing in amazement at the apartment. They were standing
in an entry way, about 9 feet deep and 20 feet long, with two
large closets, one on either end. Each closet was about 6 feet
deep and 9 feet long. In the center of the long hall was a huge
chandelier. Under the chandelier, in the center of the large
hall was a huge Christmas tree. It was just beautiful. It must
have been 10 feet tall. Dr. Pierce remarked, "This is just the
entryway," as he was taking their coats and hanging them up.
He continued, "It would help very much if everyone would
leave your shoes and boots in the front hall closets."

There was marble on the floor. Dr. Pierce asked them to
close their eyes and take hold of each other's hands, and he
would lead them into the living room. He stopped and said,
"Stand right there, and I will get the lights." When the lights
came on, they could not believe their eyes. The ceiling of
this great room must have been thirty feet high and had the
biggest chandelier anyone had ever seen. There was another
huge Christmas tree in this huge room. It looked way bigger
than the one in the entry way. There were presents under this
tree. Mother cautioned Blake, "Don't touch the trees, Blake;
as she put him down. There was a huge fireplace along one
wall, and the wall was all built-in cabinets with a huge TV
screen, built-in, about 6 x 12 feet in size. Gregory remarked,
"It would be cool watching that, it would be just like going to
the movies." On the fireplace were seven stocking holders,
with seven Christmas stockings hanging down. The fireplace
and shelves were all decorated with garlands and bows. The
furniture was just beautiful. Dr. Pierce stated, "The music
is built into every room." There were the most beautiful
pictures on the walls, and a huge mirror on the wall of the
entryway, just as you entered the great room. To the left of

this great room was the kitchen. It was just huge. There were two large commercial refrigerators, and one huge commercial freezer. There were three large built-in ovens, and two stove tops, there were two microwave ovens built into the wall. There was a large built-in grill with a huge fan over it on one end of the wall, and more cabinets than Tiffany and Grandma Woodard had ever seen. There was a huge center island with a garbage disposal, and two large sinks, and cabinets all around. There was also a deep sink in one corner with a very high faucet for filling large coffeepots. On one end of the kitchen, about 10 inches above the counter level was another counter, which was about 10 inches inside the kitchen and about 2 1/2 feet protruding out into the dining room for handing food from the kitchen right into the dining room for serving. Even the kitchen was all decorated for Christmas.

The dining room was about 24 feet long, and had a large dining room table, which must have been 16 feet long, at least. They were the most beautiful dining room table and chairs Tiffany or Grandma had ever seen. On the long wall behind the table were built-in cabinets along the whole length of the wall. It had a marble countertop, and the doors on the top cabinets were beautiful glass. Behind the glass doors was the most beautiful Christmas china and Christmas crystal glassware Tiffany or Grandma had ever seen. There was also a Christmas tree in the corner of the dining room. Not as big as the other two trees, but just as beautiful. At the far end of the dining room was a large door that led to the family room. It was not quite as big as the great room, but just as beautiful and grand, and at one end about 10 feet out from the wall, was a pool table. "Wow," Gregory said, "it sure will be fun to learn how to play pool." Dr. Pierce remarked, "I'm sure we can find time to play a game or two." On the other end of the room was a baby grand piano. There were big stuffed chairs, three quarters of the way around the piano, and a large floor space in front of the piano. Dr. Pierce mentioned, "The empty floor space is for dancing." There were also small tables placed among the chairs for drinks and snacks. There was a very large Christmas tree in this room, just as beautiful but not as big as the one in the great room.

They came to a very large doorway back into the great room. About 12 feet into the great room was a circular stairway, going up to the second-floor, which was built all the way around the huge ceiling of the great room. There was another huge Christmas tree standing in the corner of the hall at the top of the stairs. There was garland and beautiful pine cones and flowers, running along the railing all along the hall and down the circular stair railings on both sides. Tiffany looked at Conrad and said, "This is way too much, we can't stay here with all the children. Conrad, what if they broke something?" Conrad gave her a smile and said, "It will be fine, Hon, trust me." No one else could even talk yet. They were still taking everything in. As they reached the top of the stairs, the first door they entered was a huge room with a king size bed, a sofa, and overstuffed chair. It had a huge walk-in closet. At one end of the closet there was a large three-sided mirror. There also was a table and two chairs in the room. There was also a smaller tree in this room, about 6 feet tall, in one corner of the room. It was beautifully decorated also. In one corner of the room was a full-sized crib. Connected to the room was a large bathroom with a huge whirlpool bath, big enough for three or four people, and a separate shower, two large sinks, and mirrored walls behind the sinks. Tiffany remarked, "I believe I will take this room." Grandma Woodard said with a smile, "I wonder why." Tiffany opened the closet door a little, and there were all her and Blake's clothes hanging up. Some of the clothes were also in the dresser drawers. Tiffany stated, "I think I'll take a couple of minutes and get Blake ready for bed, and lay him down." "That's fine," Dr. Pierce said, "we will go onto the next bedroom. This one, I believe is for the boys." It was pretty much the same as the first bedroom, only there were two double beds. There was also a big Christmas tree in this room. Sure enough, the boy's clothes were already in the closet, just about that time Mother walked into the room and mentioned, "Well, Blake is fast asleep already. Is this where you are going to be sleeping, Jackson?" "Yah," Jackson said, "I am going to sleep with Jared." Mother replied as she rubbed his head, "Well, both double beds are plenty big enough for that, I'll bet you get the other one Gregory." "Boy," Gregory replied, "these bedrooms are almost as big as our living room." There were towels laid out for everyone in each of their bathrooms, and they were all decorated for Christmas. "If you don't mind," Gregory said, "I think the boys and I will just stay here and get ready for bed also." Mother said, "I think that's a good idea; if anyone gets scared because you are in a strange place, remember I am right next door." Gregory remarked, "Mom, they will be fine, I will be right here with you guys. You can always come into bed with me, if you have a problem." Conrad told Tiffany, "There is an intercom system in each room. You can set it so you can hear if they call for you. I will show you how to set it if you want me to." Tiffany said, "That will be fine, whatever the boys want." Jackson looked at his mom and said, "I don't think I will be scared, I am big now; I am four years old, yes I am." Mother replied, "You sure are a big boy," and she gave each of the boys, a kiss goodnight and gave them a big hug. Gregory told her he would help Jackson get ready for bed.

Jared said, "What about breakfast." Mother answered, "I will let Emma know what to fix for breakfast, I am sure you will not be disappointed." Angela looked at Dr. Pierce and said, "We had better hurry to our room. I am really tired too." "Okay," Dr. Pierce replied, "on we go." The third room was just about the same size as the others, it also had two double beds, a big walk-in closet, a sofa and chair with a small table between them, there was also a Christmas tree in this room. There was also a huge whirlpool bath and a big shower in the bathroom, and their towels had also been laid out. Their clothes had all been hung up in the closets in this room also. Angela asked, "How'd they know which room's people would be going to stay in?" Mother said with a smile, "I suppose, in whatever room they put your clothes, is where you would stay." Stephanie said, "I'm sorry I hate to have to ask everyone to leave, but I'm really tired." "Good idea," Dr. Pierce said as he turned around, "let's stop at your bedroom Tiffany, and I will show you how to use the lights, the intercom system, and the security system, just in case there is a problem."

After Conrad explained to Tiffany how everything worked, Tiffany, Grandpa and Grandma Woodard, and Conrad went downstairs to leave a note for Emma. They told her what they wanted for breakfast, and explained that they would all be eating in the dining room. "Oh my gosh," Tiffany said, "Its 11:30 p.m. already, I am going to have to sleep fast. I may have to skip my long hot bath and just take a quick shower." Grandma Woodard said, "I think I am going to do the same thing." Tiffany turned toward Conrad and said, "By the way, how many people are in Sally and Jim's family?" "Oh," Conrad said, "it's just the two of them, they have no children." Tiffany looked surprised and said, "But this huge place, I don't understand." Conrad responded, "They do a lot of entertaining. I will explain a little more in the morning." Tiffany remarked, "I have never seen anything like this in my life. I am concerned about the little boys. If they ever broke anything I would never be able to afford to replace it." Conrad replied, "Don't worry so much; there are plenty of us to keep an eye on them, and they are usually pretty good." Tiffany remarked, "But, they have never seen this many Christmas trees in one place in their lives." Dr. Pierce and Grandpa and Grandma Woodard said goodnight to Tiffany, and they walked across the hall to Dr. Pierce's apartment. Tiffany locked the door and went up the stairs to her bedroom. After her shower she got into the huge bed and reached over and just touched the light, and it went off. When Tiffany woke up at 7:00 a.m. she could hardly believe her eyes when she saw how big the room really was. Tiffany just finished getting dressed, when Blake woke up. He was so excited to see the Christmas tree. Mother said to him, "Just wait until you get downstairs, there are a lot of big trees down the stairs, but you must not touch them. You can just look at them, do you understand?" "Yes," Blake answered, "don't touch, just look." "Right," Mommy replied.

Blake could hardly walk, he wanted to just take off and run. Mommy reminded him, "Don't run inside the apartment Blake, you must walk only." "Yes," Blake said, "Me knows Mommy." He took his mommy's hand, and walked down the stairs. When Mommy and Blake got downstairs, Carrie, the maid, and Emma the cook were already there. Emma said, "I have coffee made." Tiffany remarked, "It sure smells good," as she introduced herself, "Good morning, I am Tiffany Larkin, and this is my little boy Blake." "I'm Emma and, Good morning, Mrs. Larkin, Blake would you like something to drink until breakfast is ready?" Blake replied, "Oh, yes, me would like some hot cocoa milk." Emma smiled and said, "Hot cocoa milk it is, coming right up." Carrie said as she walked in, "Good morning, Mrs. Larkin would you like a cup of coffee?" Tiffany answered, "Why yes, thank you." Blake mentioned, "me likes them, Mama, they are really nice." Mother replied, "They certainly are."

Tiffany and Blake were enjoying their drinks when the doorbell rang. Tiffany got up and was on her way to the door, when out of nowhere came Carrie and was opening the door before Tiffany was halfway there. Carrie remarked, "Good morning Dr. Pierce, and a good morning to you Mr. and Mrs. Woodard." Dr. Pierce replied, "Well, good morning to you Carrie, are you and Emma ready for this whole crew?"

Carrie answered, "Oh yes, Mr. and Mrs. Meyer have several people stay here for several days at a time quite often. I think we can handle it. It will be fun having the children around. We very seldom see children around here." "Well," Dr. Pierce responded, "they are a good bunch of kids, very well behaved and well mannered." All the children happened to be coming down the circular stairway in the great room; they all heard what Dr. Pierce had said about them, and Stephanie whispered to the rest. "We had better be really good all the time, after what Dr. Pierce said." Carrie answered Dr. Pierce with, "I am sure we will get along splendidly," as they all turned and saw the children coming down the stairs. Dr. Pierce asked Emma, "would you please come into the living room, and I will introduce both of you to the children." The children stood in a straight line, with Stephanie, Gregory, Angela, Jared, Jordan, Jackson, and little Blake at the end of the line. They looked just like stair steps. "This is Emma," Dr. Pierce said, "and she will be your cook. The nicer you are to her, the better your food will be. And I can tell you she is a really good cook." Jackson asked, "Can you make macaroni and cheese?" Emma responded with a smile, "I certainly can, and a whole lot more." Everyone laughed. Dr. Pierce continued, "This is Carrie, your maid. If you keep your clothes picked up, then she will not have to work overtime." Jordan said, "We always keep our clothes picked up, you'll see." Carrie said, "That will be just wonderful, then I may even have time to play some games with you." The children thought that would be a lot of fun. "Now," Dr. Pierce said, "if each of you children could step forward, and give your name and age that would help Emma and Carrie get to know who you are and be able to tell you apart from one another. Then if you could step back and let the next one step forward that would be helpful. We will start with you Stephanie." "My name is Stephanie, and I am going to be fifteen, on January 30th." Emma said, "My, you are quite the young lady." As Stephanie stepped back, Gregory stepped forward. "I am Gregory, and I will be thirteen, on February 24th." Carrie said, "You are a fine looking young man." As Gregory stepped back, Angela stepped forward and gave her name. "I am Angela, and I am ten years old. I will be eleven years old in April." Emma said with a smile, "You are really growing up fast." As Angela stepped back, Jared stepped forward and said, "I am Jared, and I am eight. I will be nine in May." Carrie remarked, "I bet you are quite a helper." As Jared stepped back, Jordan stepped forward. "I am Jordan. I am six, and I will be seven in July." Carrie said, "I bet you help a lot with your little brother." Jordan replied, "Yes I do," as she stepped back. Jackson stepped forward. "I am Jackson, and I am four years old. I will be five in September." Emma remarked, "I bet you can hardly wait till school starts next year." Jackson said, "That will be a lot of fun," as he stepped back. Blake stepped forward, "Me is Blake, and Me is this many, (and he put up two fingers,) as he stepped back. Jackson remarked, "He was just two in October." Blake said, with a smile, "And that's my mommy." Emma answered, "And so she is, and we have already met your Mommy," as they smiled at little Blake.

Dr. Pierce stated, "Emma, this is my mother, Mrs. Olivia Woodard, and her husband Oliver, Carrie met them late yesterday afternoon, but you were already gone." Emma responded, "Pleased to meet you all, Breakfast is in the oven, we will be eating in about ten minutes. The children took their usual places, so the older ones could help the younger ones, and after the food was on the table, Dr. Pierce asked Emma and Carrie to join them at the table. Emma remarked, "Oh, we couldn't do that." Carrie said, "Oh no, it wouldn't be allowed." Dr. Pierce remarked, "Well, it is allowed now, we would like to get to know you both better, and we are all family here, isn't that right children?" The children looked at one another, he had said it again, and we are all family.

"Oh yes," they all said together, "that is right." So Emma and Carrie sat down. Dr. Pierce said the blessing, and they all ate together. They had a wonderful time getting to know one another.

This was Saturday morning, December 18th. Dr. Pierce mentioned, "We have a big day ahead of us, I have a surprise for each of you. As you may have noticed, there are presents under the large tree in the great room. There is one for everyone from me. Each morning after breakfast, I will pick one gift from under the tree for a certain person. Each one will have their present picked on a specific day; as you will see, when whoever gets the gift today, opens it, then you will understand. Are we ready to open the first gift?" "Yes, yes, yes", answered the children. "Okay," Dr. Pierce said with a smile, "I will take one gift from under the tree. Tiffany stated, "Let's all go and sit in the great room." They all sat in a circle, and Dr. Pierce picked up the first present, and said; "Jackson, you had better get in the middle of the circle. Emma and Carrie, you both come too; the dishes can be done after Jackson opens his gift." Jackson was so excited. The package wasn't very large and Tiffany mentioned to him. "Great things come in small packages." "Yeah," Jackson said, as he pulled off the beautiful blue bow and tore the paper off. On the inside was a small train engine. Jackson loved the little engine, he said, "This will go really good with my other trains." After he took the engine out-of-the-box, he had a puzzled look on his face. Mother asked, "What is wrong?" Jackson replied, "I don't know what this is," and he pulled out some strips of paper and a note. Mother said, "Bring it here, Honey, and I will see what it is." Jackson picked up the box and walked over to his Mother. Mother looked at the strips of paper and said, "Well, this looks really exciting to me. I will read the note. Dear Jackson, I thought you might enjoy a ride on a real train, so here are the tickets for a train ride this afternoon, and also tickets to the Baltimore and Ohio Railroad Museum. We will eat lunch on the train, and you can pick out a special item you want to get at the train museum. Have a Merry Christmas, love Dr. Pierce." "Wow," Jackson asked, "are we really going on a train ride?" Dr. Pierce responded, "Yes, we are, this very day, and everyone gets to go along, if they want to." The children said, "Oh yes, we do." Dr. Pierce replied, "Emma and Carrie, we would like you to come with us." Emma said, "Oh we couldn't do that." Carrie remarked, "No." Jackson said, "Oh yes, you can, please; you will have a good time." "Well," Emma said, "we will have to get the kitchen cleaned up." Carrie mentioned, "And I have to make all the beds and lay out the towels." The children remarked, "Oh, we made our own beds." Stephanie said, "And we can help with the dishes and laying out the towels." Dr. Pierce replied, "Well, we have a half-hour before we have to be downstairs for the limo to take us to the train." You should have seen the children move. Stephanie said, "I will help with the towels." Angela replied, "Me too." Mother said, "If the rest of you children will start clearing the table, I will put the dishes in the dishwasher." Emma said, "I will whip up something to put in the oven and put the timer on, so it will be all done when we get home." Olivia mentioned, "I will help cut up some vegetables or whatever you need me to do." As Emma browned the roast, Olivia washed and cut up potatoes, carrots, and onions. Tiffany made a salad and put it in the refrigerator. By the time Stephanie, Angela, and Carrie came downstairs, the dinner was in the oven, and until the timer came on, the oven kept the food cold. Tiffany and Grandma Woodard had never seen an oven like that. Dr. Pierce said, "You gals and guys are really good," as they were all getting their coats on.

Jackson said to Blake, "We are going to ride on a real train; boy, this will really be fun." So off they went on their first adventure, and on another ride in the big limo. Jared said,

"This really is fun." The ride to the train depot was just as exciting as it was on the way from the airport. "Boy," Jackson said with excitement, "this is a really big train." Blake said, "I scared," as he looked at the train. Dr. Pierce picked them both up in his big arms and carried them on the train. Jackson stated, "This is cool," as they went from one car to the next. They finally found an empty car, so the children could all have window seats. All of a sudden there was a jerk, and the whistle blew, and the train started to move. "Wow," Jackson said again, "this is really cool." All the children's eyes were glued to the windows. After about an hour, Dr. Pierce mentioned, "we had better start making our way to one of the dining cars. We want to be sure we get some window seats. We will not be able to all sit together, but we will try to get the children window seats." They walked through three cars before they made it to the dining car. The waiter remarked, "You are just in time, we just opened for lunch, and you have your pick of the seats." Jackson asked, "Is our milk going to spill?" Gregory replied, "I don't think so." And it did not spill. They had a wonderful lunch on the train, and then they walked four cars back before they found an empty car so that the children could all have window seats. The rocking of the train put little Blake to sleep. Tiffany stated, "That's good, he really needed a nap." Before they knew it, they were back at the station, and Dr. Pierce said; "we will just walk down the block to the museum." The train museum was something to see. There were two toy trains moving around the edge of the ceiling, going in and out of tunnels, over bridges, and around buildings. There was a huge train display set up in one corner of the building. It was awesome. There were four tracks and trains going in different directions. There were lakes, and streams with bridges over them, there were tunnels and mountains and roads to go over and under and there were towns and country scenes. There were water towers, churches, and there were boats in the lakes. When a train came into a town or across a road, the whistle blew, and the signs came down so the cars could not go through, and the flashing lights came on. All the children were just staring at this display. Grandpa Woodard was pretty impressed too. In fact, none of them had even seen anything like this before in all their lives. Dr. Pierce and Tiffany could hardly break the children away to tour the rest of the museum. There was a twenty-two-sided roundhouse where twenty-two of the oldest and finest specimens of America's railroad history are on display. The sign said it was built in 1851. They all really enjoyed this part of the museum, because they got to watch the roundhouse go around from one track to the other. Blake was still asleep on Dr. Pierce's shoulder.

Before you knew it, a voice came over the loudspeaker saying that the museum would close in 15 minutes. "Jackson," Dr. Pierce said, "you and I had better go and pick out something from the store for you." Jackson asked, "Can I get anything I want?" Mother responded, "Within reason, maybe I had better come along." "No way," Dr. Pierce said, "this is a guy thing, isn't that right Jackson?" Jackson answered, "I guess," looking at his Mother to make sure it was okay. "Go ahead, Honey," Mommy said with a smile, "you don't have much time." Jackson knew exactly what he wanted the minute he walked into the store. He wanted the mountain with the tunnel under it. And he said; "that lake sure looks neat." The clerk stated, "I have a different lake on sale for 50 percent off, it is right over here." Jackson said, "But that's too much." "Hey," Dr. Pierce said, "at 50 percent off, it is practically free. We will take the mountain with the tunnel, and the lake." The clerk answered, "Done deal." Dr. Pierce mentioned, "Just have it shipped to this address," as he handed the clerk his credit card. He mentioned to Jackson, "They will ship it to Grandpa and Grandma Woodard's. The Snyders are there; they can receive it." Jackson said, "Boy, thanks a lot, Dr. Pierce, there is one more thing that would make my Christmas complete." Dr. Pierce asked, "And what might that be?" Jackson replied, "Oh! I can't tell you, it's a secret." Dr. Pierce stated, "Oh, is that right?" Just about that time, they got back to the others who were over looking at all the toy trains going every which way on the display. Dr. Pierce said, "Well, it looks like our driver is ready to go." They got back in the big limo and headed back to the apartment. It had been a very busy day. The children couldn't stop talking about it all the way home. Mother asked, "What did you get at the store, Jackson?" Jackson said, "I got a mountain with a tunnel, and the lake." Mother asked, "A what?" Conrad replied, "Oh, I had them ship it to Mom's house, it's okay, Hon, it's Christmas." Tiffany remarked, "Conrad, My house isn't near as big is this apartment, you know." Conrad said, "Oh, it's not that big, it just sounds big." Everyone laughed and before you knew it; they were at the apartment building. The driver came around to the side of the car and opened the door; he helped everyone out and tipped his hat to the ladies. They thought that was cool. After they got upstairs, they all chipped in to get dinner on the table. They had a wonderful meal. Emma said, "We didn't make any dessert, so after the kitchen is cleaned up we will make some popcorn and you can all watch a movie and have popcorn and soda." After the movie was over and the children were in bed, Oliver and Olivia said goodnight and headed across the hall to Conrad's apartment. Tiffany said, "Oh, Conrad, this was so wonderful of you to do this. The children had a wonderful time. How did you ever think of it?" "Well," Conrad answered, "last fall, I asked the children what they would like to do if they ever came to Baltimore. And you will be just as surprised with what's inside those other boxes."

CHAPTER 11

JARED AND ANGELA'S BIG SURPRISE

Conrad said goodnight to Tiffany and walked across the hall to his apartment. Tiffany went upstairs and had a long hot bath in the huge whirlpool bath, and then went to bed. Little Blake was sound asleep. Seven a.m. came early, Tiffany thought, but Blake was ready to get up, so Mommy pulled herself out of bed and got Blake dressed. Then she got dressed, and they headed downstairs. She held Little Blake's hand as they walked down the big winding stairs. Blake really wanted to open one of the presents under the big tree in the great room. Mommy reminded Blake of what Dr. Pierce had said yesterday. "Do you remember, Blake?" "No," Blake said, as they were sitting at the bottom of the stairs, looking at the big tree. Mother said, "Well, Dr. Pierce said that he will pick who the next person will be to open the next gift, and that will be right after breakfast, before we go to church." Blake replied, "Okay," as he headed toward the kitchen. Emma mentioned, "Good morning Blake." Blake answered, "Mornin." Emma answered, "I bet you could use a glass of cocoa milk, while you wait for breakfast." Blake said with a grin, "Oh boy, yes," as he climbed up into the highchair. Tiffany stated, "Good morning Emma." Emma replied, "And a good morning to you too Ma'am, coffee is ready, and breakfast will be in half an hour." Tiffany remarked, "I had better buzz the children on the intercom and get them going," as she pressed three buttons and talked to all the children at once. She said, "Children, breakfast will be in half an hour, better get going." Stephanie replied, "We are up and will be down in fifteen minutes." Gregory answered, "We are almost ready too." Just then the doorbell rang, and Tiffany answered the door. There were Conrad and Grandpa and Grandma Woodard. Conrad remarked, "just look who we found roaming the hall." There was Carrie, behind Conrad. Carrie apologized, "Sorry I'm late, but the traffic was terrible for a Sunday." Tiffany responded, "That's quite all right, I believe Emma has everything under control." Conrad said, "I need a cup of coffee." Oliver and Olivia remarked, "So do I," almost at the same time. Just then, Blake ran up to Dr. Pierce and put his little arms up for him to pick him up. Blake gave everyone hugs and kisses and said to Dr. Pierce, "who opens the present today Dr. Pierce?" "That," Dr. Pierce replied, "remains a secret till after breakfast." Mommy replied, "You see Blake, that's just what I told you." Blake responded, "I know," with a sad look on his face.

Just about that time all the other children came down the big circular staircase. Jackson asked, "Is breakfast ready? I am really hungry." Emma replied, "I believe it is." Everyone took their places around the table, and Grandpa Woodard said a prayer of thanksgiving for the food, and they had a wonderful meal. Tiffany asked, "Conrad, where are we going to go to church? I didn't notice a church right around here anywhere." Conrad replied, "No, it's a few miles away; we will have to take the limo." Jared remarked, "That will be cool, getting out of that big limo at church, people will think we are really important." Mother scolded, "Jared, we do not go to church to make people think we are important. We go to church to worship God. Don't ever forget that." Jared replied, "I know mom; I was just teasing." Well, everyone was done eating and the children got very quiet. Mother said, "Well, let's all go and sit in a big circle, and Dr. Pierce will tell us who gets to open their gift today." Everyone quickly went into the great room and sat down, as Dr. Pierce went over to the big tree and picked out the next gift. Dr. Pierce stated, "Jared, you had better get into the center of the circle." Jared could hardly believe his ears. Blake also had tears in his eyes. Tiffany took him in her arms and said, "Honey, sometimes we need to be patient and wait our turn. Yesterday was Jackson's special day, and today is Jared's special day, and one day before we go home, it will be your special day to open your gift. Do you think you can be patient and wait like the big children?" Blake answered, "Well, I guess so." Jared took the present from Dr. Pierce. It was not a very big box, and it was wrapped with bright red paper with a big green bow on it. Jared's hands were shaking. By now the children realized that the entire gift they were going to get was not in the box. Jared opened the present. Inside was a Ravens football cap, and under that was a note. Jared picked up the piece of paper, it read. "Dear Jared, I believe you really enjoy football, so right after church us guys and any ladies who would like to come with us are going to the M&T Bank Stadium to watch the Ravens play football. We are going early, because we are going to meet a friend of mine at the stadium, and he will be taking us into the lockers to meet the players before the game. Have a very Merry Christmas, love Dr. Pierce." Jared responded, "Yeah, yeah, yeah, thank you so much, Dr. Pierce, this is the best Christmas I ever had." He got up and went over to Dr. Pierce and gave him a great big hug. He had the biggest smile on his face anyone had ever seen, as his mother took his picture.

Blake said, "I don't yike football." Mother replied, "Me either." Stephanie stated, "I vote not to go." Angela remarked, "Me too." Jordan replied, "I'm not going either." Grandma Woodard answered, "Me neither." Jackson asked,

"Can I go?" Dr. Pierce said, "Sure enough, it looks like it's just us guys." Then Jared gave Dr. Pierce, another big hug as he said, "this is just awesome, thanks a lot." Dr. Pierce answered, "You're very welcome, and we will eat at the game, so we will leave right from church." Mother stated, "And just remember boys, you are at church to worship God, not to think about football." Dr. Pierce stated, "Emma and Carrie are going to fix sandwiches and salads and you will also have chips and pickles for lunch and then you are all going to have popcorn in the great room while watching a Christmas movie on the big screen." Jordan remarked, "That will be just like going to the movies." Dr. Pierce said, "When we come back, we will have pizza for supper and then play games." Jared said, "This is awesome, let's get going." Mother replied, "Not so fast champ, Dr. Pierce has to call for the limo, and I want everyone to use restrooms before we leave. After you have heard what the rest of us are going to do Jackson, do you still want to go to the game or do you want to stay home with us?" Jackson remarked, "I'm going to the game with the guys." Dr. Pierce replied, "Way to go, buddy, give me five." And so off to church they went.

The limo was waiting for them when they got downstairs, and as always, they just loved riding in that big car. Emma and Carrie went with them to church and as always, they sang all the way there. It was a huge church with two really tall steeples. And it had stained glass windows, one with angels on it, and one with Jesus and a little child, and one with a huge cross. Everyone could not get over how beautiful it was. There were people to greet them as they walked in, and Dr. Pierce introduced them as his family. The children thought, "There, he just did it again, as they looked at each other, he mentioned "his" family. Dr. Pierce helped Tiffany get the children to their classrooms, and Mother again reminded the children that they were there to worship God, not to think about football. Conrad and Tiffany met

Oliver and Olivia, Emma, and Carrie back at the front of the church, and they all went in and sat down. The church service was wonderful, and Tiffany said, "I could have listened to that Pastor all afternoon." All the children had a wonderful time also, singing songs about Jesus and God, and learning about the miracles Jesus did. "Jackson had to tell the class how God did a miracle when he got Dr. Pierce to come all the way out west to operate on him last summer. And all the children in the class really enjoyed having the children from "Way out West," visit their church. Going to church seem to make everyone happier. After church was over, everyone went outside and all the ladies and Blake got in the big limo, and the guys hailed down a taxi, and the five of them were off to the game.

When the ladies arrived back at the hotel, the driver again tipped his hat and helped all the ladies out of the car. When they got to the apartment, the children quickly went upstairs and took little Blake to change from their good church clothes and put on play clothes, while Mother, Emma and Carrie got busy getting the sandwiches and salads made, and Grandma set the table. By the time the children came downstairs, the lunch was ready, and they had a wonderful time telling about what happened in their Sunday school classes. After lunch, they all went and found a place to sit, lay, or lounge, whatever they wanted, in the great room, while Emma and Carrie made popcorn and got some sodas ready. Then they all got comfortable and Emma turned on the big-screen. Jordan mentioned, "This is just like going to the movies." Mother said, "I like it even better, because if you need to get up and walk around, you can do that." Angela remarked, "Besides, if you need anything, we have our own maids to wait on us."

Meanwhile, the guys had reached the M&T Bank Stadium. They were all pretty excited. Dr. Pierce's friend met them at the stadium, just inside the door. Dr. Pierce stated,

"This is Bill," and everyone else introduced themselves. Bill mentioned, "So you are the lucky guy today Jared, well, let's get going, the players have a lot to do to get ready for the game, so we cannot take up a whole lot of their time." Jared responded, "That's okay, just being able to come back here is awesome." Grandpa Woodard remarked, "Heavens yes, I have never been back in the locker room of a football stadium in all my life, so this is just as exciting for me as it is for you, Jared." Just as they reached the locker room, Bill said; "we will be meeting Jonathan Ogden. He has been with the Ravens since the beginning. He is an offensive tackle. Also, we will meet Chris McAllister. He is a quarterback, and Ray Lewis is a linebacker and Ed Reed, he is on the safety part of the team. We may also meet Brian Billick. He is the second head coach, and he started in 1999. A guy named Ted Marchibroda was the first head coach," and just then, Bill opened the door. Jonathan Ogden said, "Well, hello everyone, welcome to our little corner of the world." Bill introduced all the players, and Dr. Pierce introduced his family to all the players. Then the players gave everyone jerseys and sweatshirts with all the names of the players on them. Jared got an autographed football, with all the players' names on it. He was so excited he could hardly speak to say thank you, but somehow he managed. Before they left, they all had their pictures taken with the players. Time flew by so fast, and before you knew it, the coach came in and said they had work to do before the game. So they all had to leave. They each shook hands with all the players and one by one left the locker room and headed for the concession stand to get something to eat. There was an hour before the game actually started, and the concession stands were not ready to serve food yet, so they went to the private suite, where they were going to watch the game. The suite was really something. There were really comfortable stuffed chairs right outside over the football field, and inside was a nice table and chairs around it and counters all around the room. And there was a microwave in one corner and a sink in one corner, and there was a refrigerator under one cabinet. It was filled with sodas, and there was ice and also glasses.

Dr. Pierce told them they could have their food ordered in, or they could go to the concession stands. When the boys found out what the food was like on the menu for ordering in, they decided to go to the concession stand. So Grandpa Woodard and Dr. Pierce got chicken sandwiches and Caesar salads and the boys went to the concession stand and pigged out on foot-long hot dogs, nachos and cheese, popcorn, and peanuts and brought it back to the suite. The boys were really excited, because after they met and talked with the players, they felt like they really knew them and they really cheered them on. It was so much fun watching the game from the suite. You could get up and walk around, and there was a large TV screen in the room that you could watch the game from. Oliver remarked, "This sure is something." Conrad replied, "This is a huge stadium, as you can see; it seats over 70,000 people." Everyone had the time of their lives, especially Grandpa Woodard. Before you knew it the game was over, and the Baltimore Ravens won. That really made their day. They were so excited; they could hardly wait to tell the girls. They had a good time talking about the game on the way back to the apartment. Dr. Pierce called and let Tiffany know they were on their way home. So Emma and Carrie started making pizzas for supper.

When the guys got home from the game, the pizzas were ready, and they all sat around in the great room and ate their pizza and each one got to tell about their day. Jared got to go first, since it was his Christmas present. He showed everyone his sweatshirt, jersey, his signed football, and said, "Just wait till you see my picture with all the players. They are all going to sign it before they mail it out. That's really going to be special." Before you knew it, it was time to go to bed.

Everyone said goodnight and the children went up to bed; Grandpa and Grandma Woodard and Dr. Pierce went across the hall to Dr. Pierce's apartment. Dr. Pierce told Emma and Carrie to bring some clothes with them tomorrow and they might just as well stay in one of the extra bedroom upstairs. There were a couple extra bedrooms with double beds in the room, and besides, they were spending all their time there any way. So they decided to do that. Dr. Pierce told Carrie, "then you don't have to worry about the traffic in the morning." Carrie remarked, "Sounds great to me." Emma stated, "Me too," and off they went. Tiffany locked the big door and off she went to bed.

They decided to have oatmeal for breakfast in the morning, along with country sausage, toast, and fruit. The children told Emma, they liked their oatmeal with raisins, nuts, brown sugar, butter and milk. Dr. Pierce told Emma he liked his oatmeal with vanilla ice cream on it. By the time Mommy got up and dressed and got Blake dressed and the beds made and went downstairs, Emma already had coffee on, and had hot cocoa milk made for Blake. Blake said, "Oh boy, this is yummy in my tummy." Mommy replied, "Well that's good, it will warm you up on the inside." Just then the doorbell rang. Carrie answered the door, and it was Dr. Pierce. Blake went to greet Dr. Pierce; he was so glad to see him. By that time, the other children were coming down the stairs. Jordan and Jackson both remarked, "Oh boy, it sure smells good in here." Emma had the table set, and everyone was ready to sit down to breakfast by the time Grandpa and Grandma Woodard got there. Grandpa Woodard said, "We decided to sleep in." Tiffany replied, "Nothing wrong with that, I would have slept in also, if someone hadn't woke me up so early." Blake smiled and said, "I waked you up, Mommy." Mommy replied, "You sure did Honey." Emma mentioned from the kitchen that breakfast was ready, and they all sat down. Dr. Pierce said the blessing, thanked God for the food, and asked Him to bless it. They had a wonderful breakfast; the oatmeal was delicious. Emma stated, "We are going to have fried oatmeal tomorrow morning for breakfast." Angela asked, "What is fried oatmeal?" Emma replied, "You will see, it will be a surprise."

Dr. Pierce stated, "I think we all should go into the great room and sit down in a circle and see who gets to open up their gift today." Blake took off running. Mommy said, "Don't run in the house, Blake." He stopped right in his tracks, and then continued to walk to his favorite spot to sit down and wait to see who got to open their gift today. When everyone got into the great room, they sat in a circle, and Dr. Pierce said, "Angela, You had better get in the center of the circle." Angela was so excited she couldn't even talk. She was hardly able to get up and go sit in the center of the circle. Little Blake had tears in his eyes, and Mommy said. "Do you remember what Mommy told you yesterday, Blake?" Blake replied, "Yes Mommy, me have to be patient and wait like the big children do." "Yes," Mommy said, "now come over here and let me hold you so you can watch Angela open her gift. That will be fun too." Blake answered, "Okay." Angela's present was a little larger than the others had been. It was wrapped in silver paper with a large royal blue bow and ribbon on it. Angela ran up and gave Dr. Pierce a big hug and kisses and said; "this present is so beautiful, I hate to unwrap it." Then she sat back down in the center of the circle, carefully took off the ribbon and bow, and carefully undid the paper. Inside were an 8 x 10 inch picture frame and a large cloth bag.

There was also a note from Dr. Pierce. "Dear Angela, there is this place downtown called "Star Salon and Picture Gallery, where you will go in and have your hair done, and they will take your picture. They will also dress you in a dress or whatever you pick out to wear. The picture will be at the hotel on Wednesday. But first you and I will go downtown to the hospital, and see all the new babies and talk to the nurses in the nursery. Then you and I will go shopping, just for you, for whatever you want from me for Christmas. We will meet the others for lunch at Sandy's, which is a buffet downtown. We will shop throughout the afternoon, and then we will have dinner at the hotel tonight. Have a very Merry Christmas, love Dr. Pierce" Angela remarked, "Oh, Dr. Pierce, this is so neat. I will feel just like a movie star, and I have no idea what I want to shop for, except clothes, maybe. And I would just love to see all the babies at the hospital and talk to the nurses. I want to be a nurse when I grew up, you know. Thank you, thank you, thank you," as she got up and gave Dr. Pierce another big hug and kiss. Dr. Pierce replied, "You're very welcome, Now I believe I have this shopping thing all figured out. I would like Emma and Carrie to come shopping with us, and Sam (the limo driver) as the children called him will go with us for the day. The rest of you can shop for one another for Christmas. And if Sam has to come back here to drop off packages during the day, he will be able to do that." Gregory remarked, "He is cool, I really like him." Dr. Pierce stated, "He is a great guy. He has never been married, so he has no family. He spends most of his time working here at the hotel. The Limo belongs to him; it is his business. It's how he makes his living." Tiffany stated, "Well then, we should invite him for Christmas dinner." Dr. Pierce replied, "Great idea, we'll ask him this morning. And with that settled we will get back to planning our shopping trip. Carrie, Sam, Oliver, and I all have cell phones, so we can keep in touch with one another. If we can each take one of the young children, that would be great. Angela will be with me." Tiffany said, "I will take Blake." Grandpa Woodard said, "I will take Jackson." Grandma Woodard mentioned, "I will take Jordan." Carrie said, "I will take Jared." Emma stated, "Stephanie and Gregory can come with me." Dr. Pierce said, "We will all help the children get their gifts for everyone else. If we do not get everything done today, do not worry, we will have time another day." Everyone was so excited about buying gifts for everyone else. The children decided that they were going to buy gifts for Emma, Carrie, and Sam also. Stephanie and Gregory had brought their own money to spend on themselves, plus money for gifts, but they found they didn't need to spend any money on themselves, because Dr. Pierce was paying for everything, so they decided they would spend that money on Emma, Carrie, and Sam, and of course they were going to buy gifts for the Snyder family as well. It was nice of them to think of others.

So off they went on their shopping trip. The first thing they did as they got in the Limo was to ask Sam if he would come to Christmas dinner. Sam stated, "Why that is very kind of you, I would be happy to come; but there is another gentleman, who also drives a limo that I usually have holiday dinners with, and I hate to leave him all alone on a holiday." Tiffany responded, "Oh, well, you had better ask him to come along too, then." Sam said, "Well. Thank you very much; I will surely do just that." First of all Sam dropped off Dr. Pierce and Angela at the "Star Salon and Picture Gallery." Dr. Pierce mentioned "We will probably be here around two to three hours; I will call you, Sam, as soon as we are almost ready to leave." Sam said, "Yes sir," and off he went to the huge department store downtown. He told them that they would all meet back at the Limo in an hour and a half. And he will take all the packages and put them in the limo. Then they could go back to shopping, while he went and picked up Angela and Dr. Pierce. He said he would call Carrie when they were on their way back, and he would pick them up so they could all go to lunch. Tiffany stated, "Sounds like a plan." So off they went in all directions. Sam thought if he was going to go to Christmas dinner, he had better pick up a few gifts himself. All of a sudden he felt the joy and excitement of Christmas, as he thought about buying gifts for the children. What in the world would I get for the children, he thought. I had better call Joe and let him know that we have been invited to Christmas dinner.

Well, Angela was having the time of her life. She had a manicure, and they washed her hair and were styling her hair. When they were done, she looked just like a princess. There was some hair pulled up on top of her head and there was some curls at the top and ringlets coming down from the top. There were ringlets coming down, one in front of each ear, and the hair at the bottom of her head was also in ringlets. Then they took her into the back room of the shop, to pick out a dress for her to wear for her picture. Dr. Pierce was sitting with her as they brought out different dresses for her to pick out. There must have been fifteen dresses. Angela remarked, "Dr. Pierce, this is going to be very hard to do, I like them all." She picked out a bright yellow one, a rose pink one, a royal blue one, and a lavender one. The lady picked up the four dresses, and Angela followed her into the fitting room. One by one Angela came out with a different dress, and after she had modeled them all, she asked Dr. Pierce which one he liked best. He said, "I am going to put the one I like best on this card, but I want you to pick the one you like best." Angela replied, "That is easy for me, I like the royal blue one." Dr. Pierce replied, "Now look at the card." Angela got a big grin on her face, gave Dr. Pierce a big hug, (it was the royal blue one) and said, "this is so much fun; I feel like a movie star." Dr. Pierce responded, "Just wait till they start taking pictures."

Angela went back in the dressing room, and the lady helped her put on the royal blue dress. The dress had a big collar and a wide belt at the waist. It had several half slips under the skirt called crinolines, and the skirt was very full and looked like a wedding dress. It came halfway between her knees and her ankles. She had on royal blue slippers, and she had royal blue flowers in her hair. Then the lady said.

"Now; Angela, we are going into the studio to take some pictures. Are you coming, Dr. Pierce?" Dr. Pierce responded, "Oh yes, I don't want to miss this." Angela stated, "I wish Mom was here." Dr. Pierce said, "So do I, she would be so happy for you, but just wait until she sees the picture." They had her do all kinds of poses. She had so much fun. One time she laughed right out loud, she was so tickled. The photographer said, "Well, we are done. You were a delight to work with young lady, and you photograph very well. You should think about modeling, and I don't mean when you grow up. I mean right now—you are a natural. And your smile is just adorable." Angela's face turned red, and she looked at Dr. Pierce. Dr. Pierce gave her a wink, and the lady took her back to the dressing room to help her change clothes, so she would not mess up her hair. When she came out, she whispered, "Dr. Pierce, this is the most fun day of my life." "Well," Dr. Pierce replied, "it is not over yet. We are going to lunch, and then shopping and dinner." Angela said, "This is just too much," as they got into the limo.

"Well," Sam asked, as he held the door for Angela and extended his hand to help her in, "where did you get this beautiful lady? Is she a movie star?" Angela remarked, "Oh, Sam, "you know me." They all laughed. Sam remarked, "Wait till your family sees you; they will be jealous." As they took off, Sam called Carrie and told her they were on their way. They would be there in ten minutes. Carrie mentioned, "That doesn't give us much time to get together, check out, and be out front, but we will try. Thank you." Sam replied, "Do your best." Carrie knew right where everyone was, so she just went from one to the other and told them to check out and meet Sam at the front as soon as possible. Sure enough, they were all waiting for Sam when he pulled up. He was five minutes late. The first thing Sam did was to pop the trunk open and put all the packages in the trunk. There were a lot of packages. Then he helped each one in the limo.

Everyone let Angela know how beautiful she was. Tiffany had tears in her eyes as she remarked, "My little girl, all grown up. Honey, you look absolutely beautiful." Grandma Woodard responded, "You sure do." Stephanie said; "Oh, Angela you look beautiful. You must've had a ball." Angela replied, "I did, and wait till I tell you all about it." Angela was still telling everyone all about her morning, when Sam pulled up to Sandy's buffet. Well, they had all gone off in all different lines, and everyone got what they wanted to eat, and sat down. Grandpa Woodard gave the blessing. A buffet is a really fun place to eat. There was something for everyone. And you can eat as much as you want. Anyway, while they ate they discussed the rest of the day. Dr. Pierce remarked, "When Sam gets back from dropping off the packages at the apartment, he will drop Angela and I off at the hospital and then drop the rest of you off wherever you want to shop. We will be in touch by cell phone." Just as they were all done eating, (except for Blake finishing his ice cream,) Sam walked in. Sam asked, "Is everyone ready?" Tiffany said, "Yes." Dr. Pierce told Sam, "You had better get a bite to eat." Sam responded, "Oh, I picked me up a sandwich and coffee at the hotel restaurant, and ate it on my way back." Dr. Pierce said, "We sure have kept you hopping today Sam, I want you to join us for dinner, when we get back to the hotel tonight." Sam responded, "Well, thank you very much; I would like that." So off they went.

The hospital was only a few minutes from Sandy's, so they were there in no time flat. As Angela and Dr. Pierce went up in the elevator, all Angela could talk about was seeing the babies. In no time at all, they were at the nursery. The place was full of babies. There must have been forty or fifty babies. "Oh, my gosh;" Angela shouted, "How do the nurses take care of so many babies?" Dr. Pierce responded, "There are a lot of nurses," as he knocked on the glass window. A nurse heard him and looked up and smiled and motioned towards the door. The nurse said, "Well hello there, my name Kristine." "Hello, my name is Angela." Kristine said, "Well, Angela, welcome to the nursery." Angela asked, "How many nurses are there here to take care of all these babies?" Kristine answered, "There are fifteen nurses, but the babies are with their mothers most of the time during the day. Right now, the mothers are watching a movie on how to take care of a newborn baby. When the movie is over, most of the babies will go to be with their mothers. The only ones that will stay here are the ones in the incubators. Those babies never leave the nursery. Their mothers come to the nursery to see those babies." Angela got to put on a mask, and washed her hands, and then Kristine let her hold one of the babies. She was really excited and asked Kristine a lot of questions.

Dr. Pierce stated, "We had better get going Angela, if we're going to get any shopping done today." Kristine asked, "What are you shopping for?" Angela responded, "For my Christmas present from Dr. Pierce." Kristine remarked, "Oh, and what do you want?" Angela responded, "Oh, clothes, I believe." "Well," Kristine replied, "I know a dress shop for young ladies on 48th and Vine Streets." Dr. Pierce replied, "I know where that is. It is only about four blocks from here, and we can go through the skyway to get there. We won't even have to bother Sam." Kristine mentioned, "You will love the skyway Angela, it is all decorated for Christmas, and the view is beautiful. There may even be people singing Christmas carols in there." Angela said, "Thank you very much and thank you for letting me hold little Jenny, she is so pretty. And thank you for answering all my questions, Merry Christmas." Kristine answered, "You are very welcome, and you were a real joy to get to know. Thank you, Dr. Pierce for bringing Angela by the nursery." Dr. Pierce replied, "You are very welcome Kristine, and thank you for the tip on the dress shop. Merry Christmas." Kristine responded, "And Merry Christmas to you both."

Off they went down the elevator to the second floor to the
skyway. It was all decorated for Christmas. After about two
blocks, there were young children standing in one corner,
singing Christmas carols. There was a sign that said they
were the children's choir from Thompson Baptist Church.
Angela and Dr. Pierce stopped, and just stood and listened
for quite awhile. Angela had all she could do not to join in
and sing with them. Finely Dr. Pierce said, "I believe we
should get going Angela, or the shop may close before we get
there." Angela replied, "Okay, but thank you for stopping to
listen. This singing is just beautiful." Dr. Pierce responded,
"It certainly is." It was indeed a beautiful walk through the
skyway, and all too soon they were at the bank building,
where the dress shop was. Angela remarked, "There it is, oh
my gosh, Dr. Pierce, this looks like a real expensive shop.
Maybe we should go to a different store." "Well," Dr. Pierce
replied, "we should at least go in and look around. You never
know, sometimes you can get some real good deals in these
stores." "Okay," Angela said, "if you say so." They opened
the door, and a little bell rang, and a clerk came from behind a
counter and said "Merry Christmas, and what are we looking
for today?" Dr. Pierce responded, "Merry Christmas. We are
looking for something for the young lady for Christmas. It is
a present." "Well," the clerk said, "we certainly have a lot to
choose from. If you need my help, just let me know." "Thank
you," Dr. Pierce replied, "Well, Angela, let's see if we can
find something for you." They started looking through the
racks. After some time, the lady came back and said, "I see
you have found a few items, would you like me to take them
for you, or are you ready to try them on?" Angela replied,
"I believe I will try them on." The clerk mentioned, "I will
help you," and she took the dresses from Dr. Pierce and said,
"You may have a seat, Sir, we won't be long."

However, this reminded Angela of the picture gallery,
where she tried on all those dresses to have her picture taken

in. With each one she tried on, she came out to show Dr. Pierce. Angela mentioned, "Boy, Dr. Pierce, this is going to be very hard to pick one out." The clerk stated, "I have one more beautiful dress that just came in yesterday. Stephen only made two of these dresses, and I was lucky enough to get one of them. I will be back in just a moment." Angela looked at Dr. Pierce and said, "Dr. Pierce that sounds really expensive." When the lady came back into the room, Angela let out a squeal, and Dr. Pierce said, "I don't believe it." The clerk asked, "What is it? What is wrong?" Dr. Pierce replied, "That is the very dress Angela had her picture taken in at the "Star Salon and Picture Gallery." The clerk stated, "So that's where the other dress went. I must see it on you. I will help you so you don't muss up your hair." Angela was just beaming. It was her princess dress. When she came back out, Dr. Pierce, (in a French accent), said "I have my princess back." Angela responded, "Oh Dr. Pierce, that is silly," although; she did feel like a princess in the dress. The clerk remarked, "You do look just like a princess." Dr. Pierce added, "We will take it. Have it delivered Wednesday morning early to this address," and he gave her his card. Dr. Pierce mentioned, "When the pictures come on Wednesday for us to look at, I will have Emma go upstairs with you, and she can help you get dressed. And then you can come down with your dress on, and everyone will really be surprised." Angela responded, "Oh that will be so much fun, especially after I told everyone how much I really loved the dress I got my picture taken in." She went and gave Dr. Pierce a big hug and kiss. She was so happy. Dr. Pierce said, "We had better call Sam and let him know where we are, so he can pick us up." They waited about five minutes downstairs before Sam got there. Sam got on the cell phone to Carrie and asked, "How is the shopping going?" Carrie stated, "We are just about done for today, everyone is pretty tired out except for Blake. He had a nice nap in the stroller." Sam stated, "We will be there in about fifteen minutes." Carrie responded, "That will be fine; we have three people to check out yet. We will see you at the corner." Sam was there, right on time. Dr. Pierce mentioned, "We will have just enough time to freshen up and change clothes, Dinner is at seven o'clock p.m." When Sam pulled up at the hotel, everyone got out and was waiting by the trunk to carry up all the packages. Sam said, "You all go ahead on up, I will bring up the packages." Dr. Pierce remarked, "Thank you Sam," as they all headed for the elevator. Dr. Pierce stated, "We are doing real well; we will be just a little early for dinner."

A pretty young lady took them to their table and remarked, "Your waiter will be with you shortly," as she gave them the menus and left. Todd came over and took their orders for drinks, and smiled at Stephanie. Stephanie smiled back. No one seemed to notice. Before you knew it, Todd was back with their drinks and took their orders. Angela told everyone about all the babies and nurse Kristine at the hospital and the skyway and the children singing. She said she had a wonderful day. Dr. Pierce remarked, "Kristine is Todd's mother, Angela, I should have mentioned that earlier today." They had a wonderful meal, and everyone was really happy to get back upstairs, and just stretch out. Dr. Pierce mentioned, "I have plenty of paper, bows, ribbon, and gift bags and tape for wrapping gifts tomorrow." Surprisingly, everyone found their own packages they had bought and took them each to their own rooms. Everyone was very tired. Grandpa and Grandma Woodard and Dr. Pierce said goodnight and went over to Dr. Pierce's apartment. All the children and Tiffany went upstairs to bed; it had been another beautiful day.

CHAPTER 12

HAPPY BIRTHDAY

Morning came quickly thought Tiffany. She took a quick shower, gave Blake a quick bath, made the bed, got dressed and they were on their way downstairs by 7:30 a.m. Blake stopped on the stairs and leaned through the railing just a little to look at the big tree. Mommy remarked, "That sure is a big, beautiful tree isn't it Blake?" "Yes, Mommy," Blake said, "and there sure are still lots of presents under there too." "Yes," Mommy responded, "and one of them is yours." Blake replied, "Maybe today, I can open mine." "Maybe," Mommy answered, as she picked him up and gave him a big hug and kiss, and then she carried him the rest of the way down the stairs. Blake continued to look at the big tree. Emma said, "Well, there's my boy, your hot cocoa milk is ready." "Oh boy," Blake remarked, as he crawled up into the big highchair. Tiffany said, "Good morning ladies." Emma and Carrie replied, "Good morning, breakfast is in fifteen minutes," as Carrie handed Tiffany a cup of coffee. Tiffany paged the children on the intercom. They remarked, "We are about ready." Just then the doorbell rang, and Carrie went to answer it. There was Grandpa and Grandma Woodard and Dr. Pierce. Just then the children were coming down the stairs, as Dr. Pierce walked in with a cupcake in his hand and a lit candle in it. He remarked, "Happy Birthday to the most beautiful woman in the world." Tiffany asked, "How did you know it was my birthday?" Conrad replied, "Oh, a little bird told me." Jackson said, "Oh, Dr. Pierce, birds don't talk." Dr. Pierce replied, "Parrot's do." Everyone laughed.

Grandma Woodard mentioned, "I have to see how you ladies made this fried oatmeal." Tiffany replied, "Me too." Emma answered, "Well, last night, we cooked the oatmeal with raisins in it, then put it in this long narrow pan, and put it in the refrigerator. This morning, we took it out and cut it in strips about an inch wide. Then we warmed a griddle, and put a little oil on it like you do for pancakes. Then we grilled them, just like pancakes. We also have bacon, toast, and fruit. You can put butter and syrup on the oatmeal, or you can just eat it like it is. Or you can put jam on it." Grandpa Woodard gave the blessing for the food. The children were really surprised that they all liked the "fried oatmeal." The adults liked it to. Emma said, "We will get the kitchen cleaned up while you all go in and open a gift." Both grown-ups and children each got up from the table and carried their own dishes and glasses into the kitchen. Emma mentioned, "We really appreciate the help, which will make the cleanup go so much faster."

The children were already in the great room and seated in a circle by the time the adults came into the room. Tiffany went and took her place beside Blake. Blake put his head close to her, and said, "Maybe today, it will be me." Mommy replied, "Maybe today." Dr. Pierce said, "Tiffany. You had better get in the center of the room." Blake said, "Oh, Mommy, it's you," and he began to clap his little hands together. Tiffany got up, and Stephanie came over and sat by Blake. Tiffany walked to the center of the room. Dr. Pierce came around the big tree with a small gift in his hand, and handed it to Tiffany. Tiffany said, "Why, it's wrapped in birthday paper." "Well," Dr. Pierce said, "so it is." Then they all began to sing *Happy Birthday to You*. Conrad mentioned, "This is your birthday present, your Christmas present will come later." Tiffany remarked, "Let's see what we have here." Blake said, "Hurry up Mommy." Tiffany slowly opened the package. There was a bottle of shampoo, a bottle of lotion, a bottle of expensive perfume, and a note. She began to read, "Dear Tiffany, happy birthday, and be prepared for a wonderful full day today. First, we are going to get you a complete body massage, have your hair done, and do some shopping. Then we will come back here for lunch with everyone, and afterward we are going to spend the afternoon together. Then there will be dinner and the evening out with me. Have a wonderful birthday, love Conrad." Tiffany had tears in her eyes. She said, "Thank you so very much, Conrad, you are so sweet." Then she got up and gave Conrad a big hug and kiss.

Dr. Pierce mentioned, "Everyone can hang out here today, and that will give all of you a chance to wrap all the presents, you bought for each other. All the wrappings are in my apartment. Grandma Woodard will help you bring them over here." Jackson said, "This is going to be so much fun." Jordan mentioned, "Let's go get the wrappings Grandma." "Okay," Grandma answered, "but we will need more help than you, Jordan, I think all of us better go over and help carry the stuff back." So as Tiffany and Conrad left to spend the day together, everyone else went over to Dr. Pierce's apartment and brought all the supplies back to wrap the gifts. When they got everything put in the great room, Grandma Woodard said, "now before we get started with the wrapping, we're all going to go shopping for birthday presents for your Mother. Sam will drive us. We don't have much time, we have to be back here and have all the gifts wrapped before your mother and Conrad get back at 12:30 p.m." Stephanie said, "Wow, we had better get going." Emma stated, "We are going to stay here, and bake and decorate the cake and fix our lunch. Sam is waiting for you; everybody get their coats on." Jared asked, "How did Mom and Dr. Pierce go shopping if Sam is still here?" Grandma Woodard replied, "They took a taxicab." So off they went. They were trying to figure out what they were going to buy for their Mom for her birthday. Emma and Carrie were busy at the apartment baking the cake and starting to get things ready for the birthday lunch. Sam pulled up to the curb, and as he opened the door and helped everyone out, he remarked, "I will pick you up here at 11:00 a.m. That will give us time to drive back, and for all of you to get your gifts wrapped before Dr. Pierce and Mrs. Larkin get back." Everyone looked at their watches. Grandpa took Jackson, Grandma took Blake, Jordan and Angela went with Stephanie, and Jared went with Gregory. The children really had fun buying gifts for their Mother for her birthday.

The time went by so fast for Tiffany. She was so relaxed during the massage, she almost fell asleep. Before she knew it, it was all over, and off they went to get her hair done. Her hair was done up on top of her head, with ringlets hanging down in front of her ears. Conrad said, "You look just beautiful, Honey." Tiffany replied, "Thank you very much, for all the pampering. I feel just like a queen." Conrad replied, "Well, your Majesty, we had better get going, or we will be late for lunch."

Everyone was done shopping and waiting for Sam at 11:00 a.m. sharp. Sam pulled up and opened the trunk and put all the gifts in, and then he went and opened the door for all to get in the limo. The children were so excited about what they had got for their Mother and could hardly wait to get back to the apartment to get them wrapped. When Sam picked up the children he hoped that their Mother and Dr. Pierce hadn't gotten there yet. They asked Walter the elevator operator, "Has Dr. Pierce and Mrs. Larkin come back yet?" Walter said, "Nope, I haven't seen them yet, do you want me to buzz the apartment when I see them?" "Oh yes," Gregory remarked, "that would be neat if we knew when they were coming up." Grandpa Woodard stated, "That's pretty sneaky." Grandma replied, "Whatever works." They rang the doorbell when they reached the apartment. As Emma let them in, she said, "Well hello there; you have just enough time to wrap those presents. We can help if you need us." They all went to the big table in the dining room, and Emma and Carrie started helping the little ones, while the older ones wrapped their own gifts. Angela asked, "Where are we going to put these presents?" Stephanie answered, "Under the big tree in the dining room." Jackson replied, "Whoever heard of putting birthday presents under a Christmas tree." Grandma Woodard said, "Well, "maybe in this family, we will start a new tradition." "Okay," Jackson said, "let's start a new tadition, and put Mommy's presents under the tree." Jordan stated, "That's tradition, Jackson." "That's what I said," Jackson replied, "tadition." That got a laugh out of everyone. After the presents were all under the tree, they all started cleaning up the dining room. When they got the paper and bows all picked up, they all worked together to set the table for lunch. And when they were done Jackson asked; "where's the cake?" "Oh," Emma replied, "the cake is put away. We will bring it out at the right time." Just about that time the buzzer went off. Grandma remarked, "Aha, which means they are getting in the elevator right now."

Jackson and Jordan said, "This is really fun." Blake echoed, "Yeah." They all liked surprising their mom. All of a sudden, the doorbell rang. Carrie went to answer the door. There stood Mom and Dr. Pierce, as they stepped into the large entry room, everyone said all at once, "Surprise Happy Birthday to you," then they saw her hair and Stephanie said, "Wow Mom, look at you; you are beautiful." Grandpa said, "I guess we were the ones who were surprised." Carrie said, "Lunch is ready." Dr. Pierce said, "Good idea, I am hungry." Gregory replied, "Me too." Mother remarked, "Thank you so much for the compliment, it does change the way I look, I do look different." Gregory stated, "Different isn't the word for it, you look like a movie star, Mom." Mother said, "Well, thank you so much Gregory," as she gave him a hug.

They all sat down at the table, and Dr. Pierce gave the blessing. Jackson said; "and thank You, God, for Dr. Pierce, Amen." After lunch was over, all the children pitched in and helped clean up the dining room and kitchen while Mother was told she should go find a comfortable chair in the great room and, as soon as everything was cleaned up, she would open her presents. Tiffany said, "I don't see any presents in here," as she found a big chair to sit in. Blake said, "They are not in here, they are under the Christmas tree in the dining room." Tiffany stated, "You put my birthday presents under the Christmas tree?" as she let out a big laugh. Blake replied, "Yah, it's a new tression." Jared said, "That's a new tradition." "I see," Mother said with a smile on her face. Blake remarked, "That's what I said, a new tression." Everyone laughed. That was so cute. Before long, everyone was done in the kitchen and they all came in, each one carrying a gift and set them down on the floor by Mom. As always the little one's gifts were opened first. Blake's gift to his Mom was a handkerchief with #1 Mom embroidered on it. Mother said, "This is beautiful; I believe I will put it in my purse and take it with me tonight. Thank you so much Blake." Blake replied, "I knowed you would like it." Next was Jackson's gift. He was just as excited as Blake to watch as his Mommy opened his gift. It was a bright red winter scarf to go with her black coat. Mommy stated, "Oh, this is really beautiful," as she put it on. "I will wear it when Conrad and I leave, it will keep me warm. Thank you so very much, Jackson." Jackson had a big grin on his face, "you're welcome Mommy." The next gift was from Jordan, it was a bright red pair of leather gloves. Mommy said, "Are these ever beautiful," as she put them on. "They will go with my scarf. I will also wear these tonight; they will keep my hands really warm. Thank you so very much Jordan." Jared's gift was a beautiful white button sweater. Mom remarked, "This is just beautiful too Jared, I will take it with me tonight, just in case the restaurant is cold. I may have to put it on." Angela's gift was a royal blue Christmas vest with white poinsettias on it. "Oh," Mother stated, "this is so beautiful. I will wear it on Christmas Eve. Thank you so much Angela." Gregory's gift was a bottle of beautiful-smelling perfume, a bottle of body lotion, and hand lotion. Mom said, "Oh Gregory, this perfume smells heavenly. I will wear it tomorrow, because I already have on the perfume that Conrad gave me today. Does anyone else want to smell it?" Blake asked, "Can I smell, Mommy?" Jackson said, "Me too." Conrad said, "Me too." So Tiffany took the perfume and the lotions and passed them around. The girls each put on some of the hand lotion. It really smelled nice, and it made their hands so soft. Stephanie's gift was next; she got a bright red leather purse with a shoulder strap. Mother stated, "Oh Stephanie, this is beautiful, I believe I will switch purses, just for tonight and go put on my red dress and wear it tonight also. Thank you so very much Stephanie." Jared remarked, "You will be the lady in red tonight." Mother answered, "I guess I will." The next present was from Grandpa and Grandma Woodard. It was a gift certificate to the big department store downtown. "Oh," Tiffany said, "this is just wonderful. Now I can go shopping this afternoon and buy a white blouse and white skirt to go with my blue vest that Angela got me. Thank you both so very much." Emma got up and handed Tiffany, a gift. Tiffany remarked, "Oh, you shouldn't have." Emma replied, "We wanted to get you something too; this is from Carrie and me." It was a beautiful crystal angel candleholder. Tiffany said, "Thank you so very much," as she got up and gave each one a big hug and kiss and remarked, "This is a beautiful birthday party." Jackson said, "We have to have cake yet." Blake said, "Yah." Jordan remarked, "You have to come sit at the table," as she took her Mother by the hand.

They all went into the dining room, and Mother sat at the head of the table. Dr. Pierce turned out the lights, and Emma came in carrying the cake with all the candles lit on it. Grandpa Woodard said, "We had better be careful we don't start a fire." Jordan remarked, "Oh, Grandpa, we won't start a fire." "Well," Grandpa said, "that's a lot of candles." Tiffany stated, "Not half as many as I'm going to put on your birthday cake." Grandpa said, with a funny look on his face. "Oh, oh, I think I'm in trouble." Everyone sang Happy Birthday, and Mommy blew out the candles. It was a chocolate cake with cream cheese frosting. It was really good with vanilla ice cream. Dr. Pierce mentioned, "Well, we had better go Tiffany, if we are going to get any shopping done before the dinner theater." Mother said, "Oh yes, you children can work on wrapping your Christmas gifts." Jordan stated, "Oh boy, that will really be fun." After Tiffany changed her clothes and purses, she said, "We will see all of you in the morning. Don't stay up too late. Tomorrow is going to be another busy day," as she kissed them all good night. "And don't forget to say your prayers." Stephanie assured her, "We always say our prayers, don't we?" Angela replied, "Oh yes, we sure do." And tonight they would pray especially long and hard on behalf of their Mother and Dr. Pierce. They were hardly out the door, when the children said; "okay, let's get busy wrapping gifts." "Okay," Grandma Woodard said, "I will help Jordan." Emma said, "I will help Blake." Carrie replied, "I will help Jackson." Grandpa mentioned, "And I will help Jared." Angela, Gregory and Stephanie each went their own way.

Emma stated, "We are ordering pizza to be brought up from the restaurant downstairs for supper, so we can all continue to wrap gifts until the pizza gets here." Jared replied, "Cool, that sounds good already." Jordan asked, "Can we put some gifts under all the trees?" Grandpa stated, "You can put them under whatever tree you want, just don't put them in front of Dr. Pierce's gifts." So off they went. They were so excited about wrapping everyone else's gifts, they could hardly stand it. Angela said, "Part of the fun of Christmas is wrapping the gifts we bought for others." Jordan replied, "Yes, and another part of the fun is watching them open the gifts." Jackson remarked, "And the most fun part of Christmas, is opening all the gifts we get from everyone else."

It was 7:00 p.m. when the doorbell rang. Stephanie said, "I am all done wrapping, I'll get the door." Todd said, "Well, hello there beautiful," as he stood there with his arms full of pizzas. "Where can I put these?" Stephanie stated, "Oh, I am sorry," as she backed up to let Todd in. "Please just put them on the dining room table." Stephanie closed the door, and pushed the intercom button to the bedroom, where Emma was helping Blake wrap his gifts. "Emma, Todd is here with the pizzas. Can I sign for them or do you have to sign for them?" Emma said, "I will be down in a moment to sign for them; meanwhile; asked Todd if he would like to join us for pizza. I believe he is off work at 7:00 p.m." Todd replied, "Yes Ma'am, I am off work at 7:00 p.m., and yes Ma'am; I would love to stay for pizza. I will just call down to the restaurant and let them know I will drop the signed slip off when I leave the building. Thank you so much." Stephanie called the other rooms and told them the pizza was here. Todd said, "Boy it sure is quiet here for having so many little children around." Stephanie replied, "Oh, that's because we're all wrapping Christmas gifts, each in a different room. The children really love to wrap their own gifts." Jared said, "Boy, are we ever glad to see you." Jordan mentioned, "Yeah, we just love pizza." Jackson said; "And we are really hungry!" Blake said, "Me too, and I'm glad to see you too," Todd asked, "Did you get all your gifts wrapped?" Jordan replied, "Almost, we will be finished before we go to bed. And we get to put them under any tree we want." Emma said, "Pizza is ready." They all went to sit down at the table, and Grandpa Woodard said the blessing. And Jordan added; "and

God please help Mommy and Dr. Pierce get to know each other better today. Amen." Everyone looked up and smiled. Jordan remarked, "Boy, this pizza sure is good, you sure are a good cook, Todd." Todd replied, "I am not the cook, I just delivered it, but I will let the cook know." Grandma Woodard asked, "So Todd, tell us a little bit about you." "Well," Todd replied, "I am a junior in high school, and I live with my mother, she is a friend of Emma's. She works in the nursery at the hospital where Dr. Pierce works." Angela asked, "Her name is Kristine, isn't it?" Todd replied, "Why yes it is; how did you know?" Angela remarked, "I met her yesterday when Dr. Pierce took me to the nursery to see all the babies." Grandpa Woodard asked, "What would you like to do when you graduate?" Todd replied, "I guess I would like to go into the medical field, if I could get a scholarship." Grandpa said, "If you started putting your money away now, it sure would help be a good start on college." Todd replied, "That sounds good, but right now most of my money goes to help my mom, so that is out of the question." Olivia stated, "We would like to have you and your mom come and have Christmas dinner with us." Todd replied, "Oh, I don't know that we could." Emma asked, "Why not, everybody else is coming. And if they invite anybody else, we will all have to eat at the restaurant because there won't be any room up here." Everybody laughed. Todd said, "Well, if you're sure it's okay." Olivia remarked, "If it wouldn't have been okay, I wouldn't have asked. In fact, we insist on it." Todd said, "My mom will want to know what she can bring." Carrie replied, "Just the two of you; your Mom deserves a break."

Todd said, "I had better get going; my Mother will worry about where I am. Grandpa Woodard stated, "Don't forget to tell your mother about Christmas, even though Dr. Pierce will be giving her a call. Now, how do you get home?" Todd replied, "I will take a bus, but I had better call my mom and let her know I will be late." Grandpa said, "I will go down with you to tell Sam to give you a ride home, and I will pay for it." Oliver asked, "Sam, would you please give this young man a ride home. We have kept him late, and I would feel more comfortable knowing he got home safely." Jared asked, "Can Gregory and I go with you?" "What the heck," Grandpa Woodard said, "why don't all three of us ride along, then no one will be left alone." Oliver had Sam call upstairs and let the ladies know they were going with to take Todd home. Todd had never been in Sam's limo before. Todd remarked, "Mom will really be surprised." There were no lights on, so Todd's Mom was not home from work yet. Todd said, "Thank you so much for the ride home, I really appreciated it." Oliver stated, "No problem; just don't forget to let your mother know that Dr. Pierce will be calling her about Christmas dinner." By the time they got back, the little ones were in bed, and the two boys had to finish wrapping their gifts. Stephanie let them know that Angela and she had already said their prayers with the little ones, so the two boys are on their own. Gregory told her they wouldn't be very long. Before long, they were all in bed, and Grandpa and Grandma Woodard left them in the care of Emma and Carrie, and walked across the hall to go to bed. When Dr. Pierce and Tiffany got home, he opened the door for her, made sure she was safely inside, and then he went across the hall to his own apartment.

Wednesday, December 22, was the fifth day of their vacation already. It was going by fast. It was going to be another exciting day. Whose turn was it going to be to open a present today? Well, Blake woke Mommy up long before she thought it was time to get up. Mommy asked, "Why are you awake so early, Blake?" Blake replied, "Me need hugs." Mommy said, "You are a precious little sweetie," as she got up, and picked up little Blake in her arms and took him to lay with her in her big bed. He snuggled right up to her and within three minutes, he was fast asleep. Tiffany was up, dressed, and had her devotions by the time little

Blake woke up. Blake remarked, "Me sleeped with you in your big bed." Mommy replied, "Well, you did for a little while, but you can't do that every night, you have to sleep in your own bed." Blake said, "Me knows; me is a big boy." Mommy replied, "Yes you are, and we had better get ready to go downstairs. What do we get, when we get downstairs?" "Hot cocoa milk," Blake said, as he ran to her and jumped up into her arms. Mother knocked on each door as they headed downstairs. Again, Blake wanted to get down and sit on one of the stairs and stare at the big tree and the packages underneath it. Then without saying anything, he got up and headed down the stairs. Blake said, "Mornin, Emma," as he entered the kitchen. "You got hot cocoa milk?" Emma replied, "I sure do have hot cocoa milk just for you." Tiffany said, "I smell coffee." Carrie said, "Freshly brewed," as she handed Tiffany a cup. Tiffany was having her first cup of coffee when the doorbell rang.

Carrie went to the door. Of course it was Dr. Pierce and Grandpa and Grandma Woodard. They said, "Good morning," as they came in. Just then the other children were coming down the big staircase. Jackson and Gregory were in front walking on the same step, when Jackson saw Dr. Pierce, and started to walk too fast on the big stairs. He seemed to trip over his own feet, and started to fall. Dr. Pierce started to run towards the stairs, but Gregory reached out and grabbed Jackson by the back of his shirt collar and lifted him right up in the air. When Gregory reached forward to grab Jackson, he began to lose his balance, and he knew that they would both go headfirst down the stairs if he didn't get rid of the extra weight he was carrying. Just then he looked up and saw Dr. Pierce was at the bottom of the stairs, and Gregory said; "catch him." And he threw Jackson through the air, and Dr. Pierce caught him in both arms. As Gregory threw Jackson, Dr. Pierce hollered "lean backwards Gregory." Gregory threw his weight backwards, and his feet went off from under him. He bounced down the last four stairs on his behind, with his feet in the air. Dr. Pierce said, "Well done, Gregory, you did a fine job. That was very quick thinking. You saved your little brother from getting hurt really bad." Jackson said; "wow," then he started to cry. Dr. Pierce said, "You're okay," as he handed Jackson to Tiffany, "but we had better see how Gregory is doing." He bent down to check Gregory over. "Are you okay Gregory?" Gregory replied, "I think so, just a little sore on the backside." Dr. Pierce stated, "Better than coming down on your head—try walking." Gregory remarked, "I can walk fine, I think I will be okay." Dr. Pierce asked, "If there is any problem, you be sure to let me know, Okay," Gregory said, "I will, but I think I'm okay; how's my little buddy?" "Jackson put his arms around Gregory, and said; "thank you Gregory for saving me," then he turned to Dr. Pierce and said; "thank you for catching me, Dr. Pierce. You are a good catcher." Dr. Pierce said, "Maybe Gregory and I should start a baseball team, he could be the pitcher, and I could be the catcher." Jackson replied, "Yeah, and I could be the ball." Everyone laughed except Tiffany. Mother stated, "That's enough, Jackson you gave me a big scare. You could have been hurt very badly. You know, you do not walk fast going down the stairs. You tell your brother how sorry you are for causing him the pain he has because he saved you, and you promise him and me that you will never walk fast going down those stairs again. You children all know there is a very good example here. Jackson, you have caused your brother pain by sinning, and doing something wrong, by walking too fast down the stairs, and it is that same kind of sin, (disobedience) that sent Jesus to the cross. He suffered because of our sins too." Jackson said, "I am so sorry Gregory, for walking too fast and causing you all that pain." Then Jackson knelt at the bottom step and asked Jesus to forgive him for being disobedient. Gregory knelt down beside Jackson, and told him that he forgave him, and that Jesus also forgives us when we are sorry and ask for forgiveness. Then Gregory picked up his little brother and gave him a big kiss and hug. Just then, Blake called from the dining room. "Me is hungry." Tiffany said, "Oh, my gosh! He is in there all by himself." Blake asked, "What happened?" Mommy said, "There was an accident. Jackson almost fell walking down the stairs too fast. And I want you to be very careful walking down the stairs. You are to walk very slowly and hang on to someone and the railing, too. Do you understand, Blake?" Blake said, "Yes, me be careful, but me also hungry, me needs food." Carrie replied, "And food you shall get," and everyone laughed. Dr. Pierce gave the blessing, and they had a wonderful breakfast. And all the children wanted to know how Mother and Dr. Pierce's evening went. Jordan asked, "What did you do?" Mother replied, "Well, first we went shopping, and bought that white blouse and skirt to go with the beautiful vest Angela gave me for my birthday. And then I got this new coat that Dr. Pierce bought for me, and this new dress, which I will wear Christmas Day, and then we went to the city park, and rode around the park in a horse-drawn cart." Stephanie stated, "Oh that would be wonderful." "That," Jared said, "would be cold." Everyone laughed. Mother added, "Well, then we went to the "Godsspell" musical, it was at the "Lorenzo Timonium Dinner Theater." We had dinner and then watched *It's a Wonderful Life*. It was just wonderful, and then we came home." Dr. Pierce said, "And today is another day, and we had better go into the great room and sit around in a circle and see who gets to open a present this morning." Jackson was the first one there and he said, "Gregory, will you sit by me please?" Gregory said, "Okay, little buddy." Mother was carrying Blake. She put him down, and he said; "Mommy, you come sit by me, please" when everyone was sitting in a circle, Dr. Pierce went over to the big tree and bent down and picked up a present.

CHAPTER 13

BLAKE'S CHRISTMAS PRESENT

It was Wednesday, December 22nd, and Dr. Pierce said, "Blake you had better get in the middle of the circle." Blake couldn't move. He had tears in his eyes as he looked at his mommy. Mommy looked at him and remarked, "Well, go Honey, go in the middle of the room, Blake." He couldn't talk either. Jackson got up and took him by the hand and helped him into the middle of the room. Tears were coming down his little face, he had waited so long. He looked over at his Mommy; there were tears in her eyes too. He finally replied, "Don't cry Mommy, me happy, me got happy tears." "Oh, sweetheart, Mommy is happy for you, too. Do you want me to read it for you?" Blake said, "Yes, please." Mommy said, "You have to open it first, Honey, I will help get it started for you." Blake remarked, "Thank you." It was a larger present than some of the others. Mommy put a hole in the paper, and Blake tore it open. Mommy tore the tape on the box, Blake opened the box and there was a stuffed Santa doll, and a picture frame, and a note. Blake remarked, "That doll is just like the man in the store." Mommy replied, "Why, yes it is; now I will read you the note." "Dear Blake, it was not easy for me to figure out what to do for you, but I figured you'd like toys. So we are going to the biggest toy store in Baltimore. We will take a break for lunch, and then go on to one of the largest indoor parks there is. We will go on all the rides you want, and then we will get our pictures taken with Santa Claus. Somewhere in there, we will have to take time out for a nap, and then we're all going to dinner at Captain James Seafood Restaurant. I hope your special day will be a joy for you. Have a very Merry Christmas, love, Dr. Pierce." Blake said, "Oh. Thank you, thank you," as he got up and went over and gave Dr. Pierce, a big hug and kiss. Blake stated, "Can we go to toy store now?" Dr. Pierce responded, "We sure can." Mommy replied, "Not so fast, everyone take a potty break, and then we can leave." Dr. Pierce mentioned, "You are so wise," as he winked at Tiffany. Tiffany stated, "It's not that I'm so wise, it's just that I've had years of practice; otherwise, you just get in the car and then they have to go potty."

When everyone was putting on their coats, Dr. Pierce said; "if anyone has got any shopping left to do for Christmas, please feel free to take your time. The only thing we really need to be concerned about is when Blake needs to take a nap." Tiffany responded, "It would be nice, if we could put Blake down at 1:30 p.m. Conrad said, "Well, that settles that. We will be back at the hotel at 12 o'clock sharp and then we can eat, and rest, while Blake is napping. After that, we will go to the park, and then we'll go to see Santa Claus and have our pictures taken, and then we will go to dinner." Grandpa Woodard said, "Off we go."

As they entered the elevator, Walter remarked, "and just where are we off to today?" Jackson asked, "Are you coming with us, Walter?" Walter responded, "Oh no, I was just being funny, when I said, where are we going. I meant, where are all of you off to today?" "Oh," Jackson replied, "we are going to the toy store to get Blake his Christmas present from Dr. Pierce." "Well," Walter mentioned, "maybe I should come; I could use some new toys." Jackson looked at Walter with a strange look on his face and said, "you're a grown up. You don't play with toys, do you?" Walter remarked, "No little man, I am just teasing you," as they reached the main floor. Walter said, "Well, here we are, be sure and let me see what Blake picked out when you get back." Jackson said, "Okay, if you are still working when we get back." Walter stated, "Oh, I will be here, see you later."

Sam was waiting for them, as they walked up to the car. "Good morning everyone, and where are we off to today?" Dr. Pierce said, "We are going to the toy store." Sam replied, "The toy store? I won't be able to get you out of there till a week from Tuesday." Dr. Pierce laughed, "I know just what you mean, and it will be like pulling teeth, getting all of them out of there." Tiffany responded; "and just how big is this toy store?" "Boy, it's big," Sam responded, "you could get lost in there, and they wouldn't find you until tomorrow." He continued to discuss this store all the way there. Dr. Pierce mentioned, "Tiffany and I will take Jackson and Blake." Grandma Woodard replied, "I will take Jordan." Grandpa Woodard remarked, "I will take Jared." Stephanie stated, "Angela, Gregory and I will go together." Dr. Pierce mentioned, "If anyone wants to talk to us about anything, have us paged and let them know which isle you are in." Tiffany replied, "Is this place really that big?" Conrad remarked, "Yes it is."

Sam pulled up in front of the store, and opened the door. "Wow," Jared said, "you weren't kidding about the size of the store." Tiffany remarked, "Now I know what Sam meant, when he said we won't get the children out of here until a week from Tuesday." They were all pretty shocked at the size of the store. Mother said, "You make sure you stay together, Stephanie." Stephanie replied, "Yes, Mother, you can be sure we will stay together." Angela remarked, "I am even considering holding onto Stephanie's hand." Stephanie replied, "We can hold hands, if you want to Angela; that's fine with me." Mother stated, "I appreciate that." So off they went. Dr. Pierce mentioned, "We will meet back here at 11:30 a.m. sharp, does everyone have their watches synchronized?" They all looked at their watches and shook their heads yes, and off they went into the vast, unknown world of toys.

Jackson wanted to go over to where the trains were, but he knew this was Blake's special day, so he did not say anything. Blake didn't know what he wanted. He just wanted to look at everything there was. Jared and Grandpa Woodard headed for the football section. Jordan and Grandma Woodard headed for the dolls and dollhouse section. Stephanie, Angela, and Gregory headed for the music section. Angela said, "How would you ever decide what you would want in a place like this, there are so many different kinds of toys." Gregory remarked, "I feel sorry for poor little Blake, he will never be able to decide what he wants. Poor little guy, he is going to be so wound up, he won't know what he wants or what to do or which way to go." Tiffany and Dr. Pierce finally got to the toddler section of the store, and Blake could hardly stay in the stroller. Tiffany remarked, "I am going to take Jackson, and look at the trains, you and Blake enjoy yourselves, and good luck, Conrad." Conrad replied, "We will be just fine, won't we Blake?" "Yah," Blake replied, "this will be fun." Dr. Pierce asked, "Now, do you understand how this works, Blake?" Blake shook his head no. Dr. Pierce replied, "Well, you get to pick out some kind of toy to take home with you, and it will be from me to you for your Christmas present." Blake said, "Okay." Dr. Pierce stated, "Maybe we had better just walk through here, one time, and if you see something you might like to have, we can take a little closer look at it. Then when we have gone through the whole section, we will go back and look at the things that you really liked and then you can pick out something you would like to have for yourself, okay?" Blake replied, "Okay." Blake had a huge grin on his face, and all of a sudden, they went by a huge swimming pool, with a slide and he let out a squeal. Dr. Pierce said, "I think that means you kind-of like the swimming pool." "Oh yes, yes, me wants that." Dr. Pierce stated, "Well now, we have only gone about thirty feet down the aisle, and there are a lot of aisles we have not even been down yet. There might be something else we find that you might like better, and you know; you wouldn't be able to play in this pool for six months. That's way next summer and besides you have the lake you can swim in." "Oh," Blake replied, "me needs to look more." Dr. Pierce remarked, "I think that's a good idea." Then they came to a sandbox full of sand with shovels and pails in it, and Blake wanted that too. Dr. Pierce had to explain that he would have to wait a long time to play with that, too.

Then they came to the big riding cars and trucks. "Wow," Blake mentioned, "that looks like Grandpa Woodard's car, me wants that." Dr. Pierce responded, "There we go again, you can't ride that in the snow, you would get stuck. You would have to wait until spring to ride that, too." "Okay," Blake said, as they went around the corner of the aisle. Blake saw something and got really excited. He said, "Look, Dr. Pierce, they have my toolbox and tools too." Dr. Pierce remarked, "Well, so they have, I'll be darned." They went up one aisle, and down the next. Blake wanted something in every aisle. They went down one aisle, and there was a big red wagon. Blake replied, "Wow, me wants that. That's big enough for me and Jackson to ride in at the same time." Dr. Pierce stated, "It sure is." They were going down the last aisle, when Blake spied a big remote-controlled hummer. Blake got really excited and said, "Look, Dr. Pierce, a big truck. Me wants that." Dr. Pierce replied, "Well, little buddy; I think you're about four years too young for that, maybe we had better get your Mommy over here to help us. What do you think?"

Dr. Pierce turned the stroller around the corner and almost ran right into Tiffany. Blake responded, "There's my Mommy and Jackson." Conrad stated, "You're just in time, I need a little help here." "Really," Tiffany replied, "and I thought you guys were doing pretty well together." Conrad said, "He seems to want everything he is too young for, or something he can't play with for at least six months." Tiffany stated, "They always want something they cannot have. Let's go over here, Blake, and look at all these toys. Look here, Blake, this is neat, and you pull the string and the animals talk. Look at this Blake, it's a barn, with all kinds of animals, and they walk too." Blake replied, "Me wants that." Dr. Pierce remarked, "Okay, that sounds like a plan to me, we will get the barn with all the animals, and let's get a couple of these story books and a video. And we will get the round thing where the animals talk when you pull the string, and here's another round thing that tells you different shapes, and look Blake, and here's one that tells you numbers so you can learn to count." Tiffany replied, "Conrad, I believe that is enough, I think you've lost it, you've gone way overboard." "Okay," Conrad remarked, "If you say so, I will quit. Mommy says that's enough, little guy. It's time to go get some lunch. Now let's see if we can round up the rest of the clan." Blake said, "Thank you so much, Dr. Pierce, me got lots of stuff." Dr. Pierce responded, "You're welcome, little guy; let's get this stuff checked out." When they got to the register, Dr. Pierce had the others paged. They were not even completely checked out yet, when here they came, one after the other. Before long they were all checked out, and loading up the car to go back to the hotel. Dr. Pierce called Emma and Carrie, and told them they were on their way back. Little Blake was so excited to tell Jared about his farm set and the animal toy that talked when you pulled the string, and all the other stuff he got from Dr. Pierce. "Boy," Stephanie replied, "you made out pretty well there, little guy." Gregory stated, "And now, little buddy, after you nap, we are going to the indoor park, and go on the rides, and then we are going to see Santa Claus." Blake asked, "Who is he?" Jared replied, "He is the man in the red suit." Blake replied, "Oh, Me remember, just like the doll Dr. Pierce gave me, Me knows him." Mother asked, "Will you sit on his lap, so we can get a picture of you and Santa?" Blake responded, "Maybe, if Jackson does." Jackson replied, "Oh, I will, you can be sure of that—and Blake, he will ask you what you want for Christmas, so you better start thinking about that, too." Blake replied, "Me wants a Hummer, Me like big trucks." Just then Sam pulled up to the hotel. Sam mentioned, "You go right on up, I'll see that these packages get brought up." Dr. Pierce replied, "Thank you so much, Sam." Emma and Carrie met them at the door. Emma asked, "Where are all the presents?" Jared replied, "Sam is having them sent up. I'm hungry." Carrie stated, "We have grilled cheese sandwiches, tomato soup, and salad coming right up." Blake said, "Num. and hot cocoa milk?" Emma responded, "Yes, Blake, and for anyone who doesn't like grilled cheese, we have roast beef sandwiches." Dr. Pierce replied, "I don't think we will have a problem, we are all pretty hungry, and no one here is very fussy." Dr. Pierce gave the blessing, and everyone enjoyed their lunch.

Mommy fed Blake half of a grilled cheese sandwich, a little salad with ranch dressing, and hot cocoa milk and then Blake gave everyone a hug and kiss, and asked Dr. Pierce if he would tuck him in. Dr. Pierce replied, "It would be my pleasure," as he picked up Little Blake and up the stairs they went. Everyone lay down and took a nap. Even Dr. Pierce lay on the large sofa in the great room, he said, "I'm just too lazy to go across the hall." Blake slept for an hour and a half. It seemed to go by very fast, but the children were excited to get going. So off they went. Sam remarked; "If you think the last place was big, wait until you see this indoor park." The children could not believe their eyes. They just stared at all the rides. There was this one ride with this log type thing you

159

sat in, and you ever so slowly rode around this little creek like a trough. There was all beautiful scenery on both sides with animals that looked absolutely real, just like they were standing in the wild. And then you started to climb this hill and at the top, you barely leveled off, when you went almost straight down on a trough of water and splash, you landed in a pool of water at the bottom. Everyone except Grandma Woodard, Jackson, and Blake went on that one. We all got wet, too. There were so many rides; it is hard to describe them all. Everyone had a wonderful time, and all too soon the three hours were up, and they had to leave.

It was just on the other side of the park, where they were going to meet Santa. Jackson and Jordan were really excited, Blake was a little scared, but he didn't want to show it. Angela asked, "Are you scared to sit on Santa's lap?" Blake answered, "No, not much." Dr. Pierce had arranged a private showing with Santa. They all went in the back of this great big shopping center, and in a great big chair sat the jolliest old gentleman, you ever saw, all dressed in a red suit. He had a large mustache and a long white beard. "Ho, Ho, Ho," he said as they walked in the room. "Well, who do we have here? I'll bet your name is Blake, isn't it?" Blake answered, "Yes, how do you know?" Santa remarked, "I know all about, you; you like trucks. Would you come and sit on my lap, Blake? Your Mother would like to take your picture." Blake responded, "Yes sir, if Jackson comes too." Santa asked, "Well, Jackson, Will you come up here and sit?" Jackson replied, "Sure I will." Santa asked, "Now Blake, what would you like for Christmas?" Blake replied, "Me wants a Hummer, but me is too little." Santa remarked, "Is that right, what kind of Hummer you want?" Blake answered, "One that moves." Dr. Pierce replied, "A remote control." Santa said, "I see; now I understand. Dr. Pierce, would you hand me that remote control sitting on that table over there." Santa said,

"Thank you. Now Jackson, could you step down just for a moment please?" Jackson stepped down.

Santa mentioned, "Now Blake, would you take this little black box please?" Blake took the box in both of his little hands. "Now Blake, somewhere in this room is a car, now I want you to move these levers back and forth and sideways to see if you can make that car come to you." Blake tried to hold the box, and move the levers, but his hands were just too small. No matter how hard he tried, he could not do it. Blake replied, "Me can't do it." Santa asked, "Shall we see if Jackson can do it?" Jackson took the box from Blake, he remarked, "The box is just too big for me to hold, and push or pull the levers at the same time." Santa responded, "Ah ha; shall we let Jared try it?" Blake said, "Yes." Jared took the box from Jackson, and started moving the levers. All of a sudden around the corner came this little red car, it made a loud noise as it came closer to Jared. Then it stopped, turned left, and started to go around Dr. Pierce. Santa asked Blake, "Do you think you might be just a little too small, to run a big Hummer, Blake?" Blake said, "Yes, and Jackson's too small, too." Santa replied, "I think you are right, I believe you will have to wait until you are bigger like Jared to run a remote control Hummer, but is there anything else you might like to have, that you could play with now?" Blake looked over at Mommy and Dr. Pierce and said, "Me would like a sandbox and a truck to fill with sand." "I see," Santa replied, "it's pretty cold out now, sand would freeze in your sandbox now, this time of year." Blake remarked, "That's okay, me will wait, me got other toys." Santa replied, "Well then, I will see what we can do about a sandbox." Blake said, "Thank you." Santa asked, "Now do you suppose, they can take a picture of you and I together?" Blake shook his head yes. And he smiled a big smile, and the girl took a picture of Blake and Santa.

Next was Jackson's turn to sit on Santa's lap. Santa asked him what he wanted for Christmas. "I would like a pair of skates for Christmas." Santa mentioned, "I will remember that, now let's have a big smile for the camera." Mother remarked, "That is going to be a really nice picture." Next, it was Jordan's turn to sit on Santa lap. "Hello, Jordan," Santa said, "what would you like for Christmas this year?" Jordan responded, "I would like a dress-up doll and some clothes." "Well," Santa remarked, "that doesn't sound like too big of an order. I think I can handle that." "By the way," Jordan stated, "we are staying here in Baltimore for Christmas this year. Do you know where Dr. Pierce lives?" Santa replied, "Why yes I do." Jordan went on to say, "Well, we are staying right across the hall from him, so please don't leave our Christmas presents at our home in Minnesota." Santa remarked, "Oh, I wouldn't do that, "I know exactly where you are staying. You're staying in Jim and Sally Meyer's apartment." Jordan replied, "Boy, you are really smart, you know everything." "Well," Santa mentioned, "I know when children are good or bad." Jackson asked with a funny look on his face, "You really know that?" Santa answered, "I sure do, and are you ready to take a picture with me Jordan?" Jordan nodded her head yes. The lady with the camera said, "Just look right at me and say with a smile, cheese please" and she snapped the picture. Mother remarked, "These pictures are going to be so nice." Santa asked, "Whose next? I'll bet you are Jared," as Jared walked up to Santa. Santa asked, "Hello, Jared, how old are you young man?" Jared replied, "I will be nine years old in May." Santa remarked, "Well, Jared, you are quite the young man, and what do you want for Christmas?" Jared said with a smile, "Well, Santa, after using that remote control car a little while ago, I guess I would like one of those, that was really fun." Santa responded, "Take my word for it Jared, it is fun, and I will see what I can do. Now, Jared, how about a big smile for a picture with good old Santa?" "Okay," Jared answered, as he thanked Santa and gave him a big smile. The lady with the camera mentioned, "Good job," as she took the picture.

"Well, let me see," Santa remarked, "who is next? I'll bet it is Angela. Would you come up here and sit on my lap, Angela?" "Oh yes," Angela replied, "I would just love to." Santa asked, "Well, young lady, just how old are you?" "I will be eleven years old in April." Santa remarked, "You are quite the young lady, and what would you like for Christmas?" Angela replied, "I would like a horse statue for my room and a video about horses." Santa mentioned, "So, you like horses?" "Oh yes, I love horses." Santa remarked, "Well, that should not be too hard for me to fill, now can you give me a big smile for the camera?" Angela gave a beautiful smile, and the lady took the picture. "Let me guess," Santa mentioned, "I'll bet Gregory is next. Don't be embarrassed to come up here and sit on my lap, Gregory, because all the adults are coming up here, too." "Really," Tiffany responded. "Really," Santa remarked, "that's the deal, isn't that right Gregory?" Gregory answered, "If you say so, Santa," as he walked up to Santa and sat down on his lap. Santa asked, "Well, how old are you young man?" Gregory remarked, "I will be thirteen in February." Santa mentioned, "You are just about old enough to drive, well in a couple more years anyway." Gregory replied, "That seems like a long time to wait." Santa remarked, "It will go by faster than you think; now what would you like for Christmas?" Gregory replied, "I would like a pair of skates, also." Santa responded, "I believe I can handle that, now how about a nice big smile." Gregory gave a big smile and the lady snapped the picture.

Santa mentioned, "Well, I believe it is Stephanie's turn, the beautiful young lady with the beautiful blue eyes. Would you please come up and sit on my lap young lady?" Stephanie replied, "Yes," as she walked forward. Santa asked, "Well, young lady, do you have a boyfriend yet?" Stephanie responded, "No I haven't, I'm too young to have a boyfriend." Tiffany breathed a sigh of relief. Santa remarked, "It's not polite to ask a young lady her age, so I won't, but I will ask you what you want for Christmas." Stephanie replied, "Well, I would like some jewelry." Santa remarked, "Jewelry, it is, that should be easy enough, and now how about a big smile for the camera." "Smile pretty," the lady with the camera stated, "that was just lovely, thank you very much." "Now," Santa remarked, "I believe Tiffany is next. Come right on up young lady; don't be afraid. I won't bite." The little ones laughed as their Mommy went up and sat on Santa's lap. Tiffany remarked, "I did not know this was going to include the adults," as she turned and looked at Conrad. Santa replied, "Oh Honey, don't you remember when you were a little girl, why; you used to get so excited about sitting on my lap. And I remember the time you had on that beautiful red dress that had the white fur collar. Why, you looked just like me. That was a beautiful picture." Tiffany asked, "How do you know that?" Santa answered, "Well, dear, I remember everything, that's my job, and Dr. Pierce, I remember him to." "Look," Blake stated, "Mommy sitting on Santa's lap; that's funny." Dr. Pierce remarked, "It is kind of cute, isn't it?" Santa asked, "Well now, tell me what you would like for Christmas. I suppose you have outgrown the little pink bunny you got that year" Tiffany's face turned white as a ghost. Angela asked, "Do you think Mommy is going to ask for a ring Stephanie?" Stephanie responded "She doesn't want a ring from Santa; she wants one from Dr. Pierce." Santa asked again, "Well, young lady. Have you made up your mind yet, what you would like this year?" Tiffany replied, "I am so shook up, I cannot even think." Santa mentioned, "Well, while you are thinking, maybe we can take your picture with me, smile pretty." "Very good," the lady with the camera remarked. Tiffany finally said, "I know what I would like. I would like a pair of diamond earrings, and a diamond necklace to go with them. I know it's a little more than a pink bunny, but I'll bet you can do it." Santa answered, "That is a tall order, but you're right, I can do it."

Santa said, "Now, Dr. Pierce, it's your turn to sit on Santa's lap." Dr. Pierce walked up and sat down. Jackson remarked, "Dr. Pierce looks silly sitting on Santa's lap, "he's way too big." Santa asked, "Well, young man, what would you like for Christmas this year?" Conrad responded, "Well Santa, I did not know I was going to be coming up here either." Santa replied, "Remember the year you asked for a slingshot. And what happened after you got it. You went to shoot at a bird on the fence, and missed the bird and shot your Dad right on the backside, while he was fixing a fence about six feet away." Dr. Pierce got a funny look on his face, and he said; "well, my aim was not so good at first." Santa remarked, "Yes, and you got your slingshot taken away for a whole month." Conrad stated, "You have a remarkable memory." "That's why I am Santa Claus; I have to remember everything about everybody. Have you decided what you want for Christmas yet?" "Yes," Dr. Pierce replied, "I would like you to come for Christmas dinner." Santa remarked, "Now that is a tall order. I usually sleep quite a bit Christmas Day, because I work all night Christmas Eve, but I will try to be there. Smile Dr. Pierce, so we can get a good picture." The lady with the camera remarked, "Very good."

Santa mentioned, "Olivia, you're next." As Grandma Woodard was walking up to sit on Santa's lap, Dr. Pierce was walking back. Conrad asked, "Did you have anything to do with this, Mother?" Olivia responded, "Why Conrad, I have never even met, or seen this Santa before. I thought he was a friend of yours. Did you not arranged for him to be here? But I must say, he does have a magnificent memory, doesn't he?" Conrad and his mother smiled at each other, and just kept on walking. Olivia said with a smile, "Well hello there, Santa Claus, it's been a good many years since I sat on your lap." Santa replied, "It sure has, and I have missed you being here." Olivia responded, "Is that so?" Santa remarked, "It sure is, why, I remember the year you asked for a rag doll, because the dolls in the store were so expensive, you didn't think you would ever be able to get one, so you asked for a rag doll instead." Tear's swelled up in Olivia's eyes. Santa continued, "And what did I get you for Christmas that year?" Olivia responded thru tears, "I got the most beautiful china doll I had ever seen, and I still have her." Santa asked, "So what would you like for Christmas this year?" Jordan asked Angela, "Is that the china doll in Grandma's glass case that they are always talking about?" Angela replied, "It must be." Olivia answered, "I would like a slow cooker. Mine is plum tuckered out. It lasted a good many years." Santa replied, "That certainly won't be a problem, now if you can give me that same beautiful smile you had so many years ago; that's it, that will be a beautiful picture." Santa stated, "Well, Oliver, it looks like you are the last one, but certainly not the least." Oliver mentioned, "I never thought I would see the day, when I would be sitting on Santa's knee again; nope, not in my lifetime." Santa remarked, "Well, wonders never cease. Do you remember one year you asked for a train, a wooden train? You knew your Dad had a shop where he made beautiful furniture to sell to others for money, and you heard that I had a toy shop where I and my elves made toys, so you thought you would ask for a wooden train. I asked you how many cars you wanted, and you said I can only count to ten, so I guess I will take ten cars with it." Tear's swelled up in Grandpa Woodard's eyes, as he thought about that very special Christmas. Oliver stated, "That was the only happy Christmas I remember; it was the last year my Dad was with us. He died the following year." Santa remarked, "You would never talk to me after that." Oliver mentioned, "No, you're right, but I still have the wooden train." Santa asked, "So then, what would you like this year for Christmas?" Oliver replied, "There is something I have always wanted, but haven't thought about for a great many years. I always wanted one of those front-end loaders. You know the kind where you can sit on it, and you push the levers, and the front end goes down and picks up a load of dirt, and then you turn it around, and you can dump it on the other side?" Santa remarked, "I know exactly what you're talking about. Are you going to play in Blake's sandbox with it?" Oliver stated, "Oh no, but I will sit on the porch and watch Blake and Jackson play with it, and I will have a blast." Santa replied, "No sooner said than done, and now we need a big smile, just pretend you are watching the boys playing with your front-end loader." Grandpa Woodard got a big grin on his face, and the lady took his picture." The lady with the camera remarked, "good, very good, Now I would like one with everyone and Santa Claus." Everyone jumped up, and they went and stood or sat around Santa, and Blake and Jackson quickly got up on Santa's lap. Angela remarked, "This is going to be just great." Jared replied, "Yeah." Everyone had a wonderful smile on their face. It was the best picture ever. Santa remarked, "I have a lot to do, to get ready for Christmas Eve, and if I am not too tired out, I will see you all on Christmas Day." And with that said, Santa got up and started to walk out. Dr. Pierce noticed that Santa had a limp as he walked out. Everyone said, "Good bye Santa Claus." Santa called back as he left, "See you in a couple of days."

Jackson remarked, "This was the best time we had yet, but, I am hungry, let's eat." Dr. Pierce responded, "That's a good idea," as they started walking out. Sam was waiting at the exit when they all came out. He opened the door for them, and asked them what they thought of Santa. Dr. Pierce asked, "Did you see him when he came out just a few minutes ago?" Sam responded, "No one came out of that exit except you guys." Dr. Pierce replied, "Yes he did," and everyone else said the same thing. Sam remarked, "Well, I don't know where your mystery Santa went, but he never came out of that exit. I have been watching that exit door for half an hour, and you are the only ones who have come out of it." Dr. Pierce went back to the exit door. He looked down the long hall; there was not one door on either side, and he remarked, "That is the strangest thing."

Off they went to Captain James Seafood Restaurant. It was really cool. It looked just like a big ship sitting on the sidewalk. The children got excited as they drove up to it. There were round windows on the inside that looked just like portholes. Blake and Jackson thought they were actually on a ship all during dinner; they talked about how Santa knew something about each one of them from years ago. Tiffany whispered to Dr. Pierce; "how did you find out all that stuff about all of us, Conrad?" Conrad answered, "I don't know anything about any of it, I thought it was Mom, but I will call in the morning and find out what is going on." When they got back to the hotel, little Blake and Jackson were both out like a light, fast asleep. Walter remarked, "Must have been a busy day," as they got in the elevator. Dr. Pierce replied, "They are plum tuckered out, and so are we." Everyone hurried off to bed when they got to the apartment. Emma and Carrie were already in bed.

CHAPTER 14

THE DOLL HOUSE

When Dr. Pierce got into his apartment, he found that Angela's dress and pictures had arrived. "She will be excited about this," he told Olivia and Oliver. I would like to open it myself, but I had better wait and let her do it. So off to bed they went.

It seemed like morning came really fast. Little Blake was awake and playing with his toy that made animal sounds when you pull the string that he got from Dr. Pierce. When his mommy got out of the shower, she said; "Well, good morning, my little man, are you ready to get up and get dressed?" Blake said, "Yes, Mommy." So Tiffany picked him up, and they both got dressed and were on their way downstairs when the doorbell rang. Carrie answered the door. It was Dr. Pierce. Tiffany stated, "My, you are early," as she put Blake down at the bottom of the stairs. Blake ran all the way to Dr. Pierce and put up his little hands for him to pick him up. Conrad mentioned, "I wanted to talk to Angela on the intercom, before she got dressed," as he picked Blake up and gave him a big hug and kiss. Tiffany asked, "What are the packages?" Conrad replied, "They are for Angela," as he went over to the intercom and paged her room. Stephanie said, "We'll be down in a few minutes." Dr. Pierce replied, "Tell Angela to send someone down and pick up something that came for her." Angela knew that her picture and dress were here, because of the conversation they had the other day. Stephanie came down and took the package upstairs and helped her with her new dress and fixed her hair as good as she could, so it looked somewhat like it did when she had it done. Then they started down the stairs.

Mother remarked, "Honey, are you ever beautiful this morning Angela, that is such a beautiful dress, and your hair, you look just like you did on Monday. Stephanie, you did a beautiful job with her hair." Stephanie answered, "Thank you Mom." Angela also said, "Thank you Mom. Dr. Pierce, where is the package?" Dr. Pierce replied, "Right here," as he handed her the package. She was so excited. Mother remarked again, "Angela, your dress is so beautiful, honey." "Thank you again and just wait until you see this." She un-wrapped the package, and Dr. Pierce held up the picture right beside her. "Oh, my gosh;" everyone seemed to say all at once. Mother remarked, "It's the same dress. How did you do that? Did you buy the dress from the salon?" "No," Angela replied, "Kristine, the nurse at the hospital, (Todd's mom) suggested that we go to this dress shop across the skyway. And we found it there. "Honey," Mother remarked again, "it is just beautiful." Angela replied, "I will wear it only on special occasions." Just then, Emma said; "breakfast is ready." Angela asked, "Can I quickly change my dress? I wouldn't want to spill something on it." Stephanie added, "I will help you," as they headed for the stairs.

Breakfast was on the table when they got back, and Grandpa Woodard gave the blessing and thanked God for all the blessings He had given them. He also thanked Him for the food. They had blueberry pancakes, bacon, hash browns, juice, and milk. It was delicious. Everyone helped clean up the kitchen, so they could all go in the great room and sit down in a circle to see who would get the present today. Dr. Pierce said, "Jordan. You had better get in the center of the circle." Jordan let out a loud squeal and got up and sat in the middle of the circle. Dr. Pierce handed her present to her. She was so excited. She had waited a long time, a whole five days. But Jordan had been a very patient little girl. The present was about the size of a shoebox, and she tore it open as fast as she could. There was a very pretty doll in it. It was dressed in a short skirt, and she had on a pair of ice skates. "Oh," Jordan remarked, "she is a skater, I love skating. Mommy, could you help me read my note? I can read printing, but I can't read writing." Mother responded, "Of course, Honey." It started out, "Dear Jordan, I know little girls love dolls, so we are going shopping at a special store where they have every kind of doll imaginable. Then we are coming back here for lunch. After lunch, we are going to the biggest dollhouse store you have ever seen. Then we are all going out for dinner, and we are all going to the park skating tonight, under the big lights downtown. They will have music to skate by, and it is all decorated for Christmas. It is just beautiful. I hope you will enjoy your special day and have a very Merry Christmas, love, Dr. Pierce." Holding on tight to her doll, Jordan said; "Oh, Dr. Pierce, that is so super. Thank you so very much. I have never even seen a dollhouse store before, and I just love skating in the park, I think. Anyway, I have never done that before, either. Thank you so very, very much."

Then she got up and ran to Dr. Pierce, and gave him a big hug and a kiss. Dr. Pierce replied, "You are very welcome, now, who all wants to go?" Jared remarked, "I'd rather not go to look at dolls and doll houses. Do I have to go?" "No," Mother responded, "you don't have to if someone will stay here with you." Jackson replied, "I will stay here with him." Everyone laughed. "Well," Mother said with a smile, "I meant someone a little older than Jackson." Gregory mentioned, "I will stay home." Grandpa Woodard replied, "I will stay here, too, and you can leave Blake here also. If all you ladies go, we guys can just hang out here by ourselves." "What about lunch?" Emma asked, "everyone is supposed to come back here for lunch," "Well," Dr. Pierce answered, "since we don't have to come back here to put Blake down for a nap, we can eat lunch anywhere. That is fine with me. That will save us some time." Grandpa Woodard remarked, "That's sounds good to me. If we can't find anything here to eat, we will just run on down to the restaurant downstairs." "Well then," Dr. Pierce remarked, "off we go, just me and all these ladies." Jordan replied, "And Sam." Dr. Pierce stated, "You're right, Jordan, there's Sam too. We will be back to change clothes and pick you up to go to dinner and skating at the park. We will see you later. Have fun, you guys." And off they went.

"My, my," Sam stated, "all these ladies, and where might we be off to today?" Dr. Pierce gave him the address and said to Jordan; "just wait till you see this doll store. It is something else. I think your Mom, Grandma, Emma, and Carrie will really enjoy it too. Before you knew it, they were there, and Sam opened the door for them as he helped them out of the car. As they entered the door, there were the most beautiful porcelain dolls anyone had ever seen, standing or sitting on either side of the aisle, as you walked into the store. They had on the most beautiful dresses and hats to match. And some had parasols in their hands. They all had different colored dresses. Some had blond hair, some had red hair, some had brown hair, and some had black hair. On some of the dolls, the hair was put up on top of their heads in curls. On some, their hair was hanging down the middle of their backs, and some had ringlets hanging down. They were the most beautiful dolls the ladies had ever seen. They just stood there looking. No one said anything. Dr. Pierce stated, "There are more dolls as we get further into the store." There were little girl dolls and little boy dolls. There were baby dolls sleeping in beds and dolls swinging on swings.

And there were beautiful dolls dressed in beautiful dresses, standing on a bridge. There were dolls in uniforms of all kinds. There were even dolls standing in a corner, as if they had been naughty. There was every kind of doll you could imagine. Jordan mentioned, "I have never seen so many dolls in all my life." Grandma Woodard replied, "Neither have I." They all agreed that it was the biggest collection of dolls they had ever seen. There were little dolls and big dolls—and the clothes; there were so many clothes. They could hardly believe their eyes.

Stephanie remarked, "I wish I was a little girl again." Grandma Woodard replied, "You don't have to be a little girl to love dolls, I would love to have one of these dolls myself." "Me too," Mother remarked, "Well, Dr. Pierce mentioned, after a while, "have you decided which one you would like Jordan? We have been here almost 3 hours, and we have to go to lunch pretty soon, we also have to go to the dollhouse store." Tiffany responded, "Oh my, I never dreamed we had been here that long. How can anyone make a decision?" Jordan replied, "I know which one I want." Dr. Pierce asked, "Which one is that?" "Yah," Angela asked; "which one did you pick out?" Jordan answered, "I like the "Southern Bell Doll" with the beautiful purple gown with the white trim and white gloves and shoes and a beautiful purple parasol with white lace. And she has brown hair, high up on her head and hanging down in ringlets on one side in front of and behind her ear, way down past her shoulders. She had a large, beautiful purple hat with white trim and a beautiful purple bow tied under her chin." Angela replied, "Oh, that's my favorite one, too." Jordan remarked, "She kind of reminded me of the way you looked in your picture Angela." Angela responded, "Thank you so much. Jordan." Dr. Pierce said, "Well, let's go and buy it, and then on to lunch. Where would you like to go to lunch, Jordan?" Jordan replied, "Oh I don't know, why don't you pick it Dr. Pierce?" Dr. Pierce mentioned,

"Well then, maybe we will do a fast food place, and then on to the dollhouse store. I have a feeling I will have a hard time getting you out of the dollhouse store, too.

Sam, would you join us for lunch, please?" Sam replied, "I would love to join you." They all had a light lunch and took their sodas with them in the limousine. Before you knew it they were at the dollhouse store. Dr. Pierce remarked, "Now this is going to be just as fascinating for all you ladies." And to be sure, it was. There were all kinds of doll houses. They were one-story ones, two-story ones and three-story ones. Some with attached garages, some with carports, and some didn't have any garage at all. Some had swimming pools, some did not. Some had exercise rooms, some did not. Some had vaulted ceilings in the living room, some did not. Some had a plain straight stairway; some had a circular stairway. Some had doors and windows, which opened and closed, and some had electric lights and huge chandeliers, while others were very plain. Some were decorated very simply, and some were decorated like mansions. Some had no furniture, some had simple furniture, and in some, the furniture was really beautiful. You could buy the house without furniture and furnish it as you like. There were so many different kinds of furniture and rugs and carpets, lights, pictures, and candles to choose from. You could get them with wallpaper or painted or both. Some had one bathroom; some had three bathrooms. Some had tile bathrooms; others did not. Some had decks and patios; some had big front porches with pillars and steps going down. There were cars, bicycles, trucks, people, and everything you could imagine to buy to furnish a dollhouse. Dr. Pierce was getting a kick out of all the excitement of all the ladies, including his mother.

Olivia remarked, "Every little girl should have one of these once in her lifetime." Conrad replied, "I figured you would say that, Mom." Tiffany mentioned, "There are some areas where a little girl never grows up." Stephanie replied,

"Oh good, because I sure would like to have one of those, but I thought I was too old." "Well," Mom stated, "since every little girl should have one once, maybe you, Angela, and I, could save our money, and we could get one of these houses." Angela remarked, "Oh, could we?" "Well," Mom answered, "we could pick one out today and write everything we want down and then when we have saved all the money we need, we could send it to Dr. Pierce and have him pick it up for us and mail it to us." Angela asked, "Would you Dr. Pierce, please?" Mom stated, "But it would take us a year or so to save up that much money." Angela and Stephanie replied, "That's OK, we will work hard; we can babysit for people, it will be fun to do that." Dr. Pierce mentioned, "Well, now that that's settled, do you know which one you want Jordan?" Jordan asked, "You mean I get one today!" Well, yes," Dr. Pierce answered, "this is part of your Christmas present." Oh my," Jordan replied with tears in her eyes, "I don't know which one I would like." Dr. Pierce mentioned, "Well, how about if Grandma and I would help you pick one out. I know Grandma would have fun helping you, and I will have fun just watching the both of you. I will operate the cart.' Jordan asked, "Are you going to operate on the cart?" Dr. Pierce stated, "No, I am just going to push the cart, and the rest of you can pick out the houses you want to order." So off they went to try and pick out the dollhouse each one wanted. Twenty minutes later, Tiffany, Stephanie, and Angela came. Dr. Pierce asked, "Are you all done already?" "Well," Tiffany mentioned, "after we took all this time picking out the house we wanted, the clerk asked how we wanted it furnished. And I said we didn't know. We are not going to buy it for about a year yet. So he said, then why don't you just take a catalog home, and then you can pick out what you want to furnish it with, out of the catalog. So we really didn't need to make a decision today." Dr. Pierce replied, "Well, a clerk just told me that all the houses have to be put together after you receive them. You do all the decorating yourself at home." Tiffany remarked, "This is beginning to sound just like a train track to me." Conrad and Olivia had a good laugh. "Well," Conrad said, "Jordan picked out the house she wanted. Jordan said, "It is a big farmhouse, kind of like yours, Mommy, but it has four extra rooms, and a two-car garage. I'm going to decorate it just like yours, Mommy." Mommy replied. "That's so sweet, Honey." Dr. Pierce stated, "The clerk also said, if we are going to be in town a few days, and you pick out what you want, they can have all the walls and floors decorated for you, so I told them you would be here until a week from Sunday. We will call in the items we want on the walls and floors, and they will take care of it. But we should do that by tomorrow. Then they will ship the whole thing out after the first of next month." "Sounds good to me," Tiffany responded, "but what happened to having to put it together at home?" Conrad said, "That's if you order the house out of the catalog." "So Jordan," Mother remarked, "show us the house you picked out." Jordan was so excited, "it's right over here," and off she went, with everyone following right behind. It was a big three-story house, with a large porch along the whole front of the house with five steps going down in the center. She said, "I will put a swing right here." It was right where the swing sets on the porch back home, she added, "Only I added a garage, so Mommy's car won't have to stay out in the cold and wet all the time." Mommy remarked, "That is so sweet, Honey. You are so thoughtful." Dr. Pierce remarked, "We have to decide how she wants it decorated, and what kind of furniture she wants. We can do that from the catalog that you are taking home, and then it looks like we are done here. Soon as we check out, we have to find Sam."

Sam was waiting in the parking lot, and Dr. Pierce went up and asked him if he could get a hold of Joe and see if he could bring Grandpa, Gregory, Jared, and Blake to the restaurant. "Wait a minute," Tiffany mentioned, "I believe we all have to go back. We all need to change clothes to go skating." Dr. Pierce replied, "Oh I forgot about changing clothes." So off they went to change clothes and get ready to go skating. They all rushed to the elevator, and up they went to the apartment. The boys were waiting for them when they opened the door. Mother stated, "We will hurry." The girls took off running up the stairs. Mother remarked, "No running in the house," as she followed after them. "Sorry," was the reply as they slowed down and continued up the stairs at a much slower pace. In no time, everyone was at the door waiting to leave. Down the elevator they went. "My," Walter remarked, "you all must be in a hurry. Didn't I just take you up the elevator?" "Well," Dr. Pierce replied, "half of us anyway." Sam had the car door open when they came out of the building. Dr. Pierce stated, "Off to the park." Sam replied, "Right on, you kids will love the park. It is just beautiful. It is all lit up, and there are ice sculptures all over, and they have stands with hot chocolate." "Oh boy," Jackson remarked, "hot cocoa milk, yah, Blake." Grandpa Woodard mentioned, "It will be real good after we have been outside for a while." It seemed like no time at all, before Sam was opening the door for them to get out. Sam told them, "The stand to rent your skates is on your left. Have fun, I will be right here, if anyone gets cold, you can come in and warm up." Tiffany replied, "Gee thanks, I really appreciate that Sam." And off they went. They had a wonderful time skating. They skated to music. It was just beautiful. Conrad and Tiffany took turns with Blake, sometimes carrying him in their arms as they skated around the ice, and sometimes holding onto his hands as he skated between them. Stephanie and Gregory took Jordan and Jackson. Jared and Angela went around together, holding hands. Grandpa and Grandma skated hand-in-hand around the ice. The park is so beautiful, everyone kept saying. They all went and got hot cocoa milk after an hour or so on the ice. The little ones never complained, not even once about being cold. The music was just beautiful, and the ice sculptures just seem to sparkle with the lights at night. Stephanie and Gregory sang to every song and had a wonderful time. Jordan and Jackson thought it was just super to be led around by their big brother and sister. They had a blast. Jared and Angela had a wonderful time also, as they went around together holding hands, or going backwards to the music.

Before you knew it, it was 7:00 p.m. "Oh my," Tiffany remarked, "we need to get these children some dinner." "Time to go," Dr. Pierce told everyone, as he skated past each couple. Emma and Carrie had been sitting in the car with Sam. They said they just didn't like to skate. By the time they got the skates returned and got in the car, it was getting late. Dr. Pierce mentioned, "Maybe we should just go to the hotel restaurant for supper." "That's just fine with us," everyone remarked. So off they went heading back to the hotel. Blake remarked, "Me needs food." Mommy replied, "We are going to eat as soon as we get to the hotel, Honey. So, what did you boys do all day by yourselves?" Jackson responded, "We wrapped presents, and got all ready for Christmas." "Yeah," Jared remarked, "and we ordered pizza for lunch, and watched a movie about trains that Grandpa bought at the museum." Gregory mentioned, "And we watched a football movie." Blake said, "We watched a movie with baby animals, I yiked it a lot." Mother remarked, "It sounds like you guys had a wonderful time." Blake remarked, "Yup, me did," with a big smile on his face. Stephanie mentioned, "You sure know how to make us laugh, Blake," as she gave him a big hug and ruffled up his hair." Blake replied, "Me love you Steffi." Stephanie answered, "I love you too, little buddy," as she gave him another big hug, "and I missed you today." Blake said, "You comed back." Stephanie responded, "I sure did."

They arrived at the hotel, and went in and were ordering their food, when Todd came up to Stephanie and said, "and what would you have this evening Ma'am," with a towel draped across his arm. Stephanie knew him a little better by now, so she said; "what would you recommend?" Todd answered, "I recommend a special Christmas dinner for today, broccoli cheese soup, and peppered rib roast, raspberry tossed salad, cheesy hash brown potatoes, warm garlic bread, warm Christmas punch, and chocolate velvet desert." "Wow," Dr. Pierce remarked, "I don't know about Stephanie, but that sure sounds good to me." Grandpa Woodard replied, "Put me down for that also." Grandma Woodard said, "Me too." "You sure made my work easier," said Todd, "now what about you Stephanie?" Stephanie remarked, "I would love to try that." Gregory asked, "What happened to the hamburger and fries, Steph?" Stephanie responded, "This just sounds so good." "Emma and Carrie said they would have the same thing, and Mother asked the rest of the children what they would have. Stephanie asked Angela if she would split hers with her, she didn't think she could eat the whole thing by herself. Angela told her that would be fine. Jared ordered one all by himself, and the three little ones split one. Dr. Pierce said the blessing for the food. The meal was delicious. Everyone enjoyed it, even the little ones. Dr. Pierce remarked, "I sure am glad you asked what Todd recommended, Stephanie." When Dr. Pierce went up to sign the slip for the meal, he asked Todd if he and his mother would like to join them for a Christmas concert and play at his church Christmas Eve afternoon. "We would love to," Todd replied, "I will ask my mom for sure." Dr. Pierce said, "We will pick you up about 12:30 p.m.; the concert starts at 1:30 p.m." Todd responded, "Thank you so much, Dr. Pierce, Mom will call you first thing in the morning and let you know."

When they got to the apartment, Tiffany headed upstairs with the little ones to give them a bath. "Don't forget to say your prayers, children," she told the other children as she reached the top of the stairs. "We won't; we will all take showers, and then get together when Jackson is done with his bath." By the time Tiffany got Blake into bed, and came back downstairs, Emma, Carrie, and Grandma were already talking about what to have for Christmas dinner. Olivia mentioned, "We don't have any Christmas goodies made." "No problem," Emma remarked, "Carrie and I made some things the other day when we did not go along shopping with you. And, we will bake more goodies tomorrow morning, before we go to the Christmas concert and play at church. In fact, we have to make some cookies for that, too. They are going to have cookies and coffee afterwards." Tiffany replied, "I didn't know we were going to a concert and play at church tomorrow, are you sure of that?" Emma remarked, "Well, I don't know for sure either, but Dr. Pierce hasn't missed one yet, when he's in town, and he makes sure we all go. I would really be surprised if we didn't go."

"Well," Oliver mentioned, as he came into the great room with a cup of coffee, "what have you ladies decided to have for Christmas dinner? Those potatoes we had for dinner tonight were mighty good." "They sure were," Dr. Pierce remarked, as he walked into the great room. "All right," Carrie replied, "let's go for it." "I will bake a birthday cake for Jesus," said Tiffany, "with candles to boot." Emma said, "Good idea." Conrad stated, "That roast beef and ham was mighty good that I had at Tiffany's last Christmas." Olivia asked, "Are you guys going to help cook this meal too?" "Oh no," Oliver replied; "we just know what we like to eat." "Yes," Conrad added, "and what about soup? Are we going to have soup?" Emma remarked, "I have a baked potato soup recipe that is really good, we can make that in the morning also, well, let's get us a plan. Tiffany, what would you like to make?" Tiffany replied, "I will make the cheesy hash brown potatoes, the chocolate cake, and I will make cranberry sauce tonight." Emma said, "Okay, and Olivia, what would you like to make?" Olivia mentioned, "I will make a mandarin orange Jell-O dish, and I will make Oliver's favorite rolls, and help with cookies." Emma said, "Great, Carrie what would you like to make?" "I will make a squash casserole, and green bean hot dish. They can both be made ahead of time; in fact, I will cook the squash tonight in the microwave. It will only take about twenty minutes or so. And I will make the filling for a couple kinds of hors d'oeuvres for tomorrow night." "Great," Emma remarked, "and I will work on some desserts and filling for hors d'oeuvres also for Christmas evening. We have about three hours after breakfast." Olivia stated, "I will be over early to start my bread. I always start it early. Will anyone be up at 6:00 a.m. to let me in?" "I will," Emma, Carrie, and Tiffany replied, all at the same time. Emma mentioned, "If we need anything we don't have, we can always borrow it from Steven at the restaurant downstairs. He is so great to always help me out." The men had retired to bed a long time ago. It was getting late, the ladies also hurried off to bed. Tiffany lay in bed and could not help but think how Emma was so sure Dr. Pierce would go to the church concert, but before she knew it, she was fast asleep. Sometimes it takes everyone working together to get a job done on time.

CHAPTER 15

CHRISTMAS PLAY AND CONCERT

Tomorrow is December 24th, Christmas Eve. The night seemed to go by fast, but Tiffany, pulled herself out of bed at 5:00 a.m. as she left the room, she turned on the intercom, so she could hear when little Blake started to move around. When she got downstairs, she found Emma and Carrie already at work in the kitchen. Emma said; "Good morning Ma'am," as she handed her a cup of coffee. Just then the doorbell rang, and Carrie went to answer the door. Sure enough, it was Olivia who remarked, "That coffee sure smells good." Emma responded, "One cup, coming right up." About fifteen minutes before the children usually came down, Tiffany paged Stephanie's room, and asked her if she could go and get Blake up and get him dressed. Stephanie replied, "Sure mom, but right now I'm doing Jordan's hair, so Angela will go, she is all dressed and ready. Is there anything special, you want on him this morning?" Mother said, "No, not right now, maybe later, but be sure to bring down the bib." Stephanie asked, "Okay, did you get that, Angela?" Angela answered, "Yes, I will meet you downstairs." "Thanks girls." "You're welcome Mom," was the reply from both girls.

By the time the breakfast was ready, the cake was out of the oven and the bread was rising. The squash and green bean hot dish were all put together except for the toppings.

The cheesy hash brown potatoes were already for the oven. The orange Jell-O dish was done. Everything was all cut up for the soup. Breakfast was ready by the time the children all came downstairs, and Oliver and Dr. Pierce had just rang the doorbell. Gregory answered the door, and remarked, "Boy, you are just in time, breakfast is ready." Grandpa Woodard replied, "These ladies are good, are they not?" Dr. Pierce led in a blessing for the food, and asked God for His blessings on the concert at church today, as we celebrate the birth of His Son, Jesus Christ. "Amen," everyone said at the same time. Blake mentioned, "Me needs hot cocoa milk." Mommy replied, "Coming right up."

They had a wonderful breakfast, and then they all retired to the great room, as soon as the kitchen and table were cleaned up. They all sat around in a circle, and Dr. Pierce went over to the big tree, and took out a package. "You had better get in the middle of the room Gregory." "Cool," Gregory remarked, as he got up and went and sat in the middle of the circle. He took the package from Dr. Pierce and said. "Thank you so much Dr. Pierce." Dr. Pierce said, "You don't even know what it is yet." Gregory stated, "I know it will be good whatever it is." Gregory started to open the box. It was a small box wrapped in beautiful green paper with a white ribbon and bow on it. He got it opened, and there were tickets to a concert on Thursday, December 30th, and a note. "Dear Gregory, I know how you like music, so first we are going shopping, just for you. Just you and I alone, and then we will pick up Todd and his mother, Kristine, and then back here to pick up everyone else. We will eat sandwiches, chips, and pop in the Limo on the way to the Christmas concert and play at church. You'll meet a very special person at the concert at church. He is Terry Murphy, he is big in Christian music, and he goes to our church. After the concert we are all going caroling, and Terry will be leading us. After we get done caroling, we are all going out for dinner, I have already made the reservations. I hope you will enjoy your day. Have a very Merry Christmas, love, Dr. Pierce." Gregory replied, "Thank you so much, Dr. Pierce, I have heard of Terry Murphy. This will be great. And these are the tickets for the concert next Thursday?" Dr. Pierce replied, "Yes, we all will be going. It will be a big surprise for all of you. We had better get going now; I have just the store picked out for you." The little children went into the great room to watch a video on the big-screen. Grandpa Woodard said, "You children pick out what you want to watch, and I will handle the controls." Stephanie asked, "Can I help you ladies in the kitchen? I am not interested in a little kid's video." Mother said, "Sure, ask Emma what she would like you to do." Before you knew it, they were all busy cooking and making goodies for Christmas Day. Stephanie asked, "How many people do we have coming?" Emma replied, "We have eighteen altogether with us." Angela and Jared asked Grandpa Woodard, if he would like to put a puzzle together with them. Grandpa answered, "I would love to help."

Dr. Pierce and Gregory finally arrived at the store Dr. Pierce had picked out for Gregory. It was a guitar store. Gregory stated, "Wow, this is a huge store. They have everything in here." Dr. Pierce asked, "Have you ever played an electric guitar before." Gregory replied, "No, but I've always wanted to." Dr. Pierce remarked, "Well, we'll just look around for a while, and in about a half an hour Terry is going to stop in and help you pick one out." Gregory remarked, "Terry Murphy is really coming here. Wow! And I get to pick one out! You mean for me to have?" Dr. Pierce replied, "Why yes, it's part of your Christmas present." Gregory said, "Oh! Dr. Pierce, that is too much." Dr. Pierce stated, "We will look at it as an investment in your future. If you are as good as I've heard you are, you could have a future like Terry's. All you have to do is work hard, practice a lot, and pray and ask God to guide and direct your path. If that is what He wants for you, it will happen." Gregory answered, "You can bet I will work hard, Dr. Pierce, and I will practice every chance I get."

Terry walked up and asked, "Hey, Dr. Pierce, Gregory; how are you doing? Did you find anything yet, Gregory?" Dr. Pierce replied, "We are doing just fine." Gregory responded, "No, I don't even know where to start, but I am really glad you are here to help me, I really like your music. It is so awesome to meet you. " Terry answered, "thank you so much and I hear you are not half bad yourself." Terry and Gregory started looking at all the different kinds of guitars and amplifiers. It seemed to Dr. Pierce like they looked at every single guitar in the store. Terry said, "I believe we have it all figured out what we are going to get, we will get this electric guitar, with this amplifier, half staff, and this head, and cabinet. And we will need a peddle or rack set up for effects. You will need fazers and flangers."

Gregory remarked, "Wow, this is just too much, Dr. Pierce." "Don't you worry about it son, this is an investment in your future." Gregory remarked, "I can set this entire set up, up in the barn at home and practice there. This will be so cool. Now I can work on getting my own band." Terry replied, "Just don't give up on your dream, young man, and make sure whatever you do, do it for the Lord." Gregory answered, "You can bet on that. I wouldn't leave God out of anything in my life." Terry and Gregory picked out everything Gregory needed. Dr. Pierce paid for it, and gave the clerk the address where to ship it. Terry said to Gregory, "Gregory, Dr. Pierce and I have been talking and we have decided that you are going to come over to my studio every day next week and practice, and Thursday evening at the concert you are going to do a number." Gregory responded, "Are you serious, Mr. Murphy?" Terry said, "I'm very serious. It is supposed to be a surprise for the rest of your family, so tonight we are going to ask your mother if you can come down to the studio this week and watch us practice." Gregory replied, "Wow, this will be super." Terry stated, "Well, I have to get to the church to practice for this afternoon. Everyone will be wondering what happened to me. See you later." Gregory said, "Goodbye, Mr. Murphy, it was a pleasure to meet you." Conrad remarked, "Goodbye, Terry, we'll see you later." Dr. Pierce replied, "Well, Gregory, it looks like we are right on time; Sam is here. Well, Sam, let's be off to pick up Todd and his mom."

Todd and Kristine were waiting when the big limo pulled up in front of their house. All the neighbors were wondering what was going on, with this big limo picking them up and dropping them off so much in the past week. As Sam got out and went around and opened the door, and bowed before Kristine, took her hand and helped her into the car. The neighbors were all watching out of their windows. Todd felt so proud to see his mom treated like royalty. He loved her so much, and he hoped he could do more for her, so she wouldn't have to work so hard. As they took off to pick up the others, Todd's mind turned to other things, like Stephanie. He thought she was the most beautiful thing he had ever seen. He had been staring out the window, when all of a sudden; it dawned on him that someone was talking to him.

Kristine asked, "What are you dreaming about?" Todd replied. "Oh, nothing, I was just looking at all the beautiful Christmas decorations." Dr. Pierce mentioned, "They are beautiful aren't they? Where we are going caroling after the concert, the decorations will be beautiful also." Todd stated, "No one ever goes caroling where we live." Dr. Pierce responded, "Is that right? Well, maybe we should change our minds about where we go caroling tonight. I will have to talk to Terry Murphy about it." Todd asked, "You know Terry Murphy?" Dr. Pierce replied. "Why yes, he is going to lead our caroling tonight." Todd remarked, "Wow, you mean I am really going to meet Terry Murphy tonight?" Dr. Pierce said,

"Yup, and I bet he would just love to go caroling around your neighborhood." Gregory replied, "Yes, I met him this afternoon, and he is just super." Todd asked, "Where did you meet him?" Gregory replied, "At this guitar store, he helped me pick out a guitar and amplifier, and everything I need to get me set up. He is a friend of Dr. Pierce's." Todd remarked, "So you play the guitar. Do you sing also?" Gregory stated, "Yes." Todd replied, "We should get together sometime; I just love to sing too. I especially liked the song by Terry Murphy, where Jesus heals the ten lepers and only one comes back to thank him. That is a super song." Gregory responded, "Oh, I love that one too." Then they started singing, and Dr. Pierce and Kristine started clapping their hands, keeping time with the music. They had a wonderful time all the way back. Dr. Pierce called Tiffany and told her they were on their way. They should be there in about fifteen minutes. Tiffany said, "We will be downstairs waiting for you." Conrad replied, "I believe fifteen of us can fit in the limo, is that right, Sam?" Sam replied, "Yes, no problem." Everyone was waiting for them when they pulled up. They had a picnic basket full of food, pop, juice, and chips, plastic dinnerware and glasses; they were ready for a picnic. They also had two big boxes of cookies for after the play. Jackson said, "This is going to be so much fun, a picnic at Christmas time." Jordan stated, "Wait till I tell everyone at school, that we went on a picnic in the limo on our Christmas vacation. They will not believe me." Mother replied, "Probably not, but that's okay. It's the wonderful time we all are having together that counts, and the fact that what you tell them is the truth." When they were done eating, they sang all the way to church. It was a very happy time. Just before they arrived at the church, Mother reminded them that they all had to use the restrooms before they took their seats.

All of a sudden, the lights went down and up and down and up. Jackson asked, "Mommy, what's the matter with the lights?" Mother replied, "Nothing that means we should take our seats. The concert and play are about to start. They do that to get our attention." Jackson answered, "Well, they sure got my attention; I thought we were going to be in the dark." Mother said, "It will be getting a little dark, just like in the theaters, when the movie starts. You all have to be very quiet during the concert and play, unless they tell us to sing. Then you can sing, okay?" They all said, "Okay." And they all went in and took their seats. The lights slowly went down until it was so dark you could not see anything; then there was a small light high up in the ceiling, and another one, and another one, and they were moving back and forth, up and down, and then one light seemed to stop and shine down on Mary, ever so softly, while she was kneeling and praying in the garden of her father's house. The rest of the lights kept moving back and forth across the sky.

All of a sudden one of the lights got so bright and shown right in front of Mary. She was startled and opened her eyes, because of the bright light, and as she looked up. There was an angel standing in front of her, and she was greatly afraid. But the angel said to her; "do not be afraid; Mary, for you have found favor with God, and behold, you shall conceive in your womb, and bear a son, and you shall name him Jesus" (Luke 1:30-31) . The angel told her many things about the baby Jesus. "He will be great, and will be called the Son of the Most High, and the Lord God will give Him the throne of His father, David. And He will reign over the house of Jacob forever. And His kingdom will have no end. And Mary said to the angel, "how can this be, since I am virgin?" And the angel answered. "The Holy Spirit will come upon you, and the power of the Most High will overshadow you, and for that reason, the holy offspring shall be called the Son of God" (Luke 1: 32-35). They sang many beautiful Christmas songs about the baby Jesus, then the angel and the bright light was gone.

Then Mary, who was great with child and riding on a donkey, (the children liked the animals in the play) and Joseph were walking to Bethlehem to register to pay taxes, and it came time for Mary to have her baby. They came to Bethlehem, but there was no room in the inn. So Joseph and Mary had to stay in a stable. She wrapped the little baby Jesus in swaddling clothes and laid Him in a manger. "And in the same region there were some shepherds staying out in the fields and keeping watch over their flock by night, and the angel of the Lord suddenly stood before them" and the glory of the Lord shone around them; and they were terribly frightened. And the angel said to them, 'Do not be afraid; for behold, I bring you good news of a great joy, which shall be for all the people. For today in the city of David, there has been born for you, a Savior, who is Christ the Lord. And this shall be a sign for you: you will find a baby wrapped in cloths, and lying in a manger' (Luke 2:8-12). The Angels were singing and praising God. They were flying all over the room. The children could hardly believe their eyes. It was beautiful, there were different colored lights flashing all over, and the gowns of the angels seemed to change color as they flew through the lights. They were saying, "Glory to God in the highest, and on earth peace among men with whom He is pleased" (Luke 2:14). All of a sudden the angels all went back up into heaven and they were left alone. Then the shepherds said to one another. "Let us go straight to Bethlehem then, and see this thing that has happened which the Lord has made known to us"(Luke 2:15B). And they left their sheep and came in haste and found their way to Mary, and Jesus' stepfather Joseph, and the baby Jesus as He lay in the manger. And the baby Jesus was so good. He moved His little arms and legs as He lay there.

The shepherds told Mary and Joseph what had been told them by the angel concerning this child. And all who heard it wondered at the things which were told them by the shepherds. But Mary treasured up all these things, pondering them in her heart. The Angels were all over the heavens, flying in and out, up and down, and the lights were flashing on and off. It was just beautiful; there was much singing and praising God. "And the shepherds went back, glorifying and praising God for all they had heard and seen, just as had been told them"(Luke 2:20). And a very soft light continued to shine down on the baby Jesus. It was absolutely breathtaking. When the lights came back up, the angels were still flying around, and all the cast and choir were standing in front of them. It was the most inspiring thing the little ones had ever seen. Well, in fact any of them, except Dr. Pierce, Emma, and Carrie, had ever seen.

Everyone went and had cookies and lemonade and coffee. After about forty-five minutes, Terry came up to them and said. "We are ready to go caroling. There are seventy-eight of us. We will take two buses. Do you have a specific area in mind? No one else does, they said wherever we want to take them was fine with them." Dr. Pierce answered, "I do have a specific area; it will take us a while to get there, but Todd mentioned to me that no one ever goes caroling around their neighborhood. He is with us, so he would just love it if we went there." Terry replied, "Sounds like a plan." The children wanted to ride on the bus, so off they went.

Sam's big limo went first, lights flashing. Behind him were the two buses with their lights flashing. They decided to take the freeway, it was a lot faster. Shortly after they got on the freeway, a police officer pulled them over. The officer asked, "What's going on here?" Sam replied, "We are going over to West Baltimore to sing Christmas carols. There are about seventy-eight of us, men, women and children." The officer said, "Well then, I should give you an escort." And so he did, with sirens and lights flashing too, all the way across town. Conrad stated, "I never made such good time on this freeway." Everyone laughed, and the children on the buses thought it was just neat that they had a police escort. Everyone began to sing Christmas carols. When they arrived at the location, Terry said, "there are seventy-eight people; we will take thirteen for each group. Mix everyone up so there are men, women, and children in each group. Make sure there are at least eight people in each group who know all the songs. We will cover a six block area, thirteen people to a street. We will cover the north–south streets for six blocks, and then we will cross back and cover the east–west streets. We will continue in that pattern until we run out of time. We also have twelve members of our prayer team here with us, and two of them will go with each of the six groups. They will not be singing, they will be praying for the people of these neighborhoods, while we are singing." And so on they went. The police officer said he would hang around the buses and the limo.

He parked his police car about a block down from the buses and the limo and had the window down to listen to the music and was just sitting there watching, when all of a sudden he saw two men hanging around the limo. He drove up very slowly with his lights off. He pulled up behind the last bus, got out, and walked very quietly up to the front bus. He could hear the two men talking. They were trying to decide if they should take the car or not. One man said they would be too easy to spot in that big of a car. He didn't think it would be a very good idea. The other man thought it would be a good idea to just sit in the back of the limo. He had never sat in one of those big cars before.

Just then the police officer came from the other side of the bus. The Officer stated, "Okay men; spread your hands across the hood of the car." The two men turned around and saw the policeman with his gun drawn and pointing right at them. They immediately spread their hands on the hood of the car. The officer searched them and didn't find anything on them. Then he said. "Maybe we should go for a little ride into town." One of the men said, "Officer, we were just admiring the car. We meant no harm. We have never seen a car like this in this area of town." The Officer replied, "Nice try, but I just heard your whole conversation about whether you should steal the car or not. I think we should go downtown." One of the men said, "I told you it was a dumb idea to steal the car." The officer stated, "I'll tell you what, since it is Christmas Eve, I am going to have you do a couple hours of community service. I am going to take you two guys to where the people who own the car and the people from the buses are, and you two are going to join them caroling through the streets for about two to three hours. Just see if you don't feel just a little bit guilty about what you were going to do here. Come with me and get in the back of the squad car. See how you like riding in that car."

CHAPTER 16

TWO LOST SOULS

One man said, "Gee officer, I never sang before." The other man said, "I used to sing in school when I was a kid."

The officer pulled up to where the group was singing and rolled down his window and said to Dr. Pierce, "Doc, how would you like to have a couple more singers to tag along with you? Keep an eye on them. I want to see them back at the car when you are done caroling." Dr. Pierce replied, "We will keep an eye on them for you, and I bet they will have a great time." The officer drove on down the street and turned the corner.

They stopped to look at the sheet music and let everyone know what the next three songs were going to be. The different groups were all trying to sing the same songs at the same time as they crisscrossed the neighborhood. The same music would be coming from all directions. It sounded beautiful.

As the two men listened to the songs and realized the same sounds were coming from a few blocks over, they got caught up in the Christmas spirit and began to sing. The older one had a wonderful voice. After a short time, he said to Dr. Pierce, "I have never had such a wonderful time since I was a little kid." After a little while, Terry Murphy came over and said, "Doc, you have a most beautiful voice coming from your group. Who in the world has joined your group?" Conrad replied, "I don't know his name, but he is right here. Sir, I would like you to meet a friend of mine, Terry Murphy, and your name is?" The old man said, "you're Terry Murphy, the singer?" Terry answered, "Yes, I am and who might I have the pleasure of meeting?" "Frank Tyson," the older man said. "Sometimes I just hang around the Christian music store just to hear some of your songs. I can't afford to buy any, I just go in and put the headphones on and listen for while." Terry stated, "Well sir, Mr. Tyson, you have a beautiful baritone voice, and I would like to have you come down to my studio Monday. I would like to go over a few songs with you and see how you sound." Frank Tyson replied, "Oh my, I would love the chance to sing with you. I can hardly wait." Terry Murphy remarked, "Well, you have a couple or three hours to practice tonight. We had better get going, or we will be left behind." So on they went, down one street and up the next. Mr. Tyson had never had such a good time in all his life. Mr. Tyson introduced his buddy Brian Collins to Dr. Pierce. You might guess what happened next. Dr. Pierce invited both of them to Christmas dinner tomorrow. "We would love to come for dinner, Dr. Pierce, but we have no way of getting there. Besides to tell you the truth, I think we have to talk to the officer when we get back to the buses. He is not very happy with us." Frank went on to tell Dr. Pierce what happened, and Dr. Pierce said, "Well, we will just have to talk to the officer when we get back and see what happens. In the meantime, we had better get moving." Frank replied, "Yes sir," and away they went. Before you knew it, they were back at the bus. They covered that neighborhood and sang for about two hours.

All the neighbors came out of their houses and joined in singing with them. Todd was so happy, nothing like this had ever happened in their neighborhood before. After the singing was over, the people in the neighborhood were hugging the singers and thanking them. This was the best Christmas present, they had ever had. Everyone was getting back on the buses, and Dr. Pierce went over to talk to the officer. He mentioned, "Officer, are you going to take these two guys in?" The Officer replied, "What do you think; do you think they've had a change of heart?" Dr. Pierce stated, "That's exactly what I would like to find out, I would like to take them with me and Terry in the limo and have a good talk with them. If you could give me your phone number, I will call you on Monday." The Officer remarked, "Fine, you can drop them off at the mission downtown. They said that's where they sleep most nights." Dr. Pierce asked everyone if they would mind riding back on the buses; he explained the plan to them and they all agreed. Then Dr. Pierce went over to Terry Murphy and explained the plan to him, and he agreed to go in the limo with Dr. Pierce and the two older men. Then Dr. Pierce went and talked to the people in the two buses, and asked them if they would pray that the Holy Spirit would convict the hearts of Frank Tyson and Brian Collins of the sin in their lives, and convict their hearts of their need for a Savior. Then Dr. Pierce went over to Frank and Brian and told them that the officer said he could give them a ride back downtown in the limo. They were just like two little children, they were so excited. So off they went, the limo first, and then the buses. Dr. Pierce told Todd and his mom Kristine, that Sam would pick them up for church, and then they would come over for dinner after church.

Dr. Pierce asked Brian and Frank, if they would like a can of pop. "Oh yes, please," they both said. They couldn't stop talking about the car, and Frank could not get over the fact that his favorite recording artist was setting right alongside him. Life couldn't get any better than this. Or could it? Terry Murphy remarked, "So, what did you guys think about the singing tonight? How did you feel about it?" It was so quiet, you could've heard a pin drop, and then Frank spoke up. "At first I thought: what are we in for now? Then we got to where you guys were, and I heard the singing. I thought it was angels singing. It took me back to when I was a little boy singing in the choir. I felt warmth come over me and tears filled my eyes. And Dr. Pierce gave me such a warm handshake and invited me to join in, I felt like I had died and gone to heaven." Terry Murphy asked, "You used to go to church, when you were young boy then?" Frank replied, "Oh yes, I accepted Christ as my Savior when I was eleven years old. Then I grew up and got married. We had a beautiful little girl and a wonderful little boy. Life couldn't have been better. Then I went off to war, and while I was overseas, my wife ran off and left me and took our beautiful little children with her. She told my folks that I called her and told her I was going to be coming home, and that I was going to be stationed in Washington State. She told them she was taking the children out there to meet me. My mother said she thought it was strange that I had not written her about it. And when she got a letter from me three weeks later, asking her if she could find out why all my letters to my wife was sent back with, "moved—no forwarding address," she knew what had happened. She wrote me and told me what my wife had said to her. I tried to find her a year later, when I got home, but I never could. All the life was knocked out of me, and I started to drink. That's the end of the story. I could not ever get my life back together. So here I am, an old man with nowhere to go and nothing to live for."

Terry Murphy replied, "But Jesus can heal those wounds. You can't get those years back, but He can give you a new life. Would you like to give all your pain and misery to Him, and let Him heal your heart and soul?" Frank responded, "Oh yes, Me would love to give Him my pain and grief, and asked Him to forgive me for wasting the life He gave me." Terry Murphy asked, "Would you like to pray a prayer of repentance with me now?" Frank added, "Oh yes," and he prayed. "I confess to God that I am a sinner, and I have wasted these years you have given me. The hurt and bitterness I have carried all these years is weighing me down. I have sinned against you, Lord God. Please take away my desire for alcohol and cleanse me. Create in me a new heart, oh God, and renew a right spirit in me. Do not take your Holy Spirit from me; return to me the joy of my salvation. I hereby rededicate my life to You, Lord Jesus. Please cleanse me and make me whole. I ask this in Jesus' precious name, Amen." After Frank had said his prayer, he started to cry, then laugh, and then cry again. "I feel like 100 pound weight has been lifted from my shoulders. I feel like I'm alive again. Thank You Jesus."

Brian just sat there. He could not believe his eyes or what he was hearing. He had known Frank for many years, and he had never told him anything about his life. And here in front of two total strangers he had blurted out his whole life. And the tears, all the tears, all the sorrow Frank felt about wasting his life seems so real, so not like Frank. He couldn't help himself. He had to ask! "Excuse me, but what just happened here? I don't understand."

"Well," Dr. Pierce replied, "let's start at the beginning. Brian, what did you think about the singing tonight?" Brian asked, "Do you want the truth?" Dr. Pierce replied, "Absolutely." Brian remarked, "Okay, at first I thought; what did I get myself into this time? I can't sing a note. And I didn't know Frank sounded like an angel, either. All the years I have known him, and I never knew he could sing. Then I thought about this guy, Terry. If he is so famous, why is he standing out here in the cold singing in the dark? What's he doing here? Then someone said you were a doctor. Are you a doctor?" Dr. Pierce answered, "Yes, I am." Terry remarked, "He is the head neurosurgeon at the hospital downtown." Brian responded, "Oh my, so what makes you guys come out on such a cold night and freeze, just to sing to a bunch of people you don't even know?" Terry answered, "I will answer that, just as soon as you finish telling me how you felt tonight." Brian continued, "Well, I'm watching all the people, men, women, and children singing with all their hearts. They seem like they're walking on air. There are smiles on their faces as they sing, I don't get it. Why do they do it? Why do you guys do it? It seems to me that everyone here tonight has something that I don't have, and I can't figure out what it is. And I sure don't understand what happened to Frank."

Dr. Pierce responded, "Okay, I am going to try to explain this to you as plain as I know how, so that you can understand it. Do you believe in God?" Brian asked, "You mean like the God they talk about at the mission?" Dr. Pierce answered, "Yes, the God who created the world and the heavens and everything in them." Brian remarked, "I don't know if anyone like that really exists. If there is a God, He sure never showed Himself to me." Dr. Pierce assured Brian, "Well, there is a God, He is real, and He is who made all these people here tonight, different from you. God is what these people have that you do not have. He is what is different about them. You see, when God created Adam and Eve, they were perfect, and they were created to live forever. God told Adam he could eat of any of the fruit in the garden, except he could not have the fruit of the tree in the middle of the garden. For on the day when he should eat of it, he would surely die. Then God created a helpmate for Adam, and Adam called his wife Eve. Then the serpent (Satan) tempted Eve and said to her, surely God didn't mean you would die if you eat the fruit, for He knows that when you eat of the fruit, your eyes will be opened, and you will be like God, knowing good and evil.

So, when Eve saw that the food was good for eating, she took a bite, and called Adam and he ate of it also.

Immediately they knew their bodies were not covered, and they were ashamed and took fig leaves and made coverings for themselves and went and hid in the garden. God came walking in the garden and called to Adam. "Here I am Lord," answered Adam. "Why are you hiding," asked the Lord God? "Because I was ashamed," said Adam. "You have sinned," God said, "you have disobeyed me. You will be banned from the Garden of Eden forever." And with Adam's disobedience, he brought sin into the world. Man was separated from God. It's like a big canyon. You are on one side, and God is on the other, separated from each other. There is no way to get to God. So God sent his Son, Jesus Christ to be born of a virgin, that through Jesus the Christ, man could be reconciled back to God. You see we deserved death for our sin, but Jesus the Christ (meaning Messiah) came from heaven and took our place on the cross. God put our sins upon Him, and He died in our place. Jesus, then through His death on the cross, and His resurrection, becomes the bridge over the canyon, because Jesus took our sins upon Himself. We now can walk directly over that bridge to God by confessing our sins to God and asking Him to forgive us our sins, and cleanse us—and we have to accept what Jesus did for us on the cross. We must stop trying to be God. We must surrender to God, the Jesus of the Bible. And when we do this; believing it in our hearts to be true, then the Holy Spirit of God comes and lives within us and teaches us how to live for God. It is the Holy Spirit, who gives each one of the people here tonight, God's love for others. That is why they were so happy and willing to do what they did. They did it to show the love of God to others. Do you think you want to take that step now, Brian?" Brian looked over at Frank and Terry; their heads were bowed and resting on their hands. He assumed they were sleeping. Actually, they were both praying for him, just as all the others on the two buses were doing. Brian asked, "What if I go through all this and wake up tomorrow morning and nothing has changed? What if God is not real." Dr. Pierce replied, "Well, you can challenge God to find out if he is real." Brian asked, "How's that?"

"Well," Dr. Pierce remarked, "In the book of Judges, chapter 6, there was this man in the Bible, Gideon; who challenged God. God promised Gideon that he would deliver Israel thru Gideon, and Gideon said to God, "if I put out a fleece of wool on the ground, and there is dew on the fleece, but the ground is dry, then I will know that it was You, God who has spoken. And it was so, the fleece was wet in the morning; he drained a bowl full of water from it, but the ground was dry. Then Gideon said to God: "do not be angry with me. But let the fleece be dry tomorrow morning and let the ground around it be wet with dew," and it was so. So what is there in your life where you could ask God to make Himself real to you?" Brian replied, "I can't think of anything." Frank responded, "I can." Brian stated, "I thought you were sleeping." Frank replied, "Gnaw, we have been praying for you. And I might say it is a wonderful feeling to talk to God; but back to your problem. To be sure: if you wake up tomorrow without the shakes, and you don't want a drink, then you would know for sure that God is real." Brian answered, "That would be a miracle, all right" Dr. Pierce responded, "Well then, let's ask God for miracle." And they began to lay their hands on Brian and prayed for him that God would make Himself real to him. "Lord God Almighty, creator of heaven and earth, and all that is in them, please convict Brian's heart of the sin in his life, and convict his heart of his need of a Savior. And soften his heart Lord God, and make Yourself real to him. We pray that tomorrow morning, when Brian wakes up, he will not have the shakes, and he will not desire another drink, ever. We know that You are real and that You are faithful and true. But we asked You this for Brian's sake, that he may know that You are real. We thank You, right now for what You are going to do in Brian's heart, Amen."

Terry Murphy asked, "How would you guys like to stay at my house tonight, and you could come to church with me tomorrow morning?" Frank spoke up and said, "We have no good clothes to wear to church." Terry Murphy responded, "God doesn't care about your clothes, but I will call a friend of mine, who owns a men's clothing store and see if he will meet us at the store in about a half an hour." He called his friend on his cell phone and then he hung up. Terry remarked, "Everything is all set; he will meet us in half an hour at the store." Then Terry opened the little window between them and Sam and said; "please drop us off at the church, Sam." Dr. Pierce mentioned, "Then you can take me to the hotel."

Brian could not keep from thinking, what are these two guys up to? They both must be very well-to-do. Why are they bothering with a couple of bums like us? And what is it with the store owner, opening up his store on Christmas Eve to sell a couple of suits to a couple of bums. There has to be something in it for them. And Frank, he has just been grinning and praying. This is not the Frank I know.

When Sam pulled up at the church, the buses were still unloading. The children saw Sam and started running towards the car. They were not all on the same bus, so they had to wait for all of them to get off both the buses. The children were so excited when they got in the car. Jackson mentioned, "We had so much fun, Dr. Pierce. We never did anything like this before." Gregory remarked, "Thank you, again Dr. Pierce for the beautiful Christmas present, this was awesome." Dr. Pierce mentioned to Sam, "Please take us to the restaurant Sam." They had a wonderful dinner, and they discussed Frank and Brian and how God had worked in Frank's life. Grandma Woodard mentioned; "we need to continue to pray for Brian, too." Tiffany replied; "we need to get these little ones home to bed." Dr. Pierce mentioned, "Sam, time to go home."

Dr. Pierce remarked, "This indeed has turned out to be a great blessing, and when we get to the hotel, while Tiffany puts the little ones to bed, we are going to pray for Brian Collins one more time." Stephanie asked, "Yeah, what happened in the limo on the way back?" Dr. Pierce responded, "Well, Frank Tyson had accepted Christ as a little child and just rededicated his life to Jesus Christ, and we will know more about Brian Collins in the morning. They are going to spend the night at Terry Murphy's home, and he is bringing both of them to church tomorrow morning. Then they are both joining us for Christmas dinner after church." Tiffany remarked, "Praise God, we have an overabundance of food." When they got in the apartment, Gregory and Stephanie looked at each other and disappeared upstairs. Stephanie mentioned, "We will put the little ones to bed for you, Mom," as they each picked up one of the little ones and off they went. Tiffany asked, "I wonder what they are up to; it is not like them to skip out on praying." After everyone prayed they all headed off to bed. Dr. Pierce remarked, "Church is early tomorrow morning, there is a continental breakfast at 6:00 a.m., and the services is at 7:30 a.m." Conrad and Tiffany stayed up in little longer than the others, talking about tomorrow and wondering what would happen to Brian if he refused to accept Jesus the Christ as his savior. Without God and Frank he would be completely on his own and quite lost. Conrad replied, "God only knows; there is power in prayer. Let's pray."

EPILOGUE

A s the Larkin family continues on their new adventure in life after the tragic death of their father, Gregory Sr. in a construction accident and their having to move to a new town. We will continue to see how their life unfolds.

Does God answer the children's prayer in the way they want or does God have other plans for Conrad and Tiffany?

What road is Gregory going to take in his life?

What about Stephanie and Todd? Will anything come of their relationship or do they go their separate ways?

What was going on with that Santa? How did he know all those things about everyone?

How about Frank? In what ways will his life change?

What about Frank and Brian's friendship? How will that change?

What about Brian? Does God make Himself real to Brian? Does Brian accept Jesus the Christ or does he reject Jesus?

CPSIA information can be obtained at www.ICGtesting.com
Printed in the USA
BVOW011843120113

310343BV00002B/2/P

9 781625 092366